CASTING SHADOWS

BY
J. S. PILE

This is a work of fiction, and as such is presented solely for entertainment purposes. Names, characters, businesses, places, events and incidents are either the product of the author's imagination or used in a fictitious manner. Any resemblance to actual persons, living or dead, or actual events and locations is purely coincidental.

CASTING SHADOWS
First Edition

Author: J. S. Pile

Copyright © 2019 By J. S. Pile
All rights reserved. This book or any portion thereof may not be reproduced or used in any manner whatsoever without the express written permission of the author and publisher except for the use of brief quotations in a book review.

For Max and Herbert,
the greatest companions I could have ever
wished for, though you may no longer be by my
side, you will both forever be in my heart.

CONTENT

- Chapter 1: The Funeral
- Chapter 2: The Wake
- Chapter 3: Home Alone
- Chapter 4: Carnation Hall
- Chapter 5: Moving Day
- Chapter 6: New Friends
- Chapter 7: The New Statue
- Chapter 8: The Haunting
- Chapter 9: The Drowned Woman
- Chapter 10: Aftermath
- Chapter 11: Where There Is A Will, There Is A Way
- Chapter 12: The Fall
- Chapter 13: Stalemate
- Chapter 14: Toxicology
- Chapter 15: The Queen Of More
- Chapter 16: The Work Shed
- Chapter 17: Epilogue

I would like to thank my parents for their constant support and inspiration, without which this story would never have come to fruition. Also, thank you for the countless mugs of tea you provided me with throughout this endeavour, for which I am eternally grateful.

And finally, a huge thank you to Holly, my ever faithful Labrador and loving friend, who has sat by my side for many long hours whilst writing this novel.

CHAPTER 1

The Funeral

The sun was shining brightly high above St. Lucia's steeple. The old stone church was just another grey building standing against the backdrop of a pale blue sky. The brightness of the day did nothing to help fight against the icy chill from the February wind, where a small congregation had gathered in the graveyard. The wind continued to howl menacingly around the old headstones, the naked trees shuddering in its grasp. The morning light was glistening through the bare branches and casting shadows onto the frost covered ground.

A group of mourners, all dressed in black, were huddled around an open graveside. Their heads were bowed, either in sorrow or just against the biting wind, perhaps it was a little of both.

The funeral inside the church had been a simple affair. It consisted of a few Bible readings from the priest, a slightly comedic speech from an old friend about their days together on the golf course, followed by the hymn

'All Things Bright And Beautiful', being sung by the congregation.

When the service had come to an end, the group had reluctantly left the warmth of the church for the icy cold of the graveyard. Everybody gathered around the graveside to say their final farewells to a good man.

Robert Jones
(9/12/1946 – 26/2/2017)
Beloved Husband and Dearest Friend
Rest In Peace

The engravings on the polished headstone stood out boldly against the dark marble in which it was carved into. The bold letters would inform all future visitors vaguely about the life of the man soon to be buried beneath. A coffin made of dark mahogany sat snugly in the hollowed out grave, its chrome finishings reflecting the sunlight as it bled through the trees. The reflection was already beginning to fade, as the priest threw a handful of earth onto the coffin and sullied its surface whilst he spoke.

"We therefore commit this body to the ground. Earth to earth, ashes to ashes and dust to dust," the priest continued with his sermon, his voice strong as he addressed the crowd. Although he addressed many, his gaze was firmly directed at only one person, as if his words were meant for her alone. Lydia Jones, the widow, was only a short woman, but she held herself strong, even whilst consumed with her current grief. Dressed all in black, she kept her head held high, the wind whipping her scarf back around her neck and stinging at her cheeks. By her side stood Susanna, Lydia's only child. Their arms were locked together, Susanna's gloved fingers rubbing patterns gently over her mother's arm in a gesture of silent support.

The ceremonial vase was passed between the relatives, each taking a handful of earth, and using it to dust the top of the coffin. Finally, the vase was handed over to Lydia, the crowd looking on with silent encouragement, as she reached inside the vase. She clasped her hand around the slightly damp soil, tossing it into the gaping hole before her. Fresh tear tracks were now running down her face as the action was completed.

"Though he may now be gone, he will never be forgotten. Though he may be absent, his presence will forever be with us, in our memories and in our hearts. Now in my father's house, his soul will forever be home, and we lay his body down for eternal rest," the priest recited, whilst silence consumed the congregation. He continued, "please each take a moment of silence to say goodbye in your own way. The family has also asked me to invite and welcome you all back to Lydia's house for a drink, and to continue the celebration of Robert's life. Thank you." He then stepped back from the grieving crowd to give them all some privacy.

Gradually, the congregation began to diminish, as the people desperately sought the warmth of their cars and protection from the vicious wind. Soon only the immediate family remained.

Susanna was still holding tightly onto her mother's arm, and seeing fresh tears welling in her eyes she quickly pulled Lydia into her comforting arms.

"It's okay, mum. I've got you," Susanna whispered softly. Lydia returned the hug, wrapping her arms tightly around her daughter's back and resting her chin on her shoulder.

From where she stood she could see far across the graveyard, thousands of headstones, each marking another grave and another life that had been lost, *"Just like my Robert,"* she thought sadly.

Robert's death had come as a devastating shock to Lydia. There had been no prior warning signs, no lingering cough or any suspicious aches and pains. Despite his age, Robert had always been in good health, keeping himself busy in the garden or playing golf down at his local golf club. He had always kept himself fairly fit, and as far as Lydia knew, he had never even set foot in a hospital. So, before that fateful night, Lydia had no reason to believe anything could be wrong with him. It's cruel how someone's fate can change so quickly, disrupting an otherwise happy and tranquil existence in just mere moments.

***

The tragedy had occurred only three weeks earlier. The day that Robert passed away had come along just like any other. Lydia had awoken that morning to the melodious sound of birds tweeting in the garden, with the first rays of light creeping their way through the bedroom curtains. The room was pleasantly warm as Lydia yawned and stretched, almost cat-like, before sitting herself up in bed. The aroma of freshly brewed coffee had meandered its way through the air to Lydia's nose, and a knowing glance at her bedside table revealed a still steaming mug sat waiting for her. The morning coffee was a daily occurrence, a simple gesture from her beloved husband to show he cared. Robert always awoke before Lydia, his golfing habits having conditioned him well for early morning starts, whereas Lydia had never been one to rise before the sun.

Yet, with the taste of coffee still lingering on her lips, Lydia was soon rising, getting herself dressed and welcoming in the new day.

She descended the stairs of her home with surprising agility for a woman of her age, entering the kitchen, and immediately searching through the fridge for bacon. It was a Sunday morning tradition for Lydia and her husband to share a home cooked breakfast together. Nothing fancy, just simple bacon, eggs and toast, but Lydia took great pleasure in preparing it for her husband.

With several strips of bacon sizzling in a frying pan, Lydia took a peek behind the net curtain that veiled her kitchen window. The sight that greeted her eyes brought a swell of jubilation to her heart. For, outside in the back garden, she could see her Robert. He was confidently marching across the lawn, his mighty electric mower held firmly within his grasp, cutting through the overgrown winter lawn, trimming it down to a more acceptable length. Lydia enjoyed watching him work. He always took great care of their garden, and would spend many hours tending to the lawn and flower beds, no matter what the weather was like! He resembled an artist, whittling away at his never ending masterpiece.

But, the recent winter had been a long and hard one, not allowing Robert much opportunity to nurture his beloved garden. That was until today, for on this seemingly innocent Sunday morning, the sun had finally broken its way through the clouds, and despite the cool bite of the February breeze, Robert was determined to make the most of this glorious bright and sunny day. Lydia patiently watched him work with a pleasant smile, taking time to carefully cook the eggs just the way Robert liked them. He favoured a runny yolk. This enabled him to submerge his buttered strips of toast into the golden coloured nectar, whereas Lydia much preferred her eggs to be more thoroughly cooked, certainly no runny yolk leaking onto the plate! Once the meal was ready to serve, Lydia would gently tap her fingers against the window pane, catching Robert's attention, and he would down his tools to join her to eat at the kitchen table.

Breakfast time would come and go as it did every Sunday morning, and whilst they were enjoying their breakfast, the happily married pair would discuss the events of the world whilst reading the daily newspaper.

Later that day, as Lydia was busying herself working through a mountain of ironing that she had neglected throughout the previous week, Robert announced that he was going out. He entered the kitchen dressed in his padded winter coat, his scarf encasing his neck, and promptly kissed his wife upon her cheek. And, with that, Robert was out the door, even before Lydia could question his intentions. He had simply said that he was going out on an errand, but Lydia suspected he was truly sneaking away to join some of his friends at the local pub. There was an important football match being played that afternoon. Robert's favourite team were playing against their rivals, Lydia was well aware of the event, as she had just read about it in the newspaper earlier that day. She had no doubt a cheeky pint with his friends was Robert's true goal for the afternoon. In truth, Lydia didn't mind him going at all. Historically, Sundays had always been their day, a chance for them to spend quality time together amidst their constantly busy lives, especially way back when they had both been working. It was an unspoken rule that they would spend as much of 'The Lord's Day' together as possible. But, now that Robert had retired, they were able to enjoy more freedom, with the pair spending practically the whole of each day together. That is, when Lydia was not tucked away working, and, as such, their special Sundays were starting to become a little less notable. So, if Robert wanted to spend his Sunday elsewhere, then that was truly fine with Lydia. They would still enjoy an early evening roast dinner together upon Robert's return. And that is how it was, with Robert arriving home with precision timing, just as the potatoes were starting to crisp inside the oven. The cottage was filled with the wonderful aromas of home cooking, the meat roasting and vegetables bubbling away in a pan upon the stove. Robert greeted his wife with a gentle kiss as he burst through the door of their home, his lips cold due to the frosty early evening air outside. Unbeknownst to both, that kiss would be the last they would ever share.

As always, their private feast was consumed and thoroughly enjoyed in a tranquil and peaceful atmosphere. But, this peace was not to last! It was merely an hour or so later, as Lydia and Robert were sat in their individual armchairs, like the king and queen of their own little haven, that things started to take a downward turn. As the pair were watching television, Robert suddenly felt a sharp discomfort in his chest. The pain soon escalated to a tightness around his lungs and a persistent ache within his core. Robert had then risen from his chair, pacing back and forth in small steps around the living room, hoping the movement alone would cure his pain. It wasn't long before he was finding it difficult to breathe, and he dropped down to his knees, falling as though he had been struck by a heavy blow! His hand was held tightly to his chest, his fingers trembling as he feebly tried to breathe and force some air into his lungs. There was nothing Lydia could do except watch her husband's plight. She was unable to aid him, and powerless to cease his suffering. As Robert collapsed to the floor, limp and lifeless like a rag doll, Lydia lunged for the phone. She immediately called for help as quickly as her ageing and shaking fingers could press down the numbers. It was all to no avail! Lydia had been sitting on the floor of her living room, Robert's head cradled in her lap, as she waited for the ambulance to arrive. Her hands alternated between hovering over his motionless body, and running soothingly through his silver hair, overwhelmed by shock!

The ambulance arrived at their door about fifteen minutes later, but Robert had passed away long before its arrival. Lydia finally began to weep uncontrollably as the paramedics removed Robert's body. She continued sobbing as they took him from the cottage, knowing that he would never return. It was a night that Lydia would remember and be haunted by forever, and by dawn the following day, she had no more tears left to cry. Lydia's throat was now dry and her eyes were sore, and she could weep no more.

The doctors had later concluded that Robert had suffered a massive heart attack, and that there was nothing they could have done to have saved him. Knowing that her inaction could not have changed his fate, brought little comfort to Lydia. She felt like a candle had been blown out, lost to the winds and its bright and glowing light would never return.

Just like that, Robert was gone from Lydia's life forever!

***

Still looking out across the graveyard, Lydia's head was swimming as she thought about all the other graves around her and the people that they belonged to. *"What had led them here and did they all have time to say goodbye?"* were just a few of the questions to cross through Lydia's mind. It was then, whilst she was still distracted by her thoughts, her vision blurred with unshed tears, that she caught a glimpse of a distant lone figure. A woman appeared to be walking slowly between the gravestones, her movements shaky and unsteady, as if she was stumbling rather than striding. The figure seemed featureless from a distance, viewed as nothing but a blur of grey amongst the other overwhelmingly dull colours of the graveyard. Lydia only caught a momentary glance of the figure, before her view was totally obscured by her tears. She then waited for the woman to reappear further down the path, but she never did. Lydia could only assume that the woman must have stopped to pay her respects at one of the graves, or, perhaps Lydia had never actually seen her at all! She then pushed the vision from her mind, putting it down to a mere trick of the light, and the stress of the day upon her exhausted mind. Gently, Lydia untangled herself from Susanna's grasp, and wiped her eyes ungracefully upon the back of her hand to clear her vision.

"Come on, mum. Let's get you to the car. It's freezing out here!" Susanna stated. They locked arms once more, and began to make their way back towards the church, each of Susanna's steps falling unsteadily as her high heels met the uneven stone path.

Ahead of them both, Lydia could see that the priest was waiting for them. Lydia knew how the conversation was going to unfold before he even began to speak. The priest began by promising that Robert would be looking down upon her from heaven. He continued his speech by not so subtly hinting for her to make a donation to the church. *"Why is it that church roofs are always in a state of disrepair?"* Lydia almost scoffed. Disinterestedly, she ignored his fake promises and bit her tongue to contain her comments.

The church had always been Robert's belief, not hers. He may not have regularly attended church, at least not in recent years, but he had always said his prayers each night before retiring to bed. She had never joined him in prayer and sometimes even teased him about it. He had often labelled her a sceptic and promised that one day he would convert her, but they both knew that would never happen. It wasn't that she did not like the idea of a religion or having something to believe in, it was just that Lydia simply knew better.

Luckily, the priest did not linger for long. Prompted either by the miserable weather, or by the look of annoyance on Lydia's face, he retreated to the sanctuary of his church. Either way, she was relieved to see the back of him!

"Christian, are you coming?" Susanna called back to her husband, when she noticed her own family's absence.

Lydia took the moment to look back towards the graveside, where her son-in-law and teenage granddaughter, Jessica, still resided.

Christian turned, shouting out a reply to his wife. However, Lydia didn't catch his words, instead, her attention had been completely grasped by Jessica. The girl's face was sickly pale and her eyes wide open, as she stared off into the distance of the graveyard, seemingly transfixed by nothing but open space.

"Jess, sweetie, are you okay?" Christian questioned, sounding concerned. He placed a hand on his daughter's shoulder, hoping to gain her attention, "You look like you've seen a ghost!" he added with a nervous chuckle, hoping to break the tension. Luckily, his words seemed to break Jessica out of her trance, but the girl continued to ignore him. Instead, she pulled her coat tighter against herself, hoping to stop the cold from seeping further into her bones. She turned to Lydia anxiously.

"Can we go home, please?" Jess asked her grandmother abruptly, a small hopeful smile gracing her features.

"Of course we can, honey," Lydia replied, holding her hand out for Jessica to take, "I have some hot chocolate back home that will warm us all up," she promised.

They all began to amble along the path back to Christian's car. Lydia and Jess still hand in hand, a few steps ahead of Susanna and her husband.

"Do you want to tell me what happened back there?" Lydia prompted quietly as they approached the car. She was curious as to what could have caused her granddaughter to react in such a peculiar manner.

Jessica slightly paled again at her grandmother's questioning. Cautiously, she took a glance to ensure her parents were still a few paces behind and out of ear shot, before leaning in and whispering directly into her grandmother's ear.

Lydia's breath caught in her throat, and goosebumps began to prickle on her skin as the words sank in. Words that would surely haunt her for days to come.

"Grandma, I saw her too!" Jessica whispered.

CHAPTER 2

The Wake

After the funeral service had ended, an assembly of cars advanced upon Lydia's home. Wheels were rolling down the tarmac at a steady pace, until the little cottage came into view ahead. Before long, the driveway was overflowing with vehicles, some had even spilt out into the road, as the mourners gathered once more.

Lydia and Robert's home had never been a grand dwelling, but to them it had been a palace. It had been their own private paradise for the past twenty five years. Just a quiet cottage on the outskirts of a small town, where the two of them could escape, and shut out the rest of the world. An ideal haven for the happy couple, far enough away from the hustle and bustle of other people's lives, and out of earshot from the roar of passing cars on busy roads.

Lydia had actually bought the cottage alone, paid for by the meagre profits from her first published book. Also the alimony she had received from divorcing her first husband, Ray, aided her to make the purchase.

The house had not been in the best condition, having been damaged by a flood years earlier, but Lydia had seen the potential home that the place could become. It had been her aim to have the cottage restored, whilst also rebuilding her life alongside it.

Lydia had met Robert purely by chance. He arrived on her doorstep one day, armed with a toolbox and the sole intention of fixing her broken television. From that day forward, the pair had quickly become close friends. Being the gentleman he always was, and finding a woman living alone, he had felt naturally protective towards her. Robert's visits to the cottage soon became more frequent, he even started calling around after work to assist her with the decorating. It wasn't long before their relationship escalated, and they were engaged before the end of the year.

From then on, a loving marriage had graced the pair and their little cottage. They would spend long winter nights huddled together by the roaring open fireplace, flames dancing in the dark and casting the room in an amber glow. Sunny summer afternoons followed, with family barbecues on the lawn. The sounds of music and laughter filled the air, as the family gathered to enjoy the rare good weather and each other's company. Throughout the good times and the bad times, their little cottage had seen and sheltered them from it all.

They say that home is where the heart is. Right now, as Lydia Jones watched her friends and family scurry around her house, sipping sherry and ravaging the buffet, she knew that the expression was true.

She had decided to host the wake at home. Susanna had suggested having it elsewhere, perhaps at Robert's beloved golf club. However, Lydia was determined to have it at home, at the house they had both loved. There is something comforting about the familiarity of your own home, from the ever present scent of coffee brewing in the kitchen, to knowing which particular stair creaked in a certain way. After such a traumatic day, the one thing that Lydia now craved most was some comfort.

It was now late afternoon, and the sun was beginning to fade. Outside, the sky was set alight with bright ambers and pinks, like a burning sunset as the imposing darkness of night slowly approached. Lydia and Robert's home was filled with the gentle sounds of laughter, familiar voices telling stories of adventures shared, and reminiscing over times gone by. An air of merriment had filled the house, a welcome tonic to help cure the overbearing gloom the day had up to now provided.

Lydia was sitting quietly in her armchair, her favourite spot. She was listening intently to the stories being told by their friends, each one placing Robert in the starring role. Some of these tales she knew well, yet others she was hearing for the first time. She had always known that her husband had quite a mischievous side. However, only after hearing in detail of the chaos that he single handedly caused on a trip away with the lads, did she realise just how much of a rebel her husband could be. Lydia was almost in tears when the tale had come to an end. But, for the first time today, they were not tears of sorrow. So many people speaking fondly of Robert was truly heartwarming for her to hear. The tension was gradually easing from Lydia's shoulders, as the crushing weight of grief was now beginning to lift, at least temporarily.

Across the living room and through the narrow door that led into the kitchen, Lydia could faintly hear Jessica and Christian talking. The pair were quietly discussing a film that they both wanted to see, whilst they were working their way through washing and drying the pile of dishes littering the worktops. Her granddaughter no longer seemed troubled by the events of the morning. After a brief conversation in the car on the journey back from the church, Susanna had managed to convince them all that it had just been the stress of the day, and a trick of the light that had distressed her daughter so. Robert's funeral had been the first time that Jessica had ever had to visit a graveyard. They all knew that the teenager regularly entertained herself by watching horror films and reading scary stories. And, add that to an overactive teenage imagination, and it shouldn't have been a surprise that the girl had become spooked so easily back at the graveyard.

Susanna, having seen that her mother was finally alone, momentarily stepped out of a conversation about holiday destinations with some of the other women, in order to approach Lydia.

"Mum, can we talk?" Susanna requested, as she quickly claimed the chair directly across from Lydia, and she reached over the gap to take her mother's hand in her own. A gesture that was both meant for comfort, but also demanded attention.

"You can always talk to me, love," Lydia reassured her, "what is it?"

"I don't like the idea of you being alone here, mum," said Susanna, "it's too far from town, and it's too far from us," she continued. "You're not as young as you used to be, mum, and if something were to happen, like if you fell, then there would be nobody here to help you. So, Christian and I have been talking, and we think that you should move in with us. That way, we would be able to look after you and you wouldn't have to be alone!" Susanna was hopeful as she spoke, yet she already knew what her mother's answer would be, even before Lydia replied.

"It is truly lovely of you to offer," said Lydia, "but I couldn't stand to be a burden." Susanna then began to open her mouth, about to protest against the comment, but she wasn't given the chance. "Besides, I like my own space. What makes you think I want all of you getting under my feet?" Lydia replied jokingly, with a mischievous glint in her eye. Her comment had instantly lightened the tension, and forced a small chuckle from her daughter. "I appreciate the gesture, I really do, but this is my home. It's mine and Robert's home. Leaving here would feel like leaving him, and I'm not ready to do that.

At least not yet. It's too soon," Lydia explained, her voice filled with sadness, yet, she refused to let the smile fall from her lips.

"Okay, mum," Susanna sighed in surrender, "I understand, but the offer is still on the table and our door is always open if you ever change your mind." She then rubbed her fingers over her mother's hand once more, before finally breaking the contact. "Do you fancy a drink?" Susanna asked, standing up with her own empty wine glass in hand. It was then that she noticed a woman lingering behind her, seemingly in line for a chance to speak to Lydia.

"A coffee would be lovely, dear," Lydia requested. Susanna nodded in agreement, before making her way towards the kitchen.

As soon as Susanna had moved, the other woman quickly approached Lydia, taking the vacant armchair whilst Susanna was absent.

The woman was rather skinny, her wrinkled face gaunt and her greying blonde hair tied back tightly. She looked permanently tired in a way that caused her to age beyond her years. Lydia knew this woman well. Her name was Marie, and she was a regular client. She attended Lydia's readings almost every week since her son had been killed in action overseas in Iraq, about six months ago. Marie had started out as a sceptic, coming to see Lydia out of pure desperation. However, her opinion had soon been reversed after just a single session. Now she was possibly

Lydia's biggest fan, or perhaps she was addicted. Either way, Marie was good for business!

"I just wanted to say how sorry I am," Marie confessed.

"Thank you," Lydia responded on impulse. Lydia watched intently as Marie's gaze wandered around the living room, carefully scanning the people before settling on the bookcase.

"I have read your new book!" Marie exclaimed, suddenly focusing on Lydia again, "I thought it was wonderful!" she added with a shy grin.

"I'm glad you liked it," Lydia replied tiredly.

"I have told some of my friends about what you do, about what you've done for me. They would also like to come and see you when you're feeling better," Marie informed. "You are going to keep doing it, aren't you? Helping people?" Marie added, sounding concerned.

"Honestly, I don't even think I could stop even if I wanted to," Lydia stated, only partly joking.

"You've helped me so much since I lost my Timothy, I'm not sure I could have coped without you," said Marie, "but knowing that he is still here in spirit, watching over me, and keeping me company is the only thing that keeps me going . . ." she paused, her breath catching in her throat as she forced herself not to cry. "I could never repay you for what you have done for me, but if there is anything I can do for you, anything you need, just call me, I'm not far away. Thanks to you Lydia, I know I'm not alone, and you don't have to be either," Marie declared, leaning forwards and giving Lydia a shy hug.

***

It was now late, and all of Lydia's friends and family had returned to their own homes. She was now truly all alone in her little cottage. Downstairs, the house was still in disarray. The meagre remains of the buffet were going stale on the dining room table, and the kitchen sink had been left full of glasses that needed time to soak. Lydia would tend to both tasks in the morning, no longer having the energy left to clean up.

Instead, Lydia had retreated to her bedroom. The house was eerily quiet as she curled up in her bed in the dark. The sheets on Robert's side of the bed felt unnaturally cold to her touch. As her fingers traced the spot where Robert used to sleep beside her, the hollow feeling in her chest began to set in once more. The pain of grief was overwhelming, and for a fleeting moment she couldn't breathe past it. The tears once again began to fall. Lydia now let them flow freely with nobody around to see her. A damp patch formed on her pillow as her sobs echoed and faded off into the silence of the house. On the first night since burying her husband, Lydia Jones cried herself to sleep. It was an act that she had done every night since Robert's death, and an act that she would repeat for countless nights to come.

CHAPTER 3

Home Alone

The time since Robert's death had passed quickly. Hours became days, days had turned into weeks, and weeks had bled into months. Still, the grief had not faded, lingering in Lydia's every waking hour and haunting her dreams. There was nothing she could do to remove the hollow feeling she felt within. However, Lydia had quickly learned that staying busy helped to ward it off, at least for a little while. So, she threw herself into her work, hosting readings everyday to provide the human interaction she so desperately needed.

Lydia Jones was an experienced medium, and over the years she had managed to single herself out from the fraudsters and the amateurs. Now, she was viewed by her clients and others in the profession as an expert in her field. Her last published work had become a national bestseller in its genre. If it wasn't for the fact she always wrote under a pen-name, she would surely be hounded by fans day and night. Her popularity was mostly down to

Lydia's honesty in her writing. She had always been brutally honest, both in her books and with her clients. The public consistently had unrealistic expectations about what a medium could achieve during a reading. It had been explaining these facts that had made Lydia's latest work so successful!

Besides Lydia's clients, her daughter Susanna would come to visit almost every day. Her daughter would call in for a coffee after work, bring groceries, and also take Lydia out shopping at the weekends. But, even with the constant stream of people coming through her door, Lydia still felt lonely. Her house was too isolated for her neighbours to just drop in, and she had no means of going anywhere on her own. She had never learned to drive, and since both her husbands had been avid drivers, it had never before been necessary. Naively, it had never occurred to her that she might be alone one day. Now, Lydia wished that she had taken the time to learn to drive. Maybe it wasn't too late to learn. She could finally get her driving licence, and then escape the prison that her home was now quickly becoming.

Night time was always the worst for Lydia, lying in bed without Robert by her side. It felt like a betrayal against him, she felt guilty for still being here without him.

Obviously, with all her years of experience and extensive skill, Lydia had tried many times to use her gifts to contact her Robert. But, each time she tried it had been unsuccessful, and each time it broke her heart a little more. In a way, she hoped that the lack of contact with

Robert proved that he had already moved on to the afterlife. Yet selfishly, she desperately hoped he was still here by her side.

Today was to be like any other. Lydia was currently preparing her reading room for a new client. She went about lighting candles and incense sticks to help add the ambience that people associated with her craft.

The reading room had once been the dining room within the little cottage. But, since both Robert and Susanna objected to her so called 'hobby', she had commandeered the dining room for her needs. Lydia and Robert normally shared their meals in the kitchen or in front of the television, so nobody would ever eat in there anyway, hence the room was not missed. After spending a few decades in the trade, Lydia knew how to make the right impression on her clients, and her reading room was how she accomplished this. In essence, the room was clearly recognisable as a dining room, and would probably still be serviceable as such if an occasion presented itself. These days the room would be stacked with piles of books overflowing from the bookcase. Candles littered practically every surface, all at various degrees of life, dried tears of wax running down their sides and pooling at their bases where it had cooled. The walls were covered in pictures and symbols from across the globe, all representing spirituality or the occult from several religions. Long red lace curtains concealed the only window, and cast the entire room in a crimson shadow. The dining table was now home to a large spirit board, her most useful tool. Although letter dice and tarot cards also sat upon its surface, ready for Lydia to use during her sessions. The reading room was also home to several other objects of intrigue. People often claimed these objects could help contact the deceased. These items included a crystal ball which often drew the attention of her clients. The glass ball was purely for decorative purposes, as was practically everything else within the room. Lydia did not need any of this tat that resided within the room, but each item served its purpose, and gave her clients exactly what they were expecting to see. The items in the reading room, much like a gypsy's tent at a funfair, intrigued people and enticed them in. This form of showmanship helped to hold their attention until she had a chance to use her gift properly, and prove herself as a professional.

When the doorbell rang, Lydia instinctively knew that it would be her new client. She hurried off to answer the front door, desperate for the human contact that would help drain her own grief away, whilst she bathed in the sorrow of others. It was a depressing truth that anyone coming to visit a medium would not be doing so gleefully. In Lydia's experience there were three kinds of clients. Firstly, the 'curious' type, desperately looking for a sign of the afterlife or for a glimpse of a ghost. Secondly, the 'agnostics', who wanted nothing more than to expose her as a fraud. Thirdly, and finally the 'grieving', those people who are so sad or alone, that they would do anything for just a glimpse of their loved ones once more. A feeling that Lydia now understood on a more personal level than ever before.

The doorbell sounded once more, and with a composing sigh, Lydia quickly pulled open the door revealing a young woman standing on the doorstep.

"Oh, hello," the young woman greeted, giving a nervous smile. Immediately, Lydia could tell that this woman was a 'griever'. From the dull grey shades of her clothing to the still red rings around her eyes, giving away that she had recently been crying. A wave of pity then passed over Lydia. The young woman held out her hand for Lydia to take in a gesture of introduction. "I'm Amelia. I think we have an appointment. Marie sent me. Are you the psychic?" the woman asked shyly.

"I prefer the term medium, but please call me Lydia," she replied, taking Amelia's offered hand and shaking it firmly. Retreating back into her home, Lydia then led the way to her reading room and held the door open for Amelia to enter.

"What a lovely home you have," Amelia commented, having followed Lydia through the house. But, Lydia didn't miss the way the other woman became tense upon seeing the reading room. It was a common reaction as the fear of the unknown crept in!

"Please, take a seat," Lydia gestured at the dining table, "can I get you anything before we begin? Tea, coffee?"

"No, I'm fine thanks," Amelia replied, taking a seat at the table. She paused to pull a newspaper out from within her handbag, before dropping the bag to the ground by her feet. "Marie said that you like puzzles, so I've brought you this. I've finished reading it and none of the puzzles have been done," Amelia informed, holding out a folded newspaper and laying it at the end of the table.

"Ah, thank you, that's very thoughtful. I don't get out much these days, but the weekly Sudoku puzzles are my guilty pleasure," Lydia smiled kindly. She pushed the paper aside before taking her own seat. "Now, before we begin I want to ask you a few questions, and explain a few things so that we both know what we are hoping to achieve, and what to expect," Lydia informed calmly. "Who is it that we are trying to contact today?"

"My husband, Arthur," said Amelia, "he died in an accident last month. It was a hit and run caused by a drunk driver!" Amelia explained, beginning to choke on her words, as she was forced to stop and compose herself.

"Would you like a tissue?" Lydia asked compassionately.

"That's okay, I have some with me, as I need them a lot these days," Amelia replied. Lydia could sympathise with Amelia, as since Robert's death Lydia herself could not go a day without breaking down and crying, sometimes for seemingly no reason at all. The packet of tissues that she had stuffed into her pocket had quickly become a permanent fixture.

"Take your time, but can you let me know what you would like to achieve from this session?" Lydia questioned calmly.

Amelia stifled another sob before answering, "Arthur and I had always promised that if anything happened to either of us, we would do everything in our power to let the other one know that we were okay. I've tried calling out to him alone, but I didn't know what I was doing. So, I figured maybe coming to you would be the best way forward. Marie speaks very highly of you. I think she is even trying to start a fan club at the community centre in your honour," Amelia explained, a hint of amusement entering her voice as she spoke.

"Oh dear, I hope not!" Lydia replied with a chuckle. "Did you bring something of Arthur's like I asked?" Lydia added, as she continued with the session.

Amelia bent down and began fumbling through her handbag again. This time she emerged with a pair of silver cufflinks and a photograph clutched tightly in her hand. She passed them over to Lydia, who gently took both items from her. The cufflinks were nothing special, made from a bland metal that looked inexpensive and well worn. They were most likely used regularly for work. The photograph was of a young man smiling at the camera, as he held a bundled up infant child in each arm.

"Do you have children?" Lydia enquired.

"Yes, twin boys. Terry and Charlie. They'll be five in a few weeks," Amelia replied.

"How precious," Lydia said, placing the photograph onto the table. "Now, before I attempt to make contact, it is important that you understand a few things," she informed.

"Okay," Amelia acknowledged, sounding nervous.

"It's important that you understand that not all spirits can be contacted," Lydia began, "some of them don't want to be called, and others have already crossed over. In that case, there is nothing we can do to contact them. I just want you to be prepared, because there is no guarantee that we will be able to contact a spirit at all, and even if we do, it might not be Arthur," Lydia explained.

"What do you mean?" Amelia questioned.

"Well, when we call out to a spirit, it's not just the ones we call for who can hear us. Any spirit that lingers close will be able to hear the call," Lydia informed. Amelia began to look panicked by this revelation. "But, there are things we can do to increase our chances. Normally, when someone dies, their spirit will become attached to a person or a possession that they were close to, and that's why we need something personal of Arthur's," she explained.

"Is this dangerous?" Amelia requested to know, as if realising the possibility for the first time.

"No. Spirits can communicate with us, but they can't hurt us," Lydia reassured. But, this was actually a lie. Lydia had heard many stories from other people in her profession who had met malevolent spirits and angry ghosts, some of which were capable of extreme force and acts of violence. Luckily, Lydia herself had never experienced anything like that, but she had no doubt that they existed.

"Well, that's a relief," Amelia sighed, resting her hand over her heart for dramatic effect.

"The other thing to remember, is that the dead do not have a voice. That is why we have to use tools to give them a way to speak with us. Personally, I prefer using the board, but there are other methods if you have any preference," Lydia prompted.

"No, the board is fine with me. Marie mentioned that's what you normally use with her," Amelia responded.

"Okay, so now we are clear, are you ready to begin?" Lydia quizzed, holding out her hands for the other woman to take.

"Yes. I'm nervous, but I'm ready," Amelia confirmed, taking Lydia's hands firmly in her own, watching intently as Lydia took a deep breath, raising her head to stare at the darkness of the ceiling before closing her eyes.

"Spirits of the past hear my voice, be guided by my voice and come towards us. We wish to communicate with Arthur Wells. Follow my voice Arthur. Do you hear our call?" Lydia recited into the quiet room. Amelia held her breath as silence consumed the room, she looked around anxiously for any sign that they were not alone. Amelia suddenly gasped when a candle beside her flickered violently.

"We have made contact with a spirit," Lydia stated calmly, addressing Amelia.

"Is it Arthur?" Amelia questioned expectantly.

"I'm not sure," Lydia replied, her eyes still tightly closed. She continued. "Arthur, is that you? Amelia would like to speak with you. Do you wish to communicate with us?" Another candle flickered, this one resting beside the spirit board. Lydia took this as confirmation. Finally, opening her eyes, Lydia gently unhooked one of her hands from Amelia's and placed her index finger lightly onto the planchette, gesturing for the other woman to do the same. Once both of them were situated, Lydia took another calming breath, before continuing with the session. "Arthur, if that is you, please use the board to speak to us. Feel our energy and use us as a tool to give you a voice. Use our hands to write your words. Can you do that for us?" Lydia called out.

There was a pause before the planchette was swiftly pulled directly across the board by an invisible force! And, looking through the magnifying glass of the planchette where it had abruptly stopped, revealed a single word, *'Y-E-S'*!

"Oh my god!" Amelia gasped, a look of horror written across her face.

"Take a deep breath. I know this maybe overwhelming the first time, but you are safe here with me. Everything is fine," Lydia attempted to soothe, worried that the other woman would panic further and disrupt the connection. "Is there anything you would like to ask, to help confirm this is Arthur we are communicating with?"

"Erm," Amelia mumbled, attempting to think rationally through her shock, "how we met . . . ask him how we met!" Amelia decided.

It took a moment, but once again the planchette began to fly around the board, dragging their fingers with it as it jumped from letter to letter, *'P-L-A-N-E'*, the planchette spelt out circling the board once more before continuing to spell, *'D-R-I-N-K'*, before stillness took over once again.

"Plane and Drink?" Lydia questioned, "does that mean anything to you?"

"Yeah! Yes, yes it does! He's right, that's how we first met!" Amelia nodded her head repeatedly in confirmation, looking tearful once more as she explained. "I was an air hostess on a flight back from Dubai, and I spilt a drink all over him in mid flight. He said I had to go to dinner with him to make it up to him," she chuckled a little through her tears at the fond memory. "Oh Arthur, I've missed you so much!" Amelia exclaimed, looking up at the empty gloom above the board expectantly, in awe, tears flooding her eyes.

The rest of the session was pretty uneventful for Lydia. It was a scene she had witnessed many times before, and would probably see again many more. Amelia had continued to throw out questions such as, "are you okay?" and, "will we ever be together again someday?" Arthur had answered positively, but Lydia had the feeling that he had been lying for his young widow's sake. This was another thing she had seen many times before. Just because a person has died doesn't mean that they lose their ability to be untruthful. Lydia knew full well that Arthur would not discover the restraints of what was and what wasn't possible for spirits, until he chose to move on to the other place. Be that paradise or limbo, nobody still living knows.

The session had been a long one, stretching well past the one hour time limit that Lydia usually kept. But, since it had been Amelia's first session and Arthur hadn't shown any signs of fading, she had let it pass. Finally, the spirit had began to weaken and his control of the planchette became sluggish.

Lydia had explained to Amelia what was happening, that spirits ran out of energy after a time when interacting with the living. She encouraged Amelia to say her goodbyes, and the other woman had reluctantly complied, but it was Arthur who got the final say.

'I-L-O-V-E-U', the planchette wrote, before coming to a deathly stop on the board.

Amelia had left Lydia's cottage in tears, but not before arranging another session for the following week.

***

It was late in the evening now and Lydia was once again home alone, a feeling that she had become accustomed to, but could not enjoy. The dead silence of a house that had once been so full of life was unsettling. Her beloved home now felt foreign to her, and the loneliness was setting in more each day. Susanna had offered countless times to share her home, but Lydia would be damned before she became a burden on her daughter. But still, perhaps it was now time for her to move on and leave this place behind. She had done it before after her divorce, and she could do it again now.

It was the memories that were the most painful. Everywhere she looked, it was like an old film reel repeating in her head, all the good times that had been and would never be again.

Lydia was stood at her kitchen sink, washing the dishes from the pasta bake she had cooked for dinner, and then only picked at. Since Robert's death her appetite had diminished drastically. Every evening she went through the motions of cooking a meal as she had always done, but as soon as she sat down at the kitchen table alone, she instantly felt hollow with loneliness. She felt nauseous with the returning grief of loss, whilst she stared across at the empty chair sitting opposite her.

It was as she was rinsing her hands from the suds, that a familiar cold feeling sent a shiver up Lydia's spine. A cool breeze blew through the room, ruffling the old off-white net curtains that concealed the kitchen window. It moved across the kitchen catching hold of the pages of the newspaper Amelia had left, which was now sitting on the kitchen table. Lydia watched as the pages flipped over rapidly, flying by in a blur, before coming to a sudden stop as the cold breeze abruptly vanished. Irritated due to the cold that now invaded her body, Lydia marched towards the window, throwing back the curtains dramatically with every intention of slamming the window shut. However, she was unprepared to find that the window was indeed already shut tight. Looking around in shock, Lydia searched for any other location that the sudden wind could have originated from. But, there were no other windows in the room and the back door was securely bolted. Goosebumps now littered her skin, and Lydia huddled her own arms to try and alleviate them. The newspaper was now sitting still, its pages wide open and its contents sprawled out across her kitchen table provocatively. She moved closer, curiosity drawing her towards the pages and the air of mystery they leaked. Reaching out, Lydia traced her fingers over the edge of the paper, perhaps just to prove to herself that it was real. She began to scan the open page with intent, wrinkles forming at the corners of her eyes with concentration as she read one advert after another. *'A coupon for a local fast food restaurant, a seemingly endless sofa sale, and a new second hand car dealership'.* But, nothing remarkable stood out to her, until one rather large advert finally did! It was the picture that first caught her attention.

It showed the front profile of a very impressive looking Georgian period house on a gloriously sunny day. The large glass windows of the house and conservatory were reflecting in the sun, creating a mirage affect. In front of the main building was a central driveway, dividing the immaculately maintained grounds of the estate. A statue of a Roman centurion could be seen resting upon a pedestal in the centre of the lawn. The photograph was instantly mesmerising, reminiscent of a setting for a great Victorian novel. Consumed with interest, Lydia eagerly began to read the advert in detail.

'CARNATION HALL'
Assisted Living Apartments – Retirement Home
A place where senior citizens truly feel at home. A perfect home for mature adults who want to keep their independence and remain active, yet have the services they need on hand to continue living a confident and happy life.
Located in the rural countryside, our community offers each resident a quiet and peaceful place to spend their retirement.
Each resident has their own private apartment, fully equipped to their needs, to keep that feeling of independence, whilst our staff also provide additional daily services, such as meals, laundry and housekeeping, giving all our residents the chance to live as independently as they like, but with none of the stress.
Our many communal rooms and activities help residents make lasting friendships and enjoy their retirement to the full.
From daily book groups in our library, to afternoon tea on the lawn, there are many engaging and interesting activities our residents can enjoy every day.
Contact us today for more information or to request a viewing.

Once she had finished reading, a flutter began in Lydia's chest. Perhaps this would be the answer to her current predicament, an escape from her lonely existence. She then proceeded to carefully cut the advertisement from the rest of the newspaper using a pair of scissors, and once it was free, she pinned it to her fridge door using the magnet usually reserved for her weekly shopping list. The advert now held pride of place upon the fridge, just as a small child's artwork would decorate a family home. Lydia looked at it proudly, a plan forming in her head, and the beginnings of hope forming in her heart. She would begin by discussing the advert and the idea of leaving her once beloved home when Susanna next visited.

That night, Lydia was lying alone in her bed once more. A small smile stubbornly tugging at the corners of her mouth. For the first time since Robert's death, she didn't fall asleep to the lullaby of her own sobbing.

CHAPTER 4

Carnation Hall

Long shadows were being cast through the windows of Susanna's four-wheel drive. Each shadow being formed by the light creeping its way between the surrounding trees, as the car steadily rolled along the road. They had been travelling on this country road for several minutes, and as the time passed, the surrounding woodland was continuing to grow more dense. The advertisement for the retirement home informed that the property was very private, but Lydia was beginning to think that they were now lost somewhere along the way.

Susanna had graciously agreed to drive her mother to Carnation Hall for a viewing, as she was sceptical about her mother wanting to move into an 'old folks' home'. Once again, she insisted that Lydia would be far happier coming to live with her, but Lydia was a persistent woman. So, Lydia encouraged Susanna to do some research, such as finding some reviews on the internet, and maybe talking directly to a member of staff on the telephone. Susanna eventually conceded, and arranged an appointment for a viewing with Lydia, she even agreed to drive her mother there personally.

The property was apparently not too far out of town, and actually fairly close to where Susanna and her family were living. However, it now felt as though they had been driving on this back road for hours. Lydia was now contemplating whether or not to question her daughter's directional skills, since Susanna did not have such a great track record for map reading. But, before she could speak, Lydia had noticed a break in the dense trees ahead.

The first sign that they had arrived at their destination was upon reaching an extremely large and imposing iron gateway, seemingly appearing to them from nowhere in amongst the trees. The giant metal frame that was once black and shining, now appeared dull, having become amber in colour after years of corrosion. The damage clearly due to ageing and weathering. The gates were stood wide open like welcoming arms, encouraging and enticing them to enter its embrace.

Either side of the main gateway stood a tall firm pillar of support, each covered in faded stone cladding. Green ivy had began to creep its way along the columns, and entangle itself tightly around the edges of the gates. The foliage was so dense that the hedge blended almost perfectly with the trees, and shielded the property from the road like a veil. Each of the supporting pillars were topped by a stone grey statue of a raven, one on each side, but each in a slightly different pose. The raven on the left was standing tall, back straight and head up. It looked proud as it watched over the woodlands that surrounded the property. Whilst the raven on the right was a little more intimidating. It appeared to be stooping, with its wings tightly folded in as it peered down, glaring intently at anyone who would dare occupy the gateway. The raven's stare was so intense, that if Lydia didn't know any better, she would have sworn the stone creature was judging her worth as they passed through its gates.

The sound of the tyres suddenly changed as the car left the tarmac road and pulled onto the driveway, gravel now crunching under its wheels. Everything now appeared much brighter after leaving the shaded and sheltered woodland road. The sun was high in the sky and shining brightly down upon them. Directly ahead of them stood the main building, its grand and domineering presence impossible to ignore as they approached. In front of the house the gravel covered road divided, forming a loop that encircled a rather grand looking ornate flower bed. In the centre of this immense garden feature stood an elaborate-looking three-tiered fountain. On top of the fountain there was another statue, this was a stone statue of a young maiden kneeling, her features soft and relaxed as water flowed from the vase she carried. The falling water sparkled brightly in the sunlight as it continuously ran gently over the fountain's edges, raining down onto the lower tiers in a never ending cycle. The rest of the flower bed was filled with immaculately maintained rows of flowers. Vibrant reds, whites, yellows and pinks, standing out as a vast contrast to the pale grey stone of the fountain.

Susanna brought the car to a halt, directly in front of the main entrance to the property. It was obvious to see that the old wooden doors had been restored to help retain the classic and period feel of the house. The way that they were left wide open was giving the impression of an invitation to enter.

Now that they were both stood directly in front of the house, it became even more imposing. Huge Georgian windows loomed over the driveway, the glass panes mirroring the sun in such a way, that it was impossible to look within the building from outside. Lydia felt like a suspect in an interrogation room analysing the glass of a two way mirror, hoping to see a glimpse behind its cold surface. She couldn't shake off the feeling that someone was watching them from within, as Susanna guided her through the main doors and into the house.

"Well, I've got to say mum, I knew this place would be nice, but I had no idea it would be so fancy looking. It looks like Downton Abbey!" Susanna stated jokingly, as she led the way through to the grand looking entrance hall.

A wide staircase with a perfectly polished dark oak banister hugged the left wall straight ahead of them, rising up to the first floor. To her immediate right, Lydia could see through to a classy looking dining room where several tables had been laid out, presumably ready for lunch. Immediately to her left, on the opposite side of the foyer there appeared to be a large communal lounge area. Several people occupied the room, a couple reading quietly, whilst a few more gathered around the television enjoying its daytime offerings. It was at this point that Lydia caught sight of a woman, perhaps a few years senior to Susanna, walking confidently towards them. She had bleach blonde hair, immaculately combed into a bob cut which reached down to her shoulders. She was dressed in a bright floral shirt and expensive looking designer jeans. A warm smile cemented the woman's features that grew as she approached Lydia.

"Hello! You must be Mrs Jones. It's a pleasure to finally meet you," the woman greeted in a friendly tone. She then held out a hand for Lydia to shake.

Lydia took the offered gesture and shook firmly before replying, "yes, that's right. Please, call me Lydia."

"My name is Kelly. I'm the manager here at Carnation Hall. Are you excited to take a look around? I'm sure you are going to be pleased with everything here. I run a very tidy ship," the woman said enthusiastically, not taking her gaze away from Lydia. "How about we start by taking a look at the vacant apartment, then I can give you a tour around the rest of the establishment and grounds," Kelly suggested. However, the way Kelly confidently locked her arm with Lydia's, and began to lead her towards the stairs, suggested that there was no room for debate upon the idea.

"It's very nice to meet you Kelly," Susanna suddenly spoke up, her tone suggesting a slight distaste at not being addressed yet.

"Sorry! Where are my manners?" Kelly responded, still cheerful. Kelly suddenly stopped and turned around to face the younger woman, breaking her contact with Lydia as she did so. "And you are?" Kelly questioned.

"This is my daughter, Susanna. She's the one who called to arrange today's viewing," Lydia replied, stepping closer towards her daughter, and placing her hand on the small of Susanna's back in a gesture of solidarity. Even before they had left her cottage this morning, Lydia had sensed that Susanna would be determined to not like her potential new home. Her daughter was fiercely protective, and secretly still felt discouraged that her mother had refused to go and live with her. Perhaps, it was merely the thought in Susanna's mind, that another woman could be Lydia's first point of assistance from now on that she didn't like. Perhaps, it was simply that Susanna feared that she was being replaced that had Lydia's daughter so set on disagreeing with her mother's plans. Antagonising the staff at the Hall was Susanna's first act of defiance.

"It's nice to meet you too," Kelly remarked, still smiling happily. "The apartment is on the first floor, so luckily there aren't a lot of stairs to contend with," Kelly explained, as she boldly began to lead the way once more towards the staircase. "If either of you have any questions then please let me know and I'll be happy to help."

And with that, Kelly marched on, leaving Lydia and Susanna to follow in her footsteps up the old wooden staircase, they then turned left, continuing down a long hallway. Upstairs the building became significantly darker, but no less aesthetically pleasing. The hallway itself maintained the same Georgian style as the rest of the house. Dark polished wooden floors crept up and joined the wooden panelling along the walls, reaching waist height, before being replaced by elegant olive-green wallpaper. At the end of the hallway a square panelled window offered the only light source, letting a warm glow enter the otherwise gloomy passageway. A few paintings also complimented the walls of the hallway, displaying picturesque woodland scenes and landscapes of tranquil green and golden fields. The artwork was presented proudly from within rustic looking frames that hung tastefully along the walls. The corridor was also home to four wooden doors, two on each side of the hallway, and each door having a shining brass number placed upon it.

Kelly led them confidently to the end of the hallway, coming to a halt at a door presenting a bold number *'11'*.

"Here we are!" Kelly said in a singsong tone. She smiled broadly as she pulled at the handle and led the way into the room. Susanna and Lydia then quickly followed.

Lydia could feel her heart pounding in her chest from anticipation, as she followed the other two women into what could possibly be her new home.

The first thing Lydia noticed as she entered the apartment, was the transition from hardwood floor to soft cushioned carpet under her feet. The silent soft landing of her footfalls taking her by surprise.

The apartment was actually far more grand than Lydia had been expecting. In her mind, she had imagined that it would be somewhat cold and clinical, like a mix between a budget hotel and a hospital. However, the reality was nothing of the sort. The decor was light and airy, with soft creams and caramel colours. Immediately upon entering the apartment, a small reception room split into two further open doorways. On the left was the bedroom, a large double bed taking pride of place confirming this fact. The bedroom was also adorned by expensive looking white painted hardwood furniture, consisting of two bedside tables, a dresser and a substantial wardrobe. The only sign that the bedroom wasn't lived in, was the sight of a bare duvet which sat rolled up tightly at the foot of the bed.

The door on the right led through to a larger room, opening into a combined open plan kitchen and living room, with a small dining area by the window. A subtle, yet stylish fireplace centred the room with a television placed on the wall above. An elegant sofa sat opposite the fireplace with a glass topped coffee table before it. All the furniture throughout the rest of the apartment maintained the light and modern style, making each room alluring and inviting.

"I thought the apartment was supposed to be unfurnished?" Susanna enquired. Her attention was firmly locked on Kelly, who was stood casually occupying the doorway.

"Usually they do, but our previous resident sadly didn't have any family, and left all her personal possessions to the Hall. So, in the circumstances we were willing to include the furniture with the apartment. Obviously, if you would prefer to bring your own furniture, then that could easily be arranged. The choice would be totally yours Lydia," Kelly explained, looking eager as she watched Lydia wander from room to room.

"Well, whoever she was, she had good taste!" Susanna commented, admiring the expensive looking cream sofa. "What do you think mum?" she asked.
Lydia just nodded her head in agreement as she continued to browse the room. She suddenly found herself speechless as the opportunity of a future here began to form in her mind.

"When you are ready, we can continue with the tour," Kelly gleamed.

***

Lydia was quickly growing to like Kelly as the woman merrily led them all around the old house, pointing out what activities were held at the Hall, and who would organize what. The Hall was becoming more and more enticing by the second. It wasn't just a place to live, it was a community with activities and events happening daily. If Lydia decided to move here she would not only gain a new home, but she would also gain an adventurous social life, the likes of which she had never known before. She had always been a very private person, even when she was living alone or with either of her husbands. It had always been just themselves in the house day after day. Apart from shopping trips or the occasional seaside break, Lydia never really ventured anywhere. She was always restricted to being kept alone inside her home due to her inability to drive, or in the case of her first husband, an unwillingness to ever publicly socialise together. Ray had been a creature of habit, and even after they had been married several years and had a small child together, he had always insisted on spending his nights at the pub with his workmates. He never evolved from his bachelor mentality and the habits that came with it. No matter how many times she suggested that they should go out together, Lydia was never allowed to accompany him. *'The pub was a place for men'*, Ray had always told her, and their daughter Susanna needed a mother's constant supervision. Perhaps the main factor in their divorce had been the fact that they had never spent enough time together, or maybe some things are simply not meant to be.

Back in the present, Kelly was currently leading them through the lounge area that Lydia had already spied upon earlier. The room was still occupied with a few residents watching the television as before, though now a football match was flashing across its screen.

"This is our communal lounge. Although all of the private apartments do contain their own television sets, a lot of the residents prefer to spend their time here in the company of others. We even have a TV schedule, all you have to do is put your name down on the list in the foyer, and you can reserve a slot. There are occasional disagreements, but the system works well for the most part," Kelly explained, catching Lydia's gaze whilst she observed a group of men watching the football. "There are also many games and activities in here that you are free to enjoy," Kelly then added, before leading them further into the living room and then onward through into the conservatory. It was the same glass covered room that Lydia had first spotted in the advert. The conservatory was huge, an entirely glass panelled structure that glimmered brightly as it brought light flooding through its windows. The room was beautiful in Lydia's opinion. Several comfy looking wicker sofas and chairs were spread about in tasteful order, coffee tables filling the gaps between them. The conservatory was also home to a vast array of greenery, in the form of house plants that filled the room with colour. Potted plants of all shapes and sizes were used as additional decoration, many filled with blooming flowers. The entire conservatory was filled with the scent of wonderful roses and lavender, a natural perfume that could not be bested by even the most expensive of designers. Along one wall, an imposing set of double glass doors had been opened and led out into the Hall's luscious and spacious grounds. It had all been designed in such a way that the conservatory itself felt like an extension of the garden. Lydia was made speechless by its beauty. Her hand discreetly rose up to her eye, and quickly removed a tear before anyone could notice its existence.

The garden of her cottage had always been Lydia's favourite place and also Robert's great passion. She had spent countless hours enjoying its company whilst writing her book, pruning the roses or simply just taking in the fresh air and rare English sun. But, her little garden couldn't hold a candle compared to the splendour of the Hall's grounds. Deep down she knew that Robert would have adored this place, and a quick stab of guilt struck her for not having discovered it while he was still alive.

"I'll show you around the grounds in a few moments Lydia. But, perhaps first you would like to speak to one of our residents, in order to get an insider's view on what living here is like," Kelly suggested in a cheery tone that left no room for disagreement. Kelly immediately scurried them towards the back of the conservatory, where a lady about Lydia's age was sat in the sunlight reading a book. The lady didn't take much notice of their approach, as she was too engrossed in her book. The words on the pages met her eyes through a distinctive pair of thick-framed bright red glasses, that where continuously slipping down her nose.

"How are you doing today Kate?" Kelly enquired, startling the woman somewhat from her reading. The woman looked up first with annoyance, and then with intrigue upon seeing the new faces beside Kelly.

"Oh, I am very well thank you. I see you have company," the woman, apparently called Kate, stated curiously.

"Indeed we do. This is Mrs Jones, she is here regarding the vacant apartment," Kelly explained. "I was wondering if you could help me by sharing your experiences of living here," Kelly said, before turning back to Lydia and Susanna. "Kate is actually one of our newer residents, but she should be able to give you a good feel for what living at the Hall is like. Susanna, why don't you and I take a quick trip to my office, and you can take a look over some of the purchase forms for the apartments here, whilst these two get better acquainted," Kelly suggested, already beginning to walk away.

"Will you be okay here, mum?" Susanna asked, a concerned smile on her face, clearly reluctant to leave Lydia unsupervised.

"She'll be fine, don't worry, I don't bite!" Kate jumped in with a teasing grin. She then swiftly pulled Lydia down into the unoccupied chair next to her.

"I'll be fine, love. You go and look over the paperwork for me, you're much better with that kind of thing than I am," Lydia encouraged.

Susanna momentarily hesitated, before straggling off after Kelly.

"Wow, she doesn't look too happy," Kate commented, as she watched the two younger women retreat.

"She's . . . protective," Lydia asserted, finally finding the desired word. "She's my only child and she doesn't like the idea of me moving into a place like this instead of moving in with her," she explained to Kate.

"Ah okay, I understand, but she has nothing to worry about. You're going to love it here!" Kate stated, relaxing back into her own chair.

"How long have you been here?" Lydia quizzed, also becoming more relaxed in her comfortable seat.

"About six months," came Kate's reply, "I moved here after my husband died. I didn't like the idea of living alone," Kate informed casually.

Lydia nodded in agreement, but didn't comment on it further. "And everybody here is friendly?" she enquired.

"Yep, pretty much. A few of the old dears can get a bit crabby every once in a while, and you'll probably learn the hard way to avoid Francesca whenever possible," Kate warned, but her tone was light and friendly.

"Who is Francesca or shouldn't I ask?" Lydia questioned, raising an eyebrow in interest.

"Trust me, you'll know her when you meet her," Kate smiled with a mischievous wink, "but, with all things considered, I'm very happy here and I wouldn't want to be anywhere else."

"And you are free to come and go as you please?" Lydia enquired.

"Of course! It's an assisted living complex, not a maximum security prison! We are free to do what we want when we want. We are all adults here after all," Kate reassured.

"I suppose you're right. I guess my daughter has been putting ideas in my head. She seems convinced that I'm going to be living under strict rules here," Lydia expressed with a nervous chuckle.

"Well, there are no rules that I know of, other than stay out of areas marked 'PRIVATE'. Though I don't know why anybody would want to go there anyway. Mostly just store rooms and Kelly's private office. Nothing exciting there as far as I'm aware. Anything else you'd like to know?" Kate asked with a welcoming smile.

"Not that I can currently think of, but thank you for your time," Lydia said gratefully.

"My pleasure. Besides, I have a feeling we are going to get along great when you move here," Kate stated.

"I haven't actually made my decision yet," Lydia responded somewhat shyly.

"Maybe not, but I'm an optimist," Kate teased.

A few moments later Kelly returned, strutting through the conservatory with Susanna in her shadow.

"Is everything alright with you two ladies?" Kelly asked enthusiastically.

"Having a lovely time, thank you," Kate responded, sending a playful glance Lydia's way.

"How about we finish this tour, mum?" Susanna suggested, seeming eager to move on.

"An excellent idea. Only the gardens left to see, and I don't think you'll be disappointed," Kelly informed. And, without a moment's notice, she was leading them off through the double French doors that led outside.

The conservatory led out onto a paved patio area, littered with quaint tables and chairs, with a potted flower on top of each one as an added touch of class. From here the patio would break out onto the lush green lawn area.

A monotone humming sound reached across the fields, drawing Lydia's attention towards a large sit down lawn mower. The faint smell of petrol filled the air, whilst a large bulking man could be seen driving the machinery up and down the lawn with expert precision.

Another prominent feature of the garden was the collection of stone statues placed on pedestals around the estate. Lydia's eyesight wasn't clear enough for her to see each statue in detail, but the closest one to her stood out as clear as day. The statue was in the form of a Roman goddess, her dismembered torso was weathered and crawling with moss, helping to show its age. The statues were an odd sight to perceive, not something Lydia would have expected to see around such a lavish garden. However, they didn't look out of place. In fact, the detailed stone statues added an extra layer of unique class to Carnation Hall. Actually, it had been a statue that she first noticed in the original advert for the Hall, and it had intrigued her enough to read the rest of the advert. The image had stuck in Lydia's memory ever since.

"Wow! Mum, this is a far bigger garden than your cottage has. I bet you'll be practically living out here. Might as well save some cash, let the apartment go and just pitch yourself a tent," Susanna suggested with a wink, stepping out behind her mother. "Kelly, these gardens are beautiful. Who takes care of them?" Susanna called over her shoulder, noticing the other woman was still lingering in the conservatory doorway.

"That would be my husband, Mitch. He is our resident grounds keeper and handyman. Any problem around here, he takes care of it!" Kelly replied proudly, throwing a warm smile towards the man sat on the lawn mower. "And there he goes now!" she added, waving vigorously at the man as he passed the group, bobbing along on his machine.

"Really! So one man does all this?" Susanna questioned in disbelief, "I would have thought you'd have a team. How many staff even work here?" she probed.

"We don't have too many actually. This is a private property and our residents are very private people. We aim to form a very intimate relationship with our residents, so we only have a few carefully selected staff members," Kelly offered as a response.

"That doesn't really answer my question though, does it?" Susanna stated.

"Well, for most of the daily tasks, we have eight staff members who come and assist us. Cooks, cleaners, etc. However, the only resident staff members are myself and my husband. We live on the property and are always here in case any of our residents require assistance," Kelly replied, a slight strain showing in her voice now but her smile never wavering. "Does that answer your question?" she asked Susanna, her gaze fixed sternly.

"Yes, thank you," Susanna accepted, purposely not meeting Kelly's glance. "So you don't own this place then? It's just when we spoke on the phone, I got the impression that . . ." Susanna tailed off, letting the words hang in the air.

"No. The house itself is owned by a trust, it is a listed building after all. The Hall is run by a group of investors in the city, they have several buildings that are commissioned in this way I believe. I am simply the manager here," Kelly clarified.

"Well, I must say, your husband is a very talented gardener. My husband loved gardening. He spent most of his life out in our little garden, it was his pride and joy, but I'm sad to say it was never a patch on this," Lydia voiced, halting whatever polite disagreement was occurring between Kelly and Susanna. Lydia didn't give either woman a chance to respond, before beginning to wander off towards the lawn. "I've never seen anything like this . . . the statues I mean. Where did they come from?" Lydia questioned, intrigued.

"My husband makes them," Kelly announced, "it's Mitch's hobby. He casts stone statues. Keeps him out of trouble," the woman jested.

"Quite a unique hobby," Susanna said in retort.

"He's a very special man," Kelly sharply replied, the look on her face daring a disagreement which never came. "Lydia dear, is there anything else you would like to see, or shall we go and have a coffee whilst we look over the deeds together?" Kelly enquired.

"No, I think I've seen more than enough to get a feel for the place. Thank you," Lydia grinned. "Lead the way!" she added, with excitement brewing in her chest.

***

The drive home from Carnation Hall was made in relative silence. As soon as they had left the property grounds, Susanna had began to protest her dislike for Kelly, calling her a snob and a few other choice words. But, she was quickly silenced by Lydia. Kelly's warm and cheerful persona had instantly resonated with Lydia. Although possibly a little over friendly, Kelly seemed like a very kind and positive person. How could she not be, working everyday with vulnerable elderly people. Lydia stating this point quickly silenced Susanna. However, her daughter was clearly still annoyed about the experience, and it seemed she had opted to give Lydia the silent treatment as revenge. It was only now, as they were pulling up into the driveway of Lydia's home, that Susanna began to acknowledge her mother once more.

"You're really going to do this aren't you?" Susanna asked, her gaze locked somewhere out of the windscreen. The sudden sound in the silence had been enough to startle Lydia, and she jumped to attention with fright as she turned and stared at her daughter.

"Do what?" Lydia questioned cautiously.

"Leave this place," Susanna replied, gesturing with her hand to the cottage situated before them.

"I have to!" Lydia gasped, suddenly feeling overwhelmed by the words alone. "I can't stay here. I can't stay here without him," she began to cry, "it's not my home any more. It was our home, but it's not my home, not alone! Everyday I wake up and I expect to see him! I expect to hear him! I expect to feel him lying beside me! But, he's never there and I'm always alone! I feel like the house is haunted now and it's killing me! I just can't be here any more!" Lydia exclaimed with a gasp, the intensity building as she spoke, until it stole her breath away.

"And you still won't come to us?" Susanna requested once again, desperation bleeding from her words.

"You know I won't!" Lydia persisted.

"Okay then," Susanna whispered, her voice barely audible.

"Okay?" Lydia echoed, unsure of the word's true meaning.

"Yes, okay! Make the move. I support your decision," Susanna clarified defeatedly.

"Really?" Lydia asked, not quite believing her own ears.

"Well, how could I not after the speech you just threw me," Susanna teased, "but I'm serious mum, I just want you to be happy. So whatever you need, whatever you want, we'll do it together!"

At that moment both mother and daughter broke down into streams of tears. Lydia couldn't contain herself any longer, reaching across to the driver's seat, and wrapping her arms tightly around Susanna's neck with a surprisingly strong grip. Her tears began to soak into Susanna's shirt, whilst they both sobbed gently. This interaction lasted several minutes before Lydia broke away. Her eyes red and raw, while her cheeks were painted a slight crimson from the embarrassment. Lydia didn't make a habit of crying in public, she was usually such a reserved and private person.

The rest of the day would pass very quietly. Lydia took a nap before spending the afternoon in her garden, whilst Susanna returned to her own home. Neither woman would mention the special moment they had shared in the car that morning, but neither would forget it either.

Susanna would keep to her word and assist Lydia in making her move as soon as possible. Before the end of the week, a new feature had been added to Lydia's cottage, a bright yellow sign was now hanging from a post beside her driveway. Large block letters were printed upon it, impossible to miss as it swayed gently in the breeze. Its prominent writing clearly displayed two words in bold lettering:

'FOR SALE'

CHAPTER 5

Moving Day

Lydia's quiet little cottage, which would normally only welcome a few stray visitors each week, was today filled with activity. There were people in almost every room, each performing their own designated tasks. Lydia's family were busy packing the last of her prized possessions neatly into boxes, and then moving said boxes into the now very cramped hallway, ready for collection. Today was the big day, the day that Lydia would finally move into her new apartment at Carnation Hall, and she could finally begin her new life.

They say that moving home is one of the most stressful things you can do, but for Lydia the task had so far been a breeze. There had initially been some difficulty actually finding a buyer for the cottage, but eventually it had gained a lot of interest. A young couple had originally placed an offer which Lydia had accepted, but the deal had fallen through upon them realising how far out of the city the cottage actually was. The commuting to and from the city would be too much for them, so they reluctantly backed out from the purchase. However, the right buyers did come along soon enough, a lovely middle aged couple who were both tired of the busy city, and were now craving the quiet of the countryside. After that, the sale had moved with extreme speed, far too quickly in fact, as Lydia was unable to complete all of her packing before the moving day arrived. An unexpected surprise had slowed the packing process down, and despite Susanna and Jessica's best efforts to help, they had been unable to catch up with the task.

Lydia had actually come to an agreement with her buyers to leave most of the furniture within the cottage. Apparently, they liked the classic old fashioned decor which Lydia had created within the cottage. However, it wasn't until the sale had gone through that Lydia realised just how many possessions she owned. After years of collecting ornaments and trinkets for her reading room, Lydia had convinced herself that she was the most likely one to have a hoarding problem. But, it had only taken one trip down to the bottom of the garden to Robert's shed, for her to discover just how mistaken she was. The shed was packed full of garden equipment and much more. Various tools were stacked sky high, bundled on top of each other all over the place in a haphazard manner. On another occasion, Lydia had also ventured into the loft in search of some empty boxes from the last time she had moved, in an attempt to get a head start on the packing. But, upon entry to the loft, she was overwhelmed to find it also was filled with what she considered junk. She found an array of electronic devices such as video players, radios, etc.., most of them seemingly broken beyond repair. Finding out that Robert had been hoarding so many things within their cottage had been quite a shock to Lydia. In the early days of their marriage, they had often visited car boot sales together. Lydia herself was in search of more items for her 'new at the time' reading room, whilst Robert eagerly looked for any items that he could restore and resell. Restoring such items had been a hobby of Robert's for many years, but this had faded with time, his passion turning instead to the upkeep of their garden, or so Lydia had thought. It had been unsettling to discover that Robert had taken to hiding things from her, especially within their home. She couldn't understand why he would feel the need to keep something from her in this way, and could only conclude that he must have been embarrassed about his habits.

In retrospect, Robert's old habits didn't really matter much now. However, it did mean that Lydia had to deal with the excessive contents of both the attic and the shed before moving day. She had hired a skip to deal with most of the junk, and had decided to donate practically everything that was in working order to a local charity shop, along with most of Robert's clothes and other possessions. It had been a very emotional and time consuming process, but with Susanna's help they had waded through it. Dealing with the clutter had greatly reduced Lydia's time available to pack the things she had wanted to take with her. Hence now, only hours away from leaving the cottage for the final time, she found herself still packing.

When the day finally arrived, Lydia signed over her home successfully. The drab yellow *'FOR SALE'* sign that was hanging in her front garden had now been covered over with an equally vile red *'SOLD!'* sign. Now, all that was left to do was for them to finish packing in time for the removal van to arrive, and carry away her personal effects.

Despite the joyous atmosphere inside the cottage, the weather outside was not consistent with the mood. A light sprinkling of rain had persisted since the early hours, speckling the windows, and constantly reminding those indoors that it was still falling.

Outside, the rumbling of a vehicle arriving could be heard, as a large white van pulled up triumphantly into Lydia's driveway. The driver, a bulking figure of a man, quickly disembarked and made a dash for the front door. He hammered upon the door with his fist to inform the occupants inside of his presence, protected by the porch that was sheltering him from the rain.

"I'll get it!" Jessica called from within. Her smaller stature allowed her to elegantly move through the maze created from the piles of boxes blocking the hallway, reaching the door in record time. She unhooked the catch and pulled open the door, revealing a large man beyond its frame. "Oh, hello!" Jess greeted, having to tilt her head up in order to catch the man's downward gaze.

"Hi," the man replied, taking a step forward and ducking down slightly in order to enter the house. "These the boxes to go?" he questioned, gesturing with his head tilted towards the boxes in the hallway.

"Yep, think so," Jess replied, ducking out of the way to let him pass. "Grandma! The Van Man is here!" she called.

Only a moment passed before Lydia began her own fight to get into the hallway, in order to greet the new arrival.

"Hello again, Mitch, thank you for coming," Lydia said, smiling up at him.

"No problem, I'm happy to help," Mitch replied, actually flashing the older woman a small smile.

"Can I get you a coffee or something, before we pack up?" Lydia offered.

"Sure! Coffee!" Mitch stated with a nod.

"No problem," Jess interjected, "milk and sugar?" she questioned.

"Yes," Mitch returned, "please," he then added as an afterthought.

"Why don't you take a seat, everyone is just finishing up packing," Lydia said as she ushered him through a doorway leading into the lounge.

Inside the lounge Christian was already settled on the sofa. He had a cardboard box at his feet, and bubble wrap over his lap, whilst he carefully went about the task of packaging porcelain figurines for transport. An increasingly frigid cup of coffee sat by his side, demonstrating how much time the task was consuming. Mitch eyed him disinterestedly as he claimed Lydia's favourite armchair.

"Hi, you're the guy from the home, right? Michael was it?" Christian asked, looking up from his work in an attempt to make conversation.

"Mitch!" the larger man corrected.

"Right, Mitch. Sorry!" Christian apologised, "but it's really nice of you to come and help Lydia like this," he commented, noticing Jess as she entered the room carrying a cup and handing it to Mitch.

"Yeah, it's really sweet of you to take time out for my grandma," Jess smiled, "she told me you take care of all the gardens and things at the Hall. I guess that must keep you pretty busy?" the girl enquired.

"It can do," Mitch replied, slurping ungracefully at his coffee. Jess waited patiently for the man to elaborate, however, after several seconds of silence she realised that would be the only reply she would get. Then, throwing a confused look in her father's direction, which he returned, Jess excused herself. She rushed back into the sanctity of the kitchen, and assisted her mother with packing the expensive looking crystal glasses. The living room then returned to silence as everybody continued to work.

About an hour later everybody was ready to leave. The packing was completely done, and the boxes from the hallway were now all safely stacked into the back of Mitch's white van. In reality, hardly any furniture was being transported. Only Lydia and Robert's precious armchairs were making the move with her. The other boxes were mostly filled with personal belongings such as clothes, soft furnishings and family pictures. The only boxes with any real weight were those containing the contents of her reading room. In truth, Lydia was undecided on whether or not she would continue her reading sessions after the move. However, she was content with the fact that she would have time to think over the decision.

Also in the van were several boxes destined for the local charity shop, clearly labelled *'British Heart Foundation'*. Mitch had very kindly offered to drop these boxes off on his way back to the Hall, which Lydia had thanked him greatly for. Before long, his van pulled out of her driveway and sped off down the road.

Lydia was presently stood in the doorway of her cottage looking extremely pensive. She had hold of the door handle, preparing to pull it closed for the very last time. She stared long and hard down the hallway, and with the lights switched off inside, it appeared dark and dull in the gloom of the day. A wave of emotion and sadness flooded through her body as she stood there in silence, replaying the memory of the last time she had stood there with Robert by her side. That day had been cold and wet also, the pair of them struggling to unlock the door and escape the weather outside. They had rushed into the warmth of the hallway and instantly felt the heat return to their bones, as the cosiness of their home welcomed them. In those days it had been as if the house itself was alive, always offering warmth and love to all who entered. But, since Robert's death, that feeling had seemingly died with him. The cottage now felt empty and distant to her, but she hoped with all her might that the new owners could bring the feeling of love back into the old building. After all the years of happiness it had shown her, Lydia wanted to think that the house could once again become a loving home.

With a long and final sigh, Lydia closed the door, hurriedly locking it and turning away, doing all that she could to maintain her composure.

Most of her family were already placed within Christian's car, with the man himself in the driver's seat and Jessica sat behind him. Jess was watching out of the window with a sympathetic look on her young face, whilst they both sheltered from the rain within the car. Susanna was not with them, instead, she was standing beside the car. Her ever immaculate hair being protected from the rain by a large umbrella she held over head. She held out her free hand towards Lydia, beckoning her to take it.

"Come on, mum," Susanna said, her voice calm and warm, "let's go and begin your new chapter," she added with a smile.

Holding back a tear, Lydia took the offered hand, and together they walked hand in hand down the driveway for the last time. The cottage was left behind to become just another memory.

***

By the time the family arrived at Carnation Hall, the mood had significantly brightened. The trip had been filled with Lydia and Jessica in deep discussion about all of the activities that the Hall had to offer, everything from monthly trips visiting museums and art galleries, to weekly sherry tastings which the residents themselves organised.

Now that the move was actually happening, Lydia was beginning to feel a little nervous. She would now be living with other people, even though not directly, Lydia could not fight the feeling that she was going to feel left out. Like the new girl in school, it would take some time for her to become accepted and part of the group. However, at least when she had first visited the Hall, Lydia had instantly hit it off with Kate, and she was fairly sure that the other woman would welcome her warmly. It was reassuring to know she had at least one person she knew on the inside. With her fears calmed for the moment, Lydia turned her thoughts back to the road, and was surprised to see that they had already reached the imposing iron gates, signalling the entrance to Carnation Hall. She glanced out of the side window, just in time to catch the eye of the stone raven sitting above the gate post, its piercing eyes glaring down at her once more as she passed.

Christian pulled the car into the driveway, and Mitch's van took shape ahead of them, with the man himself already carting Lydia's boxes inside. In the doorway, Kelly stood supervising her husband while he worked. Today, she was dressed in a tight black and white striped dress that hugged her figure, her hair positioned in its usual bob, and a displeased look on her face as she took in the damp weather.

Christian was the first one out of the car, and using his leather jacket as a temporary shelter from the rain, he jogged over to the van to catch Mitch's attention.

"Want a hand?" Christian called, pointing to the boxes still inside the van.

"Sure," Mitch replied with a shrug, before marching off inside the building with a box in his arms.

"Good talk," Christian muttered under his breath, before climbing into the back of the van and helping himself to a box.

Meanwhile, Lydia led the way to the entrance of the Hall, looking pleased when she saw Kelly with folded arms standing there waiting for them.

"Hello again Lydia. It's wonderful to see you," Kelly called out, stepping forwards and placing a kiss on each of Lydia's cheeks as a warm greeting. "How've you been? The move wasn't too stressful I hope," she added cheerfully.

"Oh no, I'm fine, my girls both helped me through it," Lydia told her with a smile, wrapping an arm around both Susanna and Jessica at her sides.

"Well, it's lovely to know you have such a caring family," Kelly said, looking the trio over with interest. "Shall we go in? No sense in us all standing out here getting wet, is there?" she suggested, already turning to leave. Kelly clearly expected the others to follow as she marched past the men, who were still ferrying in the contents of the van, and not sparing them a parting glance.

Once inside, Kelly led them up to Lydia's new apartment. The door was already propped open, and the lights were switched on inside, flooding the usually dark hallway with a single stream of light. Upon walking in, Lydia felt joy well up inside her, as she saw that her chairs had already arrived in their new home. Though clearly out of place, and standing out slightly from the other more modern furniture within the apartment, the familiarity that the chairs brought was comforting and priceless, just like seeing an old friend again.

"How about I put the kettle on while you all get settled. Just give me a shout if you need me," Kelly announced, striding off into the kitchen as if it were her own home. Nobody commented, the prospect of a hot drink was far too enticing to risk antagonising the woman.

Whilst they waited for Kelly's return, the rest of the group delved into the boxes now cluttering Lydia's new home. This act echoed the process they had all taken this morning, but this time in reverse order.

Susanna took it upon herself to locate the packed sheets and prepare Lydia's new bed. This way, at least her mother could retire for the night when she became fatigued, without having to worry about further unpacking. Jessica also assisted in the bedroom, hanging up her grandmother's clothes into the large double wardrobe.

Lydia herself was occupied in the living room. She had chosen a box at random and found it to be her private library. Deciding that this was as good a starting place as any, the mature woman started to unpack its contents, filling the bookcase standing in the corner of the room. Little effort was put into any form of organisation, as Lydia placed the books randomly onto the shelves. When the box was almost empty, Kelly stepped back into the room, carefully placing down a steaming mug of tea onto the coffee table, so as not to spill a drop. The blonde woman watched Lydia with intent, her hazel eyes wandering over some of the book titles with growing intrigue as they caught her eye. *'The True Purpose Of Tarot Reading'*, *'Voices From The Other Side'* and *'The Power Of Psychics: Facts vs Fiction'*, standing out boldly amongst the period dramas and the gardening manuals.

"You have some very interesting literature here, Lydia," Kelly commented, "is this an interest of yours? The supernatural, that is?" she enquired, raising an eyebrow.

"I suppose you could say that," Lydia replied, her smile becoming sheepish as she refused to meet the other woman's gaze. She was unsure of what Kelly or the other residents would make of her career, especially her gifts if they ever came to light. For now she had hoped to keep that information totally private.

"Well, it must be fascinating, perhaps you can educate me about it someday," Kelly said, continuing to browse the bookshelf. "I'm afraid my curiosity is getting the better of me. What was it that you did before you retired, Lydia?" the blonde asked, her tone light and casual, but there was no doubt that she was prying.

"I was . . . or rather am, a writer," Lydia stated, taking a seat in her armchair and grabbing the mug on the way.

"A writer? Really? Wow! Have you written anything that I may have read?" Kelly asked curiously.

"I doubt it. My works are all within a specific genre," Lydia replied, turning once more to the bookshelf. Kelly followed her gaze and realisation struck her.

"Oh! So some of these are yours? You really must be an expert!" Kelly gasped with excitement. "Since I have been managing the Hall, we have had some very talented and professional people come to stay, but you are our first published writer. This is very exciting. I would love to be able to read one of your books sometime, that is if you could spare me a copy?"

"If you'd like, but I'm not sure they would be to your taste," Lydia told her.

"Nonsense, I'm sure I'd love it. You might just open up a whole new world to me!" Kelly beamed.

The rest of the day passed quickly with everybody working hard to unpack and arrange Lydia's belongings, finally making her new apartment as much like home as possible. Thanks to their efforts, most of the unpacking was complete before twilight. It was at that point that Lydia's family had all departed, the Pearson family returning to their home. Christian would once again be working the graveyard shift at the hospital later that evening, whilst Susanna still had to prepare the family dinner.

Standing in the car park outside of the Hall, Lydia waved goodbye to her family. She patted Christian on his back and thanked him for all his help, after which she gave Jessica a great big hug. Only Susanna remained, her signature high heeled shoes crunching loudly into the gravel as they walked side by side to the car.

"Thank you again for today, love," Lydia said, rubbing her daughter's arm affectionately.

"You don't have to thank me, mum," Susanna replied.

"I know, but I'm going to do it anyway," Lydia stated cheekily, "how about we all meet for lunch next week? My treat!" she offered.

"Okay, sure. That would be lovely," Susanna accepted, leaning in for a hug before stepping away and reaching for the car door. "You go in now, mum. Don't want you catching a cold."

"I'll be fine. I'll go straight in after I wave you off," Lydia dismissed, watching as her daughter slid into the passenger seat, "call me when you get home, okay?"

"Yes mum," Susanna said in a jokingly sarcastic tone, adding a wink to extend her teasing before her tone returned to normal. "I'll call you when I get in to check everything is alright here with you."

"Drive safely!" Lydia called over to Christian.

"Bye mum," Susanna said, shutting the car door.

"Take care love," Lydia responded, waving vigorously as she watched the car start up and pull away.

***

Alone once more, the day was coming to a close and Lydia felt exhausted from its trials. She was now almost fully unpacked in her new apartment, with just a few lingering boxes remaining. She had been there for less than a day, and the apartment was already beginning to feel like home. She may have opted to keep the previous occupant's furniture, but it was now her own books occupying the bookcase. It was her rug complimenting the living room floor, and it was her own personal bedsheets spread out immaculately over the bed. This was her home now and she was settling in nicely.

She had been battling through yawns for the past hour or so, and was eager to finally collapse into the soft looking bed. Whilst now dozing slightly in her armchair, Lydia had almost jumped out of her skin when the phone began to ring out loudly, cutting through the quiet evening atmosphere. With a sigh, she raised herself from her seat and unhooked the violently chiming phone, holding it up to her ear.

"Hello," Lydia began, waiting patiently for the caller to speak, "oh, hello love," Lydia said, grinning cheerfully upon hearing her daughter's voice through the receiver.

"Did you make it home okay? Oh, good. Yes, all fine here!" Lydia chattered merrily to her daughter for a few moments more, before the two women bid one another farewell and goodnight.

Lydia finally slipped into her bed, thoroughly exhausted after her busy day. She fell asleep with a smile upon her face and rested peacefully until morning.

CHAPTER 6

New Friends

Waking up for the first time amidst new surroundings can be disorientating, especially after spending so many years opening your eyes every morning to the sight of the same old familiar room. The sudden change of scenery can be quite bewildering, likened to being woken up from a prolonged period of sleep to find the entire world has changed around you, not registering at first that you are the one who has actually moved, and not the room. So, as Lydia began to open her eyes for the first time in her new bedroom, blinking in the first rays of daylight, she momentarily forgot where she now was. She was no longer within her own little cottage, with its faded wallpaper and well worn carpets, and it took several moments for her to regain her bearings. Now, as she pushed away the fog of sleep from her mind, she began to slowly sit herself up and started to scan her new surroundings. Everything felt new and foreign to her, from the freshly ironed bed sheets that she was lying on, to the yellow hue the bedroom was coated in, created by the morning light glaring against the curtains.

Hesitantly, Lydia searched the bedside table, gently feeling around for her watch as she rubbed the tiredness from her eyes in order to check the time:

'09:47'

Realising how late it had become, Lydia quickly hopped out of bed, instantly feeling her joints click, and her bones groan in protest against the sudden movement. She then headed straight towards the kitchen to begin the process of making coffee, struggling now to locate a mug due to the rehousing of all her possessions. It took her several attempts of opening and closing cupboard doors before the elusive mugs were found. Following this, she popped a few slices of bread into the toaster before returning to her bedroom and getting dressed for the day. It was only then, as she pulled a fleece around her shoulders, that Lydia pushed open the curtains for the first time, revealing to her eyes the stunning view of the gardens below. Vast lawns of emerald-green grass sat shimmering in the bright morning light. Broad flowerbeds flooded with colour, and the sounds of distant birds tweeting chimed in Lydia's ears. This place was a virtual paradise, Lydia thought, as she let out a contented sigh whilst admiring the view of her own personal 'Garden of Eden'.

Eventually, Lydia decided it was time to leave her apartment, and venture downstairs and out into the communal areas below. She was both eager and nervous to finally meet her new house mates. As she walked slowly down the stairs, holding onto the banister for support, Lydia could already hear the sound of the television blaring out from the communal lounge. The sound was soon followed by a merry chuckle of men laughing at whatever the screen was displaying. Upon reaching the bottom of the stairs, Lydia immediately took a right turn and entered the communal lounge. Just as she had expected, she discovered three elderly fellows belly laughing at a rerun of an old sitcom on the television.

For a moment, Lydia was tempted to join them and watch the end of the show, her husband Robert had always been a fan of that particular programme. She had always been amused by the disastrous escapades of other people, and also found them very entertaining. But, before she could locate a place to sit down, or start up a conversation with these gentlemen, Lydia caught sight of Kate. She was once again sat in the conservatory area with a book in her hand, and a cup of tea at her side. A flutter of excitement passed through Lydia's chest at the sight of her potential friend. She quickly made her way over to the conservatory, an extra skip in her step as she hurried towards Kate to greet her.

"Well, you were right, here I am!" Lydia announced, leaning against Kate's armchair.

"Did you ever doubt me?" Kate stated, smiling back at her, standing up and throwing her arms eagerly around

Lydia's smaller frame. "So, come on, take a seat. Tell me, how is it going so far? Have you unpacked everything yet?" Kate questioned inquisitively.

"Almost. I still have a few things I haven't found a place for yet, but I'm getting there," Lydia replied, sighing as she slumped back and relaxed into a chair.

"Need any help? Can't say that I'm the tidiest person around here, but I'll do my best," Kate asked, still smiling broadly.

"I think I can manage, thanks," Lydia returned.

"That's a shame, I was hoping to have a nosy around your apartment," Kate winked cheekily, "but are you settling in well? Have you met the rest of the inmates yet?" she questioned as she took a sip of her tea, eyes peeking over the rim of her teacup as she spoke.

"Not yet. So far you're the only person I know here," Lydia replied somewhat shyly.

"Well, let's change that right now," Kate decided. She then leant over the far side of her chair, and reached her arm out to wave at a man sat quietly in the corner of the room. "Hey, Bryan! Come and meet our new neighbour," Kate called over at the man.
The man, who Lydia had not previously noticed being in the room, seemed to jump in shock as Kate addressed

him. He was clearly a mature gentleman, perhaps a few years senior to Lydia and Kate. He was smartly dressed wearing a tweed jacket complemented by a bow tie, while a large yet neatly trimmed white beard adorned his face. The man had been sat in the corner, intently writing in a small notebook until Kate had disturbed him. The man, Bryan, had suddenly looked up from his writing with an annoyed look on his face, before his expression was taken over by curiosity at the sight of Lydia.

Huffing into the air as he stood up, Bryan returned his little notebook to his breast pocket, patting it gently to confirm its containment, before shuffling over and taking the spare wicker chair beside the two ladies.

"Hello my dear!" Bryan's deep, smooth voice joined the conversation as he offered his hand towards Lydia. She offered her hand to him, but instead of going for a handshake as Lydia had expected, he leant down to press his lips to the back of her palm. "Who says that chivalry is dead?" Bryan stated, smirking at Lydia.

"Oh, simmer down you old goat," Kate quipped, giving him a playful nudge on the shoulder. "Don't mind him Lydia. He gets a little carried away with the whole 'James Bond' act," she said teasingly.

"Ignore her, she's just jealous that she's no longer the sole object of my attention around here," Bryan teased back with a wink, "it's genuinely nice to meet you, Lydia," he added warmly.

"Bryan has been a resident here a little longer than me. He has also lost his other half!" Kate began to tell, "how long has it been now?" she enquired, turning her attention and gaze back to Bryan.

"Must be a little over a year," Bryan replied, before leaning forwards in his chair and clearing his throat. His new position suggesting that what he was about to say would be a story or a speech of some kind, and that the words would carry some importance. This sudden change instantly intrigued Lydia, and she found herself subconsciously leaning in to listen more intently.

"I used to live in the city with my wife Edith. I used to be a bank manager and Edith was a psychiatrist, so we were able to afford and live a good life. We lived in a penthouse apartment, we had a classy sports car, a couple of holidays a year to the Maldives, plus a Christmas cruise if the mood took us. That sort of thing," Bryan told, with a faint smile at the pleasant memories from his past, before continuing with his story. "We had been married for nearly forty five years when Edith became ill. Pancreatic cancer," he said sadly. "Things were okay for a time, she was receiving first class treatment, and we were able to carry on as normal. But, a few years passed and the medication no longer seemed to be as effective. That's when we found out that the cancer had spread. She underwent chemotherapy treatment and new medication, but they didn't really have any effect, and things started to go downhill from there on." Bryan's tone was slowly becoming strained, and his previously cheerful face now looked cold and downcast as his tale progressed. "Edith put up a brave fight for eight long years, but the cancer eventually took her away from me," he announced, his voice now sounding out as nothing more than a loud whisper.

The room then fell quiet, and at that moment, the sound of birdsong outside was the only thing stopping the world from becoming completely silent. Nobody said anything for a short while, until Bryan decided to break the silence and continued with his tale.

"Anyway, after that the city no longer felt like a place where I belonged. We never had any children, and I don't have any family that I speak to any more, so there was nothing left for me there. I then did some soul searching and discovered this place. Well, that was it! I sold my apartment, packed up everything I owned and made the big move. No regrets!" Bryan informed. He sounded far more calm and untroubled now that his mind was in the present. "Not a day goes by that I don't miss my dear Edith, but I can genuinely say that I'm glad to be here amongst new friends," he concluded with a gentle smile, whilst Kate leant over and patted his hand reassuringly.

"I'm sorry for your loss," Lydia offered, looking morose, before turning her gaze to the floor.

"Thank you," Bryan replied. "I suppose that is why we are all here in a way. We have all lost somebody close to us," Bryan stated, looking pensive as his gaze trailed out of the window and far away.

"Well, this is morbid!" Kate announced, instantly breaking the tension with her bluntness, "how about instead of boring Lydia to death with our tales of woe, we show the new girl around a bit," she continued, rising up out of her chair, tucking her book under her arm and then reaching out to offer Lydia a hand. "Come on!" she said.

"Where are we going?" Lydia questioned curiously, but she took the offered hand and stood up regardless.

"To the dining room. It's nearly eleven o'clock, so Kelly should have finished baking by now," Kate replied, looking gleeful at the prospect as she led the way, "don't worry, you're going to love it! Kelly is an amazing baker. You'll just die after a slice of her Victoria sponge!" And with that, Kate was away leaving Lydia and Bryan to hurriedly follow after her, giggling quietly as they went.

***

Later on that evening Lydia was stood in the kitchen of her apartment, watching patiently for the kettle to bring itself to the boil, a cup containing a tea bag already sitting before her.

The apartment was surprisingly quiet, which Lydia had not expected. It was still lingering at the back of her mind that she was now a resident in an institution of some kind, and that her nights would now be filled with the screams and wails of the other inmates. It was a very childish thought, as the reality of the situation was nothing of the sort. She knew that nothing bad would happen here, yet the thought still lingered in her mind. Perhaps it was an echo of a memory from visiting her own parents in a care home many years ago. That particular place was far more reminiscent of a hospital in comparison to Carnation Hall. The nurses would walk around the halls at all hours of the day. The orderlies would even pass unfriendly looks at the residents trapped in their beds, especially when they thought that their visiting relatives were not looking! In retrospect, she now regretted leaving her parents in such a place, firmly convinced that during their time there, they had experienced some wrongdoings. But, at that particular time in her life she had a young family of her own to care for, and her brother refused to give her any assistance, so she had very little choice over her actions.

However, it was clear that Carnation Hall had no similarity to her parent's care home. Each resident here had their own individual freedom, respect and privacy, all the things that her parents hadn't been afforded before their eventual demise.

Lydia's thoughts then returned to the present as the kettle began to sing out steam, signalling its readiness for use. Lydia poured the water into her mug, leaving it for a few seconds to brew, before transporting it into the living room and collapsing down into her treasured armchair. A gossip magazine lay at her side and she casually browsed through its pages, enjoying her tea whilst also letting tiredness take over.

Once her mug was almost empty, Lydia began to feel her eyelids gain weight. In the comfort of her new home, she allowed her eyes to momentarily fall shut, she was now far too cosy to move and drag herself to her bed.

It was as she was dozing in her armchair, her chest slowly rising and falling with each breath, that the temperature in the room began to suddenly drop!

Lydia's skin began to prickle with the chill, and goosebumps began forming on her bare arms. Lydia was unaware that her breath was turning into small clouds of vapour as she exhaled, her lips shading blue. She was totally oblivious to what was happening, as a light frost then began to crawl and crack its way around the edges of the window pane. Lydia was sound asleep as ice cold static began to fizzle in the surrounding air. She groaned as the cold air forced its chill down her throat, invading her lungs and making them ache, constricting her breathing. It felt as if a cold dead skeletal hand had wrapped its way around her neck, and had started to squeeze tightly. Above her, the lights of the chandelier began flickering rapidly, as if from excitement at the growing static tension building within the room. Finally, one of the light bulbs could take the pressure no more, and with a loud sharp cracking noise, the glass fractured, the light blinking out of existence with an electronic whine.

Lydia woke up with a jolt, a startled gasp escaping her lips as her eyes opened wide! Her heart was pounding as she scanned the room desperately searching for what had awoken her. She had the uneasy feeling that she was being watched from afar. It was only now that she felt the coldness of the room, and she hurriedly began to rub her arms hoping that the friction would ease the cold from her body. Freezing and tired, Lydia rose up from her chair feeling disorientated and confused as she stumbled to her feet. She quickly turned around, searching eagerly for the source of the chill, or for the invisible presence that she could still feel lingering within her new home. Immediately, Lydia sensed that she was not alone, she knew there was something else in there with her. She knew what it felt like to be visited by a spirit, by the hot flash of static that always hung in the air when they came close. She had experienced that feeling countless times in her life, but this time it wasn't like that, this was not the same sensation. What she currently felt was so familiar and yet so foreign all at once, it was like experiencing déjà vu for the very first time. Lydia could hear her own pulse in her ears, as her heart pounded recklessly in her chest with fear. A glimpse of movement off to her side caught Lydia's eye. She was now drawn towards her living room window, where the curtain was blowing wildly in the midnight wind. Instantly, the feeling of cold faded away and was replaced by a hot flood of embarrassment. Lydia couldn't help but let out a laugh at her own childish superstition. The tiredness from the day, the stress of moving, and the new environment were clearly all playing tricks on her mind. She hadn't sensed anything, she was just jumping to conclusions. She had gone through a stage like this after she had moved to the cottage, and was living all alone for the first time. For the first few months she had been jumping at shadows, unable to turn off any lights at night, and after a phase of her telephone mysteriously ringing with no caller on the other end, she had convinced herself that the house was haunted. However, she had eventually settled down, no longer fearing her own footsteps in the house, and the telephone issue had been discovered to be a fault of bad wiring. It had not occurred to Lydia that her paranoia would grasp her once again, but she was now determined to ignore it.

"I just need some sleep!" Lydia told herself, still giggling slightly as she closed the window and tugged the curtains closed. She now felt relieved as the room began to rapidly warm up.

With a sigh, Lydia proceeded to march in a regimental manner confidently back for her mug, taking it into the kitchen sink, before allowing herself to return to the bedroom and claim her bed.

The apartment was now deadly silent as Lydia stood rigid in her bedroom doorway, reaching out for the light switch. She was frozen in place as she watched the hairs on the back of her outstretched hand prickle and stand to attention. Seconds later, she watched as a lone cloud of breath suddenly left her mouth. The sensation of an ice cold bolt was racing down her spine. She could now feel the return of eyes seeming to be burning into the back of her head.

Suddenly, a loud bang echoed around the apartment with surprising force, and Lydia screamed in shock. She spun around, half expecting to catch sight of an assailant behind her, but there was nobody there. The room was empty and every trace of the cold had vanished. The only evidence that she had not just imagined the event, was that now in the living room, a picture frame had fallen from her mantelpiece, and was now lying face down on the floor.

With a rush of adrenaline soaring through her body, she marched across the room. She bent down and grasped the picture frame, cautiously picking it up. Lydia held her breath as she flipped the picture over, already knowing what the other side would display. The pain of loss hit her once more at the sight of Robert's smiling face. He was staring back at her through the shattered glass of the picture frame, and a lone tear started to roll down her cheek.

"Robert?" Lydia called out loudly into the open room, still looking around for any sign, before turning back to the picture. "I've missed you so much my darling!" she managed to whisper, before her legs gave out from the weight of emotion, and she crumpled to the floor, quietly crying herself into exhaustion with both despair and joy.

As Lydia fell into a deep sleep, her last fleeting thought was that she was no longer alone. Little did she know just how right she would turn out to be!

CHAPTER 7

The New Statue

At some time during the night, Lydia had finally awoken to find herself huddled on her living room floor. Robert's picture was still held tightly in her grasp, and the sticky remains of tear tracks were still marking her face. Half asleep, she managed to pull herself up from the floor and drag herself towards the bed. She momentarily paused, just long enough to return Robert's photograph to its rightful place atop the mantelpiece. She then collapsed onto her bed and slept quite peacefully throughout the rest of the night.

Luckily, the events of the previous night were now beginning to fade for Lydia. The unsettled feeling that an unknown presence had been in the room was also nothing more than a blurred memory. It had been completely consumed by the joy and relief that, for a brief moment, Lydia had been reunited with her beloved Robert, or at least with his spirit. The following morning arrived, and the first thing that Lydia had to do after waking up was to dig out her spirit dice. Using every piece of knowledge she had, Lydia again had called out to her husband. Alas, in the light of the new day, there were no signs of a presence within the confines of her apartment. Lydia had spent a long time kneeling beside her bedside table, just staring down at the dice, the bold white letters standing out brightly against the black painted wood, whilst she silently and desperately willed them to move. A good half an hour then passed without any change in the situation. The dice had refused to move and her patience had now dwindled. It was clear that Robert's spirit was no longer there. This actually didn't concern Lydia a great deal, as she had conducted her reading room sessions for long enough to know that spirits were not constantly present. Lydia herself had once explained in her book that 'Human spirits are like batteries, some are far more powerful than others, but eventually all of them need to recharge'. It was still a mystery to other so-called 'experts in her field', as to how spirits regained their energy. It was usual for spirits to disappear for a time, so she had surmised that the spirits must need to rest in some way in order to regenerate their strength.

With this in mind, Lydia had silently promised herself that she would try to contact Robert again later that day, but after last night, she was now convinced that he would make contact with her when 'he' was ready to do so!

***

It was now later in the morning, and Lydia was once again in Kate's company. The pair were currently taking a stroll through the grounds of the Hall, walking side by side as they merrily chatted away, both enjoying the fresh air.

"You're becoming quite the celebrity around these parts you know! Kelly has been busy telling everyone about the resident author we have living with us," Kate stated suddenly, nudging Lydia in the shoulder gently with her own. "When were you going to let me in on this?" Kate demanded, her voice sounding hurt and offended, but the wide smirk on her face showed it was only a jest. Lydia groaned in displeasure.

"Honestly, I hadn't thought it was that important, and Kelly is possibly over exaggerating somewhat. I've only ever had two books published, and even one of those was a disaster," Lydia sighed, trying to explain.

"But you've still had one successful work published, right?" Kate pushed. Lydia nodded shyly in reply. "Well, there you go. You're officially our resident author. Embrace it!" Kate declared, causing Lydia to glance away in embarrassment. "So, what were these books about?" she added curiously, drawing attention back to her.

"Nothing you'd be interested in," Lydia replied sternly.

"Try me," Kate challenged.

"Believe me, it's a very specific genre," Lydia said.

"So what, are you some kind of specialist in this so-called specific genre?" Kate demanded to know.

"I suppose so," Lydia conceded.

"Well, Lydia, you don't half know how to sound mysterious!" Kate teased, again nudging the other woman gently, "are you really going to make me beg? I'm not proud, but I will do it!"

Ahead of them, some way off from the cobbled path they were currently walking on, Mitch could now be seen. A faint rumbling sound accompanied him as he went riding across the grass on his mini tractor, a rusty metal trailer in tow. In the trailer there was a large black plastic sheet, flapping in the wind concealing whatever lay beneath it.

Lydia was grasped by intrigue, and they both paused to see what Mitch was up to. Moments later he finally pulled up in his tractor at his intended destination. The broad figure of the man clambered down from the vehicle with surprising speed, before marching off towards the back of the trailer. He lowered the tailgate, and yanked off the plastic cover with unnecessary force. It was like watching a magician performing a trick, as a large and bulky stone statue was revealed, lying peacefully on its side within the trailer.

Lydia continued to watch as Mitch hauled the heavy looking statue from the trailer, displaying his brute strength as he managed to carry it away. Just a few paces away from the trailer there appeared to be a stone pedestal waiting. It was only when Mitch placed the statue down onto the pedestal, that Lydia could actually determine its shape. The new statue was that of a Lion sitting rather proudly. Its majestic mane framing the grand looking head of the noble creature. It had an expression of calm and peacefulness, despite a hint of several dangerously sharp teeth being displayed beneath.

Once the statue was in place, Mitch returned to his trailer, retrieving a trowel and a plastic container filled with pots of brightly coloured flowers, which he obviously intended to plant around the base of the pedestal.

"Looks like Mitch has been busy again," Kate said, following Lydia's gaze.

"What do you mean?" Lydia questioned curiously.

"Mitch usually makes a new statue whenever we lose a resident. He's got a work shed down by the pond," Kate informed, pointing further down the path. Lydia could just catch sight of a rooftop further down the garden, clearly belonging to a large shed or outbuilding of some kind. "Anyway, it seems he's been working on this one for quite a few weeks. It's nice to see that it's finally finished," Kate continued.

"I'm guessing that when you say lose, you mean . . ." Lydia trailed off.

"They've died. Yes!" Kate filled in bluntly, "Kelly and Mitch like to think of everyone here as a large family, so when we lose someone, Mitch makes a new statue. As a sort of tribute to them I suppose. Luckily, this is only the second new statue I've seen since I arrived here. We lost old Tom a couple of weeks ago. He had a heart attack apparently. It was quite a shock as I'd actually seen him just that morning, and he seemed perfectly fine. It's sad really, he was a nice man," Kate told, lowering her head, perhaps in respect or maybe just in thought.

"You knew him well then?" Lydia asked, keeping her tone calm and quiet.

"After a while, you get to know everybody here," Kate replied, perking up quickly, "just you wait and see. It's like living in a soap opera! But you'll soon get used to it. Plus, you now have me to look out for you," Kate said, grabbing Lydia's arm and pulling her along down the path.

"I must be honoured!" Lydia mocked.

"Oh, you are. Not everybody gets my seal of approval!" Kate laughed, "so, now that we are officially 'besties', are you going to tell me about your book?" Kate questioned excitedly.

"Maybe later," Lydia replied.

"Ooh, you big tease!" Kate complained, "I will get to the truth one of these days!"

"I'm sure you will," Lydia responded, unable to hold back a smile at the other woman's enthusiasm.

The pair were now nearing the patio around the back of the house, where the conservatory breaks out into the garden. As they approached the house, Kelly suddenly burst out from the patio doors, rushing towards them as quickly as her heels would allow.

"Kate!" Kelly called loudly, refusing to step off the end of the patio and onto the grass. She was stood looking down over the older women due to the natural slope of the lawn. "Phone call for you!" Kelly explained, having grasped the woman's attention, "front desk!" she added, before turning back towards the house.

"I'll be back in a minute. Shouldn't take long," Kate stated, unlocking her arm from Lydia's and hurrying along the path back up towards the house, then rushing inside behind Kelly.
Alone, Lydia allowed herself to take in the view. It was only now that she took notice of just how many statues the garden contained. From where she stood, she could see about a dozen, all of various sizes and

indeterminate age. With a glance to the right, Lydia could still see Mitch. He was on his knees, digging out the ground with a trowel and carefully planting some flowers. It was obvious that Mitch took great pride in his work, as he carefully laid the colourful flowers down into their resting places. Curious once more, Lydia noticed that there was another statue standing not too far away. And, unable to resist the temptation, she stepped off the cobbled path and waded over to the statue's side. Now standing much closer, Lydia was able to take note of its form. This statue was of a young woman wearing an almost sheer dress, holding a basket of flowers before her in both hands. The statue's head was turned upwards, as if she was staring up at the sky, and her facial expression held a rather sad looking smile. The amount of detail displayed in the work was impressive, however, the statue itself was aged, with the surface now looking rough and worn due to many years of being battered by the weather. The grey cement had now turned dark and dull due to the damp, even some cracks appearing in some places.

There was something very enticing about this statue, maybe even more so than the others she had spied upon so far, as it emitted a kind of sorrowful beauty. Lydia felt the urge to touch it and to feel its stony surface against her skin. She tried to imagine who the statue had been made for, and why Mitch had felt compelled to create a memorial for someone's absence.

Like a small child being left all alone with an open sweet jar, Lydia was unable to stop herself from reaching out, not stopping until her fingertips firmly pressed against the hard cold surface.

As soon as the concrete touched her skin, Lydia almost cried out, as she felt an immense energy flow free from the statue and pass through her body. Starting from where her fingers were pressed against the statue's arm, it suddenly felt as though tiny tendrils of ice had been passed from the statue and into her body. Each worming their way into her nerve endings, and crawling their way up through her wrist and then through her arm. She felt her heart beating rapidly, becoming more sporadic, as if her body was attempting to fight back against this invisible threat. The sensation was becoming more painful as the feeling spread. It was now creeping its way across her elbow and reaching for her shoulder. Lydia felt completely frozen as she was shrouded in silent agony. Using all of her will, she managed to regain her composure, enough at least to yank her hand away from the statue. She used far more force than was actually necessary, and almost stumbled over as she backed away to free herself.

She was now no longer touching the statue, and all traces of its assault on her had faded away completely. She could no longer feel its icy grasp or barely even remember what the sensation had felt like. It was as if the event had happened within some sort of dream, and now that she was awake, it was little more than an echo in her mind. Lydia knew that she had been awake throughout the whole ordeal, and she knew it had not merely been her imagination. Stealing herself, she reached out her hand once more, this time far more cautiously, and let her skin touch the stone ever so slightly. Nothing! She felt nothing at all! No energy or power buzzed from its surface, and no pain inflicted her body. She felt nothing but rough cold and lifeless concrete against her fingertips.

It was now that Lydia really began to worry about her own mental health. Susanna had been pestering her for months, ever since Robert's death, to go and visit her doctor and get checked out. Lydia had so far ignored the plea, adamant that she was fine. But, now she wasn't so sure. Could she have imagined the effect the statue had on her? Or, had whatever presence was there simply moved on? Throughout all of her life, Lydia had personally experienced many varied paranormal types of energy and forces. But, she had never once felt anything as powerful as she had from within that statue. Then again, perhaps she really had felt nothing at all, and it had all been within her mind. Lydia had always known that her abilities were passed down from her mother's side of the family. It had somehow skipped her own mother and chosen to enlighten her instead. Her very own grandmother had told her about her abilities as a young child, along with stories to match. Stories about the people her grandmother talked to, and the people she had been able to help throughout her life. Those stories had been what had inspired Lydia to follow the same path. However, she was also aware that on her father's side of the family there was a history of Alzheimer's disease. For her father in particular, this had caused him to suffer many hallucinations throughout his old age. It concerned Lydia greatly to think that this may be the start of the same affliction for her. Worry was a great motivator, and Lydia instantly made a mental note to make herself an appointment to see her doctor at the earliest convenience.

Still standing before the statue with a puzzled look upon her face, Lydia's mind waged war between reality and fantasy. She could now feel a headache brewing in her temple, and she was completely unaware of the approaching footsteps behind her.

"Making new friends in my absence?" Kate asked loudly, announcing her return, and causing Lydia to jump slightly from the shock.

"What?" Lydia gasped, her confusion evident in her expression.

"You and the statue! It looked like the start of a cosy relationship between you two there. Mind if I butt in, or is three a crowd?" Kate declared, never missing an opportunity to jest.

"Come on, let's go. She wasn't very talkative anyway," Lydia attempted to joke back.

"Aww, did she give you the cold shoulder?" Kate asked, with a wink.

"Hilarious," Lydia replied, her voice dripping with sarcasm.

"I am, aren't I?" Kate smirked, raising her chin in an expression of mock pride. Lydia was unable to hold back a laugh as the pair began walking down the path once more. Kate then steadily led her away from the statue.

"Well, since you're so interested in my career, how about we both share?" Lydia suggested, "what did you do before coming here?"

"Unfortunately, my life isn't nearly as exciting and mysterious as yours," Kate teased with a jesting smile, "not a lot to tell really. I was a florist for most of my life. I owned my own little shop. Good location, always keeping busy. My husband Bernard worked as a teacher, or really I should say 'third' husband. I went through a few husbands to find the right one," she laughed. "Anyway, we had a nice house, nothing lavish, but nice enough and we eventually both retired. We just enjoyed our time together, you know. I kept my shop going, found a manager for it and that was that. We were then free as birds. We used to enjoy going camping and such, until our joints started to fail us that is. But, we tried to keep active as much as we could, long walks and such . . ." Kate suddenly paused. "It was an accident that took Bernie. I'd just been down to the shops and came home to find him lying at the bottom of the stairs. Silly old bugger had fallen trying to carry the Christmas decorations back up to the loft. I called an ambulance but it was no good, it was too late!" Kate finished her tale, her tone having turned very subdued, compared to her usually jaunty demeanour.

"I'm really sorry for your loss," Lydia replied. Her go-to phrase for all new clients with a sad tale to tell.

"Don't be," Kate returned, "wasn't your fault. Wasn't anybody's fault. Just one of those things," she stated, with a shrug. "Anyway, after that I went back to work for a while. It kept me busy, but my heart was no longer in it. Then, one day the man who owned the restaurant next door came into the shop. He told me that some big investors were sniffing around, and that they were willing to pay a small fortune to buy up all the property on the street. Gonna knock the whole lot down and build some fancy supermarket apparently. Well, I had no other family, no children or siblings, so I went for it. Sold the whole lot. My shop, my house, everything! Then I moved here for a fresh new start. That's what I wanted and it's what I found," Kate explained, looking back fondly towards the main house.

"So, Kelly and Mitch were running this place when you moved here?" Lydia enquired.

"From what I've heard, Kelly has been running this place long before any of us moved here," Kate answered.

"You know, when I first followed up the newspaper advert, I spoke to Kelly on the phone, and she kind of gave me the impression that she actually owned the Hall, not just managed it," Lydia said quietly, as if telling a school yard secret.

"I think she has convinced herself that she does! She can certainly get on her high horse at times. But, she's a good soul once you get to know her. I actually don't know what this place would do without her. You can tell she really cares about us all. You can ask anything of her and you know she'll do it. Mitch isn't a bad egg either. Not the most chatty man around, but he's always happy to help. He takes a few of us out shopping once a week if you'd ever like to go. It saves forking out for a taxi, and he genuinely doesn't mind. Personally, I think he just likes to get away from Kelly for a few hours," Kate remarked grinning. "I think we're planning another trip this Friday if you'd like to join us?" she added, looking hopeful.

"Thanks, I could probably do with getting some odds and ends in actually," Lydia replied.

"My pleasure. All part of the service from your official Carnation Hall guide!" Kate said, bending into a mocking bow that sent both women laughing once more, as they continued their walk.

CHAPTER 8

The Haunting

The day so far had been rather eventful. Lydia and Kate had spent several hours together just chatting and reminiscing about their past lives. It started with a brisk walk through the gardens discussing the merits of good housekeeping, followed by a deep natter about the trials and tribulations of a messy husband. The latter being conducted whilst fully indulging in a cup of Earl Grey tea, and a sneaky piece of cake or two in the dining room. This concluded with the appearance of Bryan, joining the pair in the communal lounge. He was intent on discussing the events of the latest cricket match, a topic that did not interest either of the women, but one which they accepted in return for the added company.

By the time Lydia had arrived back at her apartment, the hour was just getting past seven in the evening. This was a shock to Lydia, as she was yet to prepare her dinner. She had fully intended to return to her apartment mid afternoon, allowing some time to sort out more of her belongings, and create some sense of order within her new home. But, as with all the best laid plans, that idea had clearly gone astray. She had been far too engrossed in conversation with her new found friends, and their captivating tales of old to break away and return to the solitude of her apartment.

Feeling quite lazy after a surprisingly active day, Lydia was eternally thankful for the ready-made meals that Susanna had stuffed into her freezer.

The evening hours passed quickly, and before long, Lydia had decided to turn to her bed with the company of a good book to entertain her.

Slipping into her pyjamas, Lydia took a moment to check the spirit dice that were still sitting on her bedside table. They had not moved! A slight pang of disappointment struck Lydia, burying itself deep into the pit of her stomach, before she pushed the feeling away. This meant nothing. It could take days yet, maybe even weeks for Robert's spirit to contact her again. There was nothing unusual about the lack of activity in such a short time. Determined not to be discouraged, Lydia climbed into bed, settling back against the plump pillows and opened her book, turning to page one she then began to read.

About an hour or so passed before Lydia was once again disturbed, but this time by a sudden loud ringing noise. It ripped her from the enticing pages, depicting a tale of hidden desire from a young couple in Victorian London.

With a sigh of annoyance, Lydia untangled herself from the bed sheets and swung her feet free from the bed, before moving to the living room in search of the phone.

"Hello!" Lydia spoke into the receiver, her tone reflecting her irritation at being disturbed, as she finally put a stop to its infernal ringing!

"Hi mum, sorry for calling so late, I just couldn't sleep until I knew how you were getting on. I didn't wake you up, did I?" Susanna's voice responded to her own, sounding tentative.

"Oh no, it's fine love. I was just reading," Lydia replied, having now softened at discovering it was only her daughter calling.

"I wouldn't have disturbed you, it's just you said you would call me when I got home from work, and . . ." Susanna tailed off, her voice sounding concerned even through the static distortion of the phone. "Is everything alright?"

Lydia could have kicked herself. She had made the promise to phone her only child after their previous phone call, but after events of the night before, and the unusual and busy day she had just experienced, the arrangements had faded from her mind. She felt a moment of guilt at unintentionally worrying her family, but it was too late for her to correct the situation now. Instead, she would have to settle for being truthful, although Lydia knew that it was best if she kept the strange happenings from the past few days to herself, at least for now. Susanna was already sceptical and unappreciative of Lydia's gift. There was no sense in adding any unnecessary concern to her daughter's life.

"I'm sorry, hun! I totally forgot! I ended up having such a busy day with Kate, that it just completely slipped my mind," Lydia explained, sounding remorseful.

"It's fine. I'm honestly glad you're settling in and making new friends. I'll have to call in at the weekend and you can introduce me properly," Susanna sympathised.

"I'd like that! Maybe you could bring Jess and Christian. I could make us all a special roast dinner. Kate was telling me there's a really good butcher's shop in town. I can buy a lamb joint for us all. I know it's your favourite, and it would be so lovely to host a dinner for you all again," Lydia tempted, smiling happily at the thought of having her family around once more for a special dinner. It would be like the good old days that she remembered. Whilst living in their cottage, Lydia and Robert would cook up a Sunday roast practically every fortnight. They took great pride in cooking and caring for their little family. Those Sunday evenings would forever hold a special place in Lydia's heart, thanks to the endless laughter and warmth that those occasions had provided over the years. The last time she had been surrounded by her family for such a dinner, was just a week before

Robert had died. Since then, she had not been able to face hosting such a gathering for her family. But now, after everything that had happened, her new home, new friends and a fresh start, she finally felt ready to begin the habit once again. She was absolutely confident that Robert would approve!

"Sounds great! I'm sure we would all love that," Susanna agreed, "listen, mum, I'd best let you go, it's getting late, but I'll call and confirm lunch before the weekend. Okay?"

"Alright love. Have a good evening," Lydia said.

"Goodnight mum, sleep well," Susanna wished, before cutting off the call, leaving Lydia alone with only the dull answering tone for company.

Feeling a sudden hollowness at being all alone once more, Lydia returned to her bedroom, intent on finishing the next chapter of her book, and then sleeping until late morning. But, before she could clamber back into the comfort of her bed, a gentle knocking noise caught her attention. The sound was so slight that Lydia was unable to confirm whether she had actually heard it at all. Frozen with indecision, Lydia paused, holding totally still as she waited for the sound to return. She could literally hear the seconds pass her by as her bedside clock continued to tick. It became unbearably loud in the complete silence of the night.

The silence persisted, then Lydia let out a deep breath and allowed herself to move once more. She seemed satisfied that whatever she had just heard was just a trick of the mind, or an echo from something far away. She climbed back into bed taking up her book once more. She barely had time to turn the page before the knocking noise sounded again, but this time much louder, sounding more frantic and violent! It was not possible to ignore it!

Somewhat startled, Lydia crawled from her bed and quickly put on her dressing gown, before rushing straight towards the door. Feeling her annoyance flair again at the thought of being unnecessarily disturbed, she faced the door, unlocking the clasp and then the safety chain. She paused for a moment in apprehension before finally pulling the door open. The clock on the mantelpiece suddenly informed her that it was now eleven, a time that is universally inappropriate for any visitors. It was now that she began to feel the worry brewing within herself. If somebody was demanding her attention at this unsociable time, the situation may be dire. Perhaps one of her neighbours was in need of assistance, they could have been hurt or been struck down with a sudden illness! Perhaps that was the sound she had heard earlier. That could have been the reason for the knocking before, and she had chosen to ignore their plea! Suddenly, with guilt and worry fuelling her, Lydia pulled open the door. The hallway was completely empty! Now confused, Lydia leant forwards, stretching her neck out from the safety of her apartment, looking around in search of whoever or whatever was making the noise. But, the hallway was completely dark and abandoned. The full moon was shining through the window to her left at the end of the corridor, keeping the looming shadows at bay.

Lydia's mind was tired and becoming irritated, thinking now that she was possibly the victim of some sort of childish prank! She was just about to retreat back into her room when a bright flash caught her eye. She suddenly turned to her right and glanced down the hallway, back towards the landing area at the top of the staircase. She could see the hallway lights flickering and then slowly fade to darkness, before powering back up with an electronic whine. A lump grew in Lydia's throat as she watched the lights continue to dance, menacingly strobing on and off whilst the temperature began to decrease rapidly around her. A growing feeling of dread now began to flow through Lydia's body, as she felt that she was being watched! That feeling she had experienced the night before had returned once more. With growing unease, Lydia wanted nothing more than to step back within her apartment, slam the door shut and wish the feeling away. But, her own natural curiosity refused to let her leave the scene. Instead, Lydia continued to stand firmly rooted in her doorway, her fingers grasping the door frame tightly, as if the wooden frame would somehow anchor her to reality, and stop her from floating away into the thick rising tension within the corridor.

With strobe like effect, the flashing lights were now beginning to hurt her eyes, and she could already feel the throbbing headache from this morning planning its revenge. The temperature in the hallway had now dropped considerably, and Lydia was shocked to see her own breath was now clouding the air in huge puffs. Her arms were now prickling painfully within her dressing gown sleeves, and goosebumps were starting to cover her flesh.

All of her senses were now ablaze. The familiar tingling feeling returned, as it normally would when she was in the presence of a spirit. But now it was starting to scream inside her head, even more powerful than it had ever been before. It was almost unbearable! The way it was buzzing and humming within her own consciousness was causing tears to well in her eyes with its uncomfortable sensation.

It was then that Lydia saw something, or at least she thought she saw something! She caught just a hint of movement down the hallway. A split second of what looked like static light fleeting around the corner. If Lydia didn't know any better, she would have sworn that she had seen someone's arm. A human arm wrapped around the wall, with long overgrown fingernails clawing at the wallpaper as it was slowly dragged back and out of sight. The movement had been so slight, that Lydia was unable to even confirm whether she had actually seen it at all, or whether it was simply a trick of the erratic and menacing lights!

Unable to contain herself any further, Lydia stepped over her threshold and tentatively crept along the corridor, heading directly towards the epicentre of flickering lights and icy cold air. Although intensely afraid, she was determined to discover if what she had just seen had been fantasy or reality.

Lydia moved as quickly as her age and slippers would allow, her feet tripping and stumbling as she scurried along the hallway, then slowly turning the corner with her breath firmly held. She almost felt her consciousness flee at what she then saw directly ahead. Standing immediately in front of her at the top of the staircase was a cold lone figure, human like in shape! It appeared to be a woman, but the figure was clearly not at all human, or at least human no longer! She was tall and impossibly thin, wrinkled from advanced age, and her features were gaunt and sickly as if she was malnourished. She looked as though she was wasting away. She had long hair that covered part of her face, venturing down past her shoulders and along her back. But, it was not this appearance that shocked Lydia, it was the fact that the entire figure was emitting an intense sort of blueish-grey light. For a split second, Lydia pondered whether this figure could be an angel, and perhaps Robert had been right all along. It was perhaps her time now to join him in paradise. But, as her eyes caught up with her mind, the more disturbing features of this spectre began to register. The figure was completely translucent, the staircase banister being clearly visible through its torso. Its body was constantly flickering and jerking, mimicking the erratic lights, and creating a static white noise in tune with its own movement. The figure was wearing an old and faded nightgown that appeared torn and sodden. Lydia could see ethereal water dripping down from the hem, pooling at the creatures feet in a way that didn't quite seem to touch the floor. Its hair was also noticeably wet, dripping and running down her face and body like an endless waterfall.

The spirit also seemed unable to hold itself in a solid state of being, as if it were caught between two different worlds. The body was distorted as it jolted and quivered rapidly. This inadvertently reminded Lydia of an old broken television she once owned, having similar images that broke apart and faded in and out rapidly. Looking at the woman more deeply, Lydia could decipher an even deeper vision of suffering. Her eyes were deep and hollowed, held wide open as if she were pleading, whilst her lips were moving rapidly, as if whispering a mantra, but no sound was being emitted. At this moment they were both shrouded in silence, except for the faint buzzing of energy filling the hallway. Lydia was no longer able to tell if the noise was originating from the flickering lights or from the creature itself. There was no doubt in Lydia's mind that this 'thing' standing before her was definitely a ghost!

They had both been standing facing each other for what seemed like hours, but in reality had only been just a few seconds, when as suddenly as it had appeared, the spirit faded away! It then reappeared at the bottom of the staircase, seemingly having teleported the distance in an instant! It then turned back towards Lydia with its wide eyes burning into her, as it continued whispering to itself.

Lydia was unable to explain why, but she could not stop herself from taking a step closer towards the ghostly figure. She now felt compelled to follow and discover its origin. She needed to know what it was, and where it had come from. The burning question was, why exactly was it demanding her attention? In all of her dealings with the supernatural, Lydia had never before actually seen a ghost. As far as she had been aware, spirits were not able to hold a shape of any kind, and practically everybody in her field agreed. But, after the events of tonight, her entire belief system may have to be rewritten. She thought perhaps that this was all just a bad dream, and in a few moments she would find herself waking up in the morning, having imagined the whole episode.

Lydia continued to move carefully down the staircase, and as she neared the bottom, the ghostly woman's form jolted once more. It then faded out in a shift of static, before re-emerging even further away in the foyer. Now, standing at the reception area, it shakily raised its arm, its fingers appearing to drip steadily with water, as it pointed directly down the hallway. Lydia gasped a breath of air, feeling as though she could no longer breathe normally as the ghost stared at her! Lydia had steadily felt the panic rising within her body during her journey down the staircase, but now it was reaching boiling point. It was removing all of Lydia's self control to fight off the instinct to just run and hide somewhere. She could not shake off the sense of impending danger and doom that plagued her, yet the spectre had showed no signs of aggression towards her. So why could she not fight the feeling that she herself was in mortal peril!

The figure was still standing before her, its hand still pointing towards the end of the corridor, as if instructing direction upon its guest. Lydia was unfamiliar with this particular corridor. During her initial tour of the Hall, this area had been described as administration only. She never felt the need to explore further, and she had accepted it as such.

Lydia had just made up her mind to follow the ghostly figure's lead, when the spirit once again phased, appearing halfway further down the hallway, its grizzly hand still pointing dead ahead! But, before Lydia could follow any further, the lights suddenly stopped flickering. Someone's footsteps echoed down the hallway and the lighting suddenly powered up completely. The hallway was now fully illuminated, and seconds later Kelly appeared from around the corner. She entered the corridor and looked startled at the sight of Lydia standing before her.

"Lydia?" Kelly called out, now marching right towards the older woman, "is everything alright? What are you doing up so late?" Kelly enquired with some concern.

Lydia was too shocked to respond. She was frozen still and wide eyed. Kelly walked towards her, stepping right through the ghostly figure, seemingly unfazed and unaware of its presence.

"Lydia talk to me! Are you unwell?" Kelly demanded to know, reaching her hand out and grasping Lydia's shoulder gently.

But the older woman continued to ignore her. Her attention completely grasped by the figure behind Kelly. Their eyes were locked together, tired hazel meeting cold stone grey. By now, the figure was fading more rapidly and it was taking longer between each jitter to reform itself. Lydia could see cracks in the figure, actual physical cracks appearing in its translucent skin. She could almost hear the sound of grinding rocks as the spectre began to disintegrate. The deep crevasses that spread throughout its body began to crumble and flake away. It was as if the ghost had become petrified! Part of the spirit's head then started to implode, caving in and crumbling away. The rest of the body then soon lost the strength to hold itself up, and as quickly as Lydia could blink, it completely lost stability, the cracked pieces turning into dust and falling in on itself. It then completely disappeared into an invisible wind, leaving no trace that it had ever been there at all!

Lydia was left expecting to see just a pile of dust upon the wooden floorboards, but all that remained was the static in the air, and the deafening ringing in Lydia's ears as Kelly began shaking her by the shoulders.

"Hey, are you with me?" Kelly almost shouted, but held herself back upon seeing Lydia's gaze finally find her own.

"I'm fine! Sorry . . . sorry, I just . . ." Lydia trailed off, trying to reassure the other woman, but finding it hard to speak.

"What happened? What are you doing down here? It's the middle of the night!" Kelly questioned, looking both annoyed and worried. It's clear from her expression that she was trying to contain herself from losing her temper.

"I was . . ." Lydia began, before changing her mind. She was certainly not a fan of lying. However, she doubted that telling the truth in this situation would do her any good. If anything, it would almost certainly get her evicted and sent straight to the mental asylum! "I thought I heard somebody walking around in the hallway outside my apartment, but I couldn't see anything, so I thought I'd take a look around. Just in case somebody was sleepwalking or something," she stated, sounding surprisingly convincing even to her own ears.

"Well, I've just been down this way and I haven't seen anybody at all! I'll have Mitch take a walk around before bed, just in case," Kelly informed, seemingly relieved by the explanation. She wrapped her arm around Lydia's shoulders, and began guiding her back towards the staircase. "Don't want anybody getting lost now, do we?" she smiled, "you go back to bed now dear and I'll check in with you in the morning. Goodnight Lydia," Kelly brushed her off quite abruptly. However, taking into account the time of night, and the fact that Kelly had been working all day, Lydia couldn't blame the other woman for being abrupt.

"Night," Lydia replied, suddenly feeling exhausted. She quickly returned back to her room, no longer feeling comfortable wandering the hallways all alone in the dark. She was now sitting on the edge of her bed, all ready to collapse into the cushions and sleep, that is, if her reeling mind would allow. But, at that moment something else abruptly caught her eye. The dice that she had left on the bedside table for Robert had moved! They were no longer displaying a random conjointment of letters, but, instead they had themselves spelt out one clear word:

'FOLLOW'

Feeling overwhelmed and terrified, Lydia dived under the duvet seeking its protection, just as a child would try to escape from the monster lurking under the bed. She then closed her eyes and just wished that the world would return to the simplicity of the previous morning!

CHAPTER 9

The Drowned Woman

The next morning, Lydia had awoken in an extremely confused state of mind. She had been unwilling to drag herself out from her bed, and instead, she remained curled up and cocooned within her duvet for as much as the day would allow. Around noon, Kate had been knocking on her door, but Lydia had brushed her off, feigning illness. This was a move that she would soon regret, as not an hour later, Kelly was practically knocking down her door. She was insisting to know if Lydia required a doctor, or if her daughter Susanna needed contacting. Lydia declined both, and thankfully the entourage had disassembled.

The truth was that Lydia was still in shock. She felt cold and shaky, a migraine still constantly pounding away behind her eyes, and just the thought of seeing daylight made her groan in detest.

The events of the previous night would not stop repeating themselves within her mind. The images of the ghost with its grotesque and jittering features kept making her feel nauseated, as they echoed through her mind over and over. While its pleading and desperate face filled her with constant looming dread, she just wanted the memory to fade away. She wished to wake up the following morning to discover that it had all been a fever induced dream. But, deep down she knew that would never happen. She had witnessed a ghost, not just a disembodied spirit, but an actual ghost. And now, nothing she could ever do would take that experience away from her. Her entire belief system would now have to be rewritten.

She couldn't recall ever hearing about a spirit taking an actual physical form. The only incident that had ever even been considered was in Japan. A local medium reported that he had been visited several times by the spirit of a woman, thought to have been murdered by her husband. The medium claimed that the woman was trying to lead him to her remains and to the scene of the crime. She appeared to him many times, her body dismembered and bloody, with the force of her anger growing with every visit. She even went so far as to start displaying some poltergeist like traits, slamming doors and throwing furniture. Terrified, the medium reported the events to the police, and after weeks of searching, a human arm was eventually discovered in a wooded area near to where the spirit had indicated. DNA testing proved that the woman's husband was the murderer. The rest of her body was never recovered, and the medium had been hailed by the authorities, yet his claims could never be officially confirmed. Many other mediums had since visited the same scene, but had found nothing, so the case had eventually been filed away as a grey area by fellow psychics and mediums. They were all left to make up their own minds about the facts of the case.

Lydia had always believed the event to be a coincidence, or perhaps an exaggeration of the truth, but now she had a completely different outlook. She now believed that the events could have been genuine, and that the man really could have been visited by a formed spirit. Perhaps the woman's anger had fuelled her with enough energy to take a physical form. If this was the case, then what exactly could have happened to the woman who visited her last night?

As the day moved on, Lydia's fear and shock began to be replaced by intense curiosity and wonder. She was still very afraid, and who wouldn't be after being visited by a potentially furious ghost? But, short of almost initiating a heart attack, the spirit had shown no signs of wanting to harm her. Instead, its gestures appeared to be beckoning her, possibly wanting to lead her to a specific location. But where, and why? This intrigued Lydia exponentially, and she vowed to herself that she would try to discover more if the spirit were to return soon.

***

Over the next few days, Lydia slowly returned to herself somewhat. She had eventually ventured out from her apartment a few times, spending most of her mornings with Kate and Bryan, either drinking coffee in the conservatory, or mulling around the gardens of the Hall.

Mitch had offered to drive Lydia into the local town and she had accepted his gracious offer. She visited the butcher's shop recommended to her by Kate, discovered where the supermarket was to enable her to restock her dwindling fridge, and also familiarise herself a little more with the town for future reference.

Upon returning from her shopping trip into town, Lydia had decided to seek out Kate. She wanted to thank her for recommending the local butcher and delicatessen, and had brought back some delicious looking baked goods that she intended to share with her friend.

However, upon locating Kate, seated in her forever favourite spot within the conservatory, Lydia was surprised to find that she was not alone. Instead, Kate was sat talking to Kelly of all people. The pair were apparently reading through documents of some kind, with Kelly gesturing to certain parts of the page with her pen, both women smiling cheerily.

Lydia was getting the distinct feeling that whatever was happening between the two women was a very private matter, so she deliberately held back. She took a seat near the doorway, and patiently waited for the meeting to conclude, whilst nibbling away at a sausage roll, herself lost in deep thought.

A few minutes later the meeting was concluded and Kelly came marching past, a stack of papers cradled under her arm and a Cheshire cat-like grin adorning her features.

Without hesitation, Lydia jumped up and made her way over to Kate's side. She immediately settled herself into the still warm vacant armchair, placing her box of treats down between them both.

"Are they for me?" Kate asked casually, looking at the collection of baked goods on offer.

"Help yourself," Lydia encouraged.

"Thank you!" Kate grinned, helping herself to a fruit tart.

"Thank you for the recommendation," Lydia returned.

"What are friends for?" Kate said around a mouthful of pastry, muffling her words somewhat.

"Sorry to keep you waiting, that took a little longer than I expected," Kate stated after finishing her cake and licking her fingers clean of the crumbs.

"No worries. Is everything okay? It looked kind of official," Lydia replied, trying not to pry too openly.

"Everything's great. I had just asked Kelly to help me write my will, that's all. I didn't realise there would be so many papers to sign. My hand is tired now," Kate joked, making herself chuckle in the process.

"Your will? Kelly can do that?" Lydia enquired, suddenly curious.

"Sure she can, she has all the official papers. She knows how to fill them in and also knows a lawyer to send them to. Plus, she keeps a copy in the office here so I can't lose it upstairs. It's a win-win situation for me," Kate grinned.

"And you trust her to do this for you?" Lydia asked apprehensively.

"Of course! Why wouldn't I? I know Kelly can seem a little snobbish sometimes, but she's really good at helping with this sort of thing. She's been helping me sort out my finances over the past few weeks, and now, today, we finally got my will finished and signed. I went with my husband years ago to have our will drawn up, and the process was tedious, but Kelly made it a breeze!" Kate expressed merrily.

"Maybe I should talk to Kelly about getting a will made up for me then," Lydia said pensively.

"You really should. You never know what's around the corner," Kate said, raising her eyebrow mischievously. The words made Lydia's heart sink somewhat, as the memory of the drowned woman waiting down the hallway for her was still running through her head. But, she brushed it aside, determined not to fall into the world of nightmares that had found her once again.

She had been so distracted by the memory, that she barely noticed that Kate was still talking to her.

"It was actually Bryan that recommended I should get Kelly to help me with it you know. Apparently, she has been doing this sort of thing for the residents for years. I had never been that bothered about writing a will, but I saw a really interesting programme on the television a few weeks ago. It was all about what happens when people die and they haven't written a will. It seems an awful lot of people come crawling out of the woodwork, sniffing around to see what they can get. So, I decided that it's better to be safe than sorry," Kate rambled on.

"I don't mean to pry, but I thought you didn't have any family left?" Lydia questioned, feeling guilty at how unpleasant her words may have sounded.

"I don't have any family here, but I do have a nephew, Gary, out in Australia. I haven't seen him since he was a boy, but he's still the closest relative I have right now. So, all my meagre possessions will be left to him. Lord knows if he will even remember me, but still he's all I have," Kate stated, "so, are you going to do it?" she added, suddenly sounding cheery again.

"Do what?" Lydia asked.

"Get Kelly to help you make a will," Kate prompted.

"I'll think about it," came Lydia's reply.

***

The next several days passed calmly and quietly, with no unusual events or supernatural experiences plaguing Lydia at all.

Her time was spent constantly checking her spirit dice for new messages from beyond. Each of her nights were spent on edge, sitting in her armchair reading or watching the television. She found herself constantly checking the corners of her vision for movement, or listening intently for the quiet sound of estranged fingers tapping against her door, but nothing came! The only thing haunting her was the silence of the quiet nights all alone, with the lingering memory of what she had previously witnessed.

It had now been almost a week with no further unusual activity, when Lydia abruptly found herself once more standing before the statue in the grounds. It was the same statue as she had been drawn to previously. Its stone features now looking even more familiar to her. Its image was both peaceful and tragic to behold. Yet, there was now something a little more sinister about the statue in Lydia's eye. Although it held completely still, lifeless and petrified in its pose, she could now sense a certain energy pulsating from within. Even without moving closer she could feel it. Her heightened senses were now drawing her nearer to it, and she could sense the waves of forceful intent fizzing and boiling beneath its calm-looking surface. Like a volcano about to erupt and devour the surrounding terrain, such was the anger lurking deep within.

Yet, here it was, rejoicing in calmness and peace upon the grounds where it was positioned. Flowers beautifully maintained around its base, whilst the sun beamed down upon its grey skin, warming and pleasant.

Lydia heeded the statue's gaze, feeling the temptation to reach out and touch it once again. It was as if the statue was magnetised to her, beckoning her closer, and tempting her to discover its hidden secrets.

It was only now that it suddenly occurred to Lydia, she had touched this very statue on the exact same day that the spectre had come knocking at her door. It surely could not have been a coincidence, the events must have been linked in some way.

At that moment, Lydia felt like she should slap herself! Because, one of the things that she had discovered a long time ago, was that before a spirit could take on such a physical form, and then come knocking on your door in the middle of the night, something else needed to happen. She knew, that if a spirit wanted to enter the realm of the living, it had to have its soul attached to something. Most of the time it would be a personal item such as a piece of jewellery, or even a person that they had been close to during their lifetime. But, on rare occasions, spirits could also become attached to a certain place or object. So, perhaps this spirit that was trying to contact Lydia had somehow attached itself to this particular statue. Perhaps the dead silence over the past week was indicating that it now needed a power source, a taste of human life force in order to leave its concrete prison once more.

With that theory in mind, a sudden rush of curiosity and realisation raced through Lydia, she acted rashly and immediately placed her palm flat against the statue's arm. She felt a sudden cold burn within her skin! An uncomfortable and extremely invasive feeling, but it was nowhere near as agonising as it had been the last time she carried out this same action. Previously, she had felt as though she had been dying, literally having the life bled out of her by a ghostly leech. But, this time she just felt cold, hollow and exposed, whilst the unnerving presence of being watched from afar worked its way through her bones.

She had only made contact for a few seconds when the pulsating feeling started to dwindle, and she was left feeling all alone once more. Lydia could not shake off the feeling that she had just somehow empowered a supernatural presence, and confidence dug its way into the back of her mind that she would once again be visited by the creature. An act by which she was both pleased and terrified, as pangs of regret now ached in her heart due to her sudden actions. But, she contented herself with the knowledge that she had encountered this spirit before, and it had yet to make any move towards hurting her. If the spectre had wished to harm her, surely it had already had plenty of opportunity to do so.

Taking a deep breath to steady her nerves, Lydia took a calming glance around the rest of the visible garden, only to discover she was practically surrounded by statues. It was like an army of soldiers holding their posts, waiting for their orders that would never arrive. It was almost breathtaking how many statues there were. She could see easily more than a dozen, just from where she was standing alone.

Kate had once told her, that Mitch had constructed the statues as monuments to their dear departed residents. A very personal gesture it would appear, so if the spirit of the woman that Lydia had just seen had become attached to this statue, then it was very likely that she was once a resident here, and that this statue was her legacy. Lydia's mind raced with this realisation! It then also occurred to her that this statue may not be alone! There could be others within these grounds that held similar connections to the afterlife.

Fuelled with a sudden surge of adrenaline, Lydia marched across the field, her slip-on shoes sliding across the dew-coated grass, until she arrived at the base of a far more recent statue. It was a grand lion, the exact same one that she had seen Mitch with just a week before.

She proceeded to stand face to face with the decorative animal. She then raised her hand, feeling empowered as it hovered above the surface of the statue, but not quite touching.

She suddenly felt agitated about her plan. If she had already inadvertently summoned one spirit, was it then a wise move to beckon another one? Nevertheless, her hand lowered itself, brushing against the stone, seemingly in disagreement with her will. It was as if something invisible from within had reached out and was pulling her closer. She gasped as the callous texture grazed her soft hand, and an instant chill then surged down her spine. It felt like ice was fusing each segment of her vertebrae. Lydia swiftly pulled herself away, her hand wrenching itself clear of the invisible grasp in the process. This had been a terrible idea. She now felt exhausted and drained, so she quickly scampered back towards the safety of the Hall. If anybody within the communal lounge had taken note of the look of panic in Lydia's eyes, or the haste in her step as she passed, they chose not to mention it!

***

It had taken a few hours, but, after taking a shower, and consuming several cups of camomile tea, Lydia had forced her nerves to settle. She had already acted, so there was nothing she could do now to escape her fate. There was a chance that she was being completely misguided by the events of the morning, and that nothing would actually come of it, or at least that's what she persistently told herself. She was trying to ignore the swelling feeling of dread brewing within her chest.

At one o'clock, Lydia had arranged to meet Kate for tea and cake in the communal dining room. Apparently, Kelly had spent the day baking, and a delicious sounding lemon meringue pie found itself on the dessert menu. Even after living at the Hall for only a few weeks, the one thing Lydia had picked up quickly was that Kelly's baking was to die for! So, lured by the prospect of some sweet treats, Lydia made her way down to the dining room.

She found Kate already seated, having snagged the much desired window table, and was patiently reading her ever-present book while she waited.

"I thought I was coming to tea, not book club!" Lydia teased, announcing her arrival.

"Well if you'd left me waiting any longer, I probably could have written my own book," Kate joked back, "come and sit yourself down. Everything okay?" Kate questioned, with a more serious tone, looking the other woman over.

"Everything is fine! Why wouldn't it be?" Lydia asked with uncertainty.

"You look a little pale, that's all," Kate replied, taking a sip of her tea whilst she pondered a change of subject, "I hope you're hungry."

"Starving!" Lydia told.

"So, if you're not interested in my book. Then why don't you choose the topic of conversation," Kate suggested obligingly, but the smirk on her lips said differently.

"Actually, there was something I wanted to ask you," Lydia admitted.

"Oh, this sounds interesting. What would you like to know from my deep well of knowledge?" Kate questioned, leaning forwards with interest.

"The statues in the garden. You said that Mitch makes them for the residents who are . . ." Lydia tailed off searching for the right words to continue her sentence.

"Dearly departed?" Kate offered.

"Exactly!" Lydia agreed, thanking the other woman with her eyes, "so, do you know who each of the statues were made for . . . each person's name I mean?" Lydia enquired.

"Anyone you're after in particular?" Kate raised an eyebrow.

"Yes actually! Near the conservatory, down the path towards Mitch's work shed. It's a woman holding a flower basket," Lydia described it as best she could.

"I know the one, always found it a bit creepy to be honest," Kate admitted, "all I can tell you is that one was up before I moved here. Maybe one of the old boys might remember who it was made for, or you could ask Kelly or Mitch," Kate suggested. "Can I ask what this is about?" she added eagerly.

"Later!" Lydia replied, "I'll tell you about it later," she insisted.

"Fine! But the enigmas surrounding you are really starting to build up, Lydia," Kate leant back in her chair, apparently her curiosity had been defeated for the moment. Until suddenly she straightened again, a gleam of excitement in her eye that had Lydia instantly on edge.

It was only then that Lydia picked up the sound of heels clicking across the hardwood floor. That sound had now become familiar to her since moving to the Hall. There was only one person she knew of who wore stiletto heels around the old house, so when she glanced back over her shoulder to find Kelly approaching, carrying a cake stand towards their table, it was no surprise!

"Good afternoon ladies," Kelly greeted, laying the cake stand down between them. "Lydia, it's great to see you out and about again. You didn't half have us all worried. Feeling better now I hope?" Kelly smiled sweetly, her voice dripping with concern.

"I'm fine now thank you. Must have been something I had eaten," Lydia returned.

"Well, I can assure you, there won't be any of that after my cooking!" Kelly announced confidently.

"The only side effect is how moreish everything is. I swear I've grown two dress sizes since I moved in here!"

Kate stated cheerfully, already lifting another slice of lemon meringue from the cake tray and onto her plate.

"Well, enjoy, and if there is anything else I can get you, please let me know," Kelly spoke sweetly to the pair as she prepared to step away.

"Actually Kelly!" Kate called out around a mouthful of pie, stopping the younger woman in her tracks.

"Yes?" Kelly questioned curiously.

"Lydia has something she wanted to ask you," Kate confirmed, ignoring the displeased look Lydia was shooting her way. "What? Strike while the iron's hot and all that jazz . . . go on . . . ask her!" Kate said, pushing her friend metaphorically into submission.

"What is it Lydia?" Kelly jumped in, sounding intrigued as to what awaited her, yet annoyance could also be heard tickling at the edge of her voice.

With a deep sigh, Lydia thought through her words before voicing them carefully. Still slightly put out by Kate forcing her into this situation, somewhat unprepared. "I wanted to ask you about the statues," Lydia finally stated, "I was told that they are made as memorials for deceased residents. Is that true?"

This line of questioning must have taken Kelly by surprise, as the usually unbreakable smile was replied with a look of confusion and surprise.

"Yes, it's true, but really they are just decorative," Kelly stated bluntly, "I'm aware they're not to everybody's taste, but Mitch enjoys making them, and we both feel it's a nice gesture to our guests," she continued, somewhat defensively.

"That's not why I'm asking. I don't dislike the statues, they interest me, that's all. One statue in particular. Do you, or does Mitch have some kind of record for who each of the statues were constructed for?" Lydia quizzed.

"We might have it written down somewhere, but really, it has always been a pretty unofficial gesture. For the most part, I can recall most of the residents we've had stay during our time here, and the statues my husband has made," Kelly informed.

"Does that mean you can remember which statue belongs to who?" Kate asked, seemingly giddy with the prospect.

"Mostly, yes," Kelly replied calmly, "I'm guessing this means you've got a favourite in mind," she enquired.

"Yes. We would like to know about the one near the conservatory. A young woman with a basket. Do you know which one we mean?" Kate exclaimed.

"I know it, yes," Kelly answered, her gaze meeting Kate's.

"And do you know who it was in memory of?" Lydia prompted.

"I do," Kelly sighed, leaning back against the table directly behind her, clearly no longer intent on leaving the conversation, "her name was Elizabeth Holland, but she insisted we all call her Lizzy," Kelly informed, looking down at her hands folded in her lap.

"Can you tell me anything about her?" Lydia encouraged, growing more eager with the new found information.

"Well, like most of them, she moved in here after her husband had passed away. She didn't have any family, so we all took her in as one of our own. She was also a successful artist. Most of the paintings you see around the hall are her creations actually. She and I became good friends, and she was always donating her works to the Hall," Kelly paused, as if pondering whether to continue or not, "she lived in apartment 'eleven', Lydia. She was the previous resident before you."

Kelly refused to meet either woman's gaze, as Lydia paled considerably at the realisation, her voice going small as she attempted to summon it from within her.

"How did she die?" Lydia forced the words out, voice choked as she did so. Not wanting to know the answer, but determined to know the truth.

Kelly looked disheartened as the question hit her ears, but she didn't shy away from it. Instead, she raised her head and looked Lydia straight in the eye. Perhaps in a show of strength, or, as a subconscious way to somehow punish Lydia for dragging up the past.

"She suffered an aneurysm in the bath and she drowned," Kelly spoke, her tone melancholy and her face downturned.

"I'm so sorry," Lydia whispered, feeling guilt at the sadness she had caused to rise in the usually cheerful woman.

"There are reasons we don't discuss the past, especially in a place like this," Kelly stated, before making her hasty departure.

"Did you find the answers you were looking for?" Kate questioned, once more digging into her pie, the previous conversation seemingly pushed from her mind.

"Some of them at least," Lydia replied solemnly, no longer feeling hungry.

***

By the time night fell, the weather had darkened greatly. Outside, a heavy rain fell upon Carnation Hall. It caused a huge torrent of water to flow from the rooftops, spilling over the edge and cascading down like a waterfall onto the ground below. The water puddled and flowed out towards the gardens, leaving the lawns swimming, and flooding the flowerbeds.

Inside apartment number 'eleven', Lydia Jones sat huddled in her bed. She was listening intently to the wind screeching through the air and pounding against her windows. The storm had been raging for hours, and so far held no sign of letting up. If anything, it seemed to be growing worse. The air was flowing under the old doors and around the windows of the manor house. It gave the Hall an impression of sentient life, as if the building had lungs, each creak and groan of the walls and floorboards was like an echo of the Hall breathing deeply, perhaps in slumber.

It was past midnight and into the early hours when Lydia felt her eyes finally begin to fall. Once again, she heard the same gentle knocking sound emanating from the area of her door. The sound was almost inaudible against the tumultuous weather outside, but this time Lydia had somehow been expecting its arrival. This time, she was poised and ready to greet its call, and welcome the terror of the spectre back into her life. There had to be a reason why this ghost was demanding her attention, and Lydia was determined to understand its motives. Was it in some way trapped? Unable to move on without aid? Lydia had spent most of her life committed to helping the living move on from the dead. Maybe now it was her turn to help the dead move on from the living. She just had to figure out what this spirit wanted from her, then perhaps she could set it free and end this nightmare she now found herself in.

Creeping out of bed, Lydia's feet found their way inside her worn slippers, this time with expert precision.

Dressing gown now thrown around her shoulders, Lydia felt an echo of the previous week, when the dead had last come knocking for her. She finally reached the door, already playing out in her mind the scene that was expected to greet her when she opened the door. The thought of the flashing lights down the hallway from the previous time was already irritating her eyes in anticipation.

Without any hesitation, Lydia readied herself and threw open the door, instantly recoiling in horror! Instead of seeing the expected empty hallway, she was standing almost directly face to face with the drowned woman! She was standing immediately outside her threshold. The ghost stood cold and static at the entranceway, its pale eyes rolling up and back into its head as it continuously mumbled silently to itself. The way it moved and jerked, even whilst standing still, reminded Lydia of a person suffering an endless seizure, a thought that settled uncomfortably deep within Lydia's mind.

Staring at the spectre now guarding her door, Lydia felt sick with fear. Previously, she hadn't been so close to its ethereal body, and eternally wished she had managed to keep it that way. But, knowing she had no choice now but to proceed, Lydia placed a hand on her own chest, exhaling deeply to fuel her courage, before taking a step forward towards the ghost, now standing barely inches away.

The spectre did not react to Lydia's movements, nor did it move or teleport itself away as it had done at their previous meeting. Instead, it continued to simply block her doorway, seemingly unable or unwilling to enter. It did not even acknowledge Lydia's presence. Instead, it just stared upwards and sightlessly at the ceiling, repeating a mantra that nobody would ever hear. This stalemate continued for a few moments, and Lydia could feel the terror and uncertainty building within her. She wanted to move. She wanted to get away from this disturbing visage now! She wanted to close her apartment door and never open it again! However, she knew that was not going to be an option. If this spirit demanded her attention so strongly, then she knew that it would haunt her until the day she died. She had to discover what it wanted. She felt a tiny morsel of courage return to her, and she swallowed down the rising need to retreat. Lydia raised her hand, and waved it around in the air, in much the same way as you would to attract the attention of an old friend from across the street.

"Hello!" Lydia spoke out, her voice barely above a whisper. The spectre did not react, though Lydia was convinced it had heard her. "My name is Lydia," she continued, still gaining no response, "I want to help you!"

Lydia stated, forcing herself to speak louder and with more assertiveness, "last time we met, I believe you were trying to show me something. Is that true?" There was no reply! The lack of any sort of acknowledgement was quickly beginning to irritate Lydia. If this ghost needed her help, then surely she had awarded it enough chances to ask for it. So, perhaps this ghost didn't need her help after all. Perhaps it was only here to torment her, and she had been playing into a sick game. Feeling a slight burn of anger, Lydia planted her feet before the creature and looked into its distorted face as best she could.

"Can you even hear me?" she questioned coldly.

Silence!

"I said . . . can you hear me? Answer me!" Lydia demanded.

More silence!

"I know who you are! You are Elizabeth! Tell me what you want!" Lydia practically shouted at the ghost with pure frustration. But, as soon as the drowned woman's name had left her lips, the spectre reacted immediately. Its head tilted downwards, the ugly blue veins of its translucent skin seemingly about to burst in the pale light of the hallway, whilst its deathly eyes bore directly into Lydia's soul. A look of confusion passed over the creature's features for a split second, before the ghost raised its hand, flailing it in the air, as if to strike the living woman. This caused Lydia to cower back in fear! But, before it could make any contact, the jittering spirit faded away, reappearing back into existence near the top of the staircase. Its arm was now stretched out once more, pointing downstairs to the foyer, water still dripping endlessly from its fingertips.

"You want me to follow you . . . is that it?" Lydia questioned apprehensively, as she leant around her doorway. An internal war raged within her head as her natural curiosity fought against her fear and anxiety for dominance. In the end, it was her natural instinct to investigate that won the battle, as her slippered feet gently began to shuffle along the hallway floor.

The ghost continued to stare at her, its dead glare chilling her to the bone as it gently nodded its head. This was either to confirm her question, or perhaps it was just pleased with her actions as she approached. A second later it disappeared again, this time completely from view!

Lydia was now standing at the top of the staircase, rapidly looking around for a glimpse of the creature. She could see the spectre now standing on the ground floor, aiming its skeletal hand down the hallway, pointing the way into the darkness.

Hesitantly, Lydia began to follow, cringing as the old stairs creaked beneath her feet with every downward step.

As she reached the bottom of the staircase, she could only watch as the spectre faded yet again.

Realising that this was the same hallway she was led down last time, when Kelly suddenly appeared and interrupted her apparent spirit guide, Lydia decided to continue on this path. Whatever it was that Elizabeth's spirit was trying to show her, it was obviously important enough to literally wake the dead for, and Lydia was determined to get to the bottom of this mystery.

However, as Lydia stumbled down the long dark hallway, there was no sight of the spectre. She was now alone, and the eerie silence of the night was creeping in, making every footfall echo in her own ears.

It was just as she was passing the door at the end of the hallway, labelled *'PRIVATE'* in bold letters, that a loud noise sounded from within. It was like a thunderbolt or a hammer striking against the wall. Lydia jumped out of her skin, and was left rigid as a shocked gasp poured out from her lips. She turned to the door, feeling her heart pounding violently as she reached out her hand to grab the handle. It started to turn within her grasp, but refused to open! The lock was clearly holding the door in place, preventing Lydia from entering.

Another loud bang then sounded from within the room! This caused Lydia to step back from the door with fright at the violence of the sound.

"Elizabeth . . . is that you in there?" Lydia whispered, "the door's locked, I can't follow you!" she added, attempting to jiggle the handle once more, on the off chance it may permit her access. But it was no use, and seething with frustration, Lydia leant her forehead against the door in defeat. Silence loomed once more, and Lydia assumed that the spectre had now departed. Her heightened senses were informing her that its presence was no longer nearby. However, she could not shake the feeling that she was still not alone.

It was just as she decided to retreat back to her room that a new sound caught her attention. It was subtle compared to the backdrop torrent of wind and rain, but there was no doubt in Lydia's mind that she had heard it. A scuttling, scratching noise was irritating her ears, as if something was crawling around the floor of the dark hallway. Growing dread began to form within Lydia, her breathing quickened as she felt ice sinking deep into her stomach. The sound was growing louder. It was as though her body was preparing itself for a threat that she could not yet see.

She slowly turned around to look in the direction from where the noise was originating from, even though every instinct within her body begged her not to. A new terror now revealed itself before Lydia. She was frozen in place as pure horror worked its way through her veins, stealing the air from her lungs. What she saw was a grotesque figure, once more jittering its way in and out of existence in rapid succession. But, this figure was not that of Elizabeth, even though Lydia wished it had been. No, this was a totally new creature! This was a man, and he was far more disturbing to behold than Elizabeth had ever been. It did not stand as the drowned woman had. Instead, it was creeping and slithering on its belly across the floor, dragging itself forwards by its long, jagged and chipped fingernails. Its skeletal-like fingers bending awkwardly under the force. Lydia felt her breath hitch high in her throat, as she discovered the reason why the man was moving in such a strange and disturbing way. His legs from above the knee were completely absent, seemingly ripped off! Pieces of skin and flesh were hanging loosely from his missing limbs in a grotesque display. Seeing this disturbing scene caused a wave of nausea to wash through Lydia, which she was barely able to swallow down.

The ghost, or man-like creature then continued to slowly drag himself towards Lydia! She stood petrified, unable to move as the fear cemented her feet in place! She was fixed with her back held up against the wall, as she desperately tried to move away from the creature advancing upon her. Its face was distorted with wild fury as it approached, its eyes bellowing, as a cold dead hand reached out to grab her in desperation! Lydia was frantic, trying desperately to move and get as far away from this beast as possible. Yet, she found herself frozen, rooted to the spot by a seemingly invisible force. Tears were now bellowing in her eyes as she fought against it, desperate to escape!

Lydia was unable to hold back her screams as bone-like fingers grasped hold of her ankle. Its hand felt like ice-cold death against her skin. She could feel the sensation work its way through her skin, worming through her nerves and igniting them with hot agony. The creature had only grasped hold of Lydia for a brief second, before the edges of her vision narrowed inwards. She was unable to stop herself from collapsing down to the hallway floor, her body too weak to hold her up any longer. More darkness encroached, and as strong as Lydia's will was, there was nothing she could do to prevent her world turning black, as she sank into unconsciousness.

***

Lydia had no idea how much time had passed when she suddenly awoke. But it was still dark, and she was still lying on the hallway floor. Her eyes finally opened, her unsteady vision was now locked onto the *'PRIVATE'* sign above her. She then remembered where she was, and how she had come to be lying there in such an unusual position. It took several attempts before she was able to push herself up and onto her elbows, almost blacking out again with the head rush that accompanied the movement. Once securely propped up, she was now able to take stock of her surroundings.

Lydia's heightened senses informed her that she was now completely alone. No spirits or ghosts were hiding in the shadows waiting to tempt or attack her, and she was eternally grateful for that.

Her head was pounding, and she felt nauseated and exhausted as she sat upon the floor. Her back was against the wall to keep her vertical, as she willed her world to stop spinning and allow her stiff body to move once more.

There was a persistent throbbing coming from her ankle, and with more effort than it should have taken, Lydia managed to pull up her trouser leg to reveal an ugly dark bruise that lay beneath. It was a hideous injury to behold. Various shades of blue, yellow and purple had worked their way through the bruise itself, as if it was some chaotic child's artwork painted upon her skin. The flesh around the bruise was still glowing red from the irritation and abuse, a stark contrast from the rest of her pale skin. What was making Lydia now shake with fright and look away with repulsion, was seeing the bruise itself with its perfect outline of a handprint. Just more proof that what had occurred this night was real, not a bad dream or hallucination . . . although she dearly wished that it had been!

Lydia wanted to cry. She wanted to scream. She wanted to run away from this horrible place and return to the comfort of her little cottage, forgetting that this place ever existed. She wanted Robert by her side again. She wanted to feel his love and protection surrounding her whilst she cried. She felt it wasn't fair! Her entire world had been ripped apart when he had been taken away from her, and now she found herself desperately clutching to any small pieces she could to hold herself together. Her search for happiness was now being torn away again in the worst possible way. Perhaps Robert had been right, perhaps there was a god, and now he was punishing her for her lack of belief. She was a sinner, and purgatory had laid claim to her soul. That's where she was now, abandoned by her soulmate and was being tormented in limbo by the spirits of the dead. Lydia could have laughed at herself for having such thoughts. She was not the kind to doubt herself. She was not weak and helpless, yet here she was, crying openly into the night, wishing life had dealt her a better hand. She had never felt more pathetic in all her life.

She sat there sobbing for what felt like hours, but in reality, barely a minute had passed by. The fog of exhaustion and pain started to fade from Lydia's head, at least sufficiently for a new sound to assault her sensitive ears. It was familiar and constant in the way it demanded her attention. She recognised the sound instinctively, and pushed away the dark depressing thoughts that had been plaguing her mind and fuelling her tears. She was suddenly overcome with concern as the sound continued to spill out. It was the whooping and wailing of a nearby siren that filled her with dread.

A sudden rush of adrenaline gave Lydia the strength to move. She stumbled up to her feet using the wall as support, and she urged herself on down the hallway as quickly as her aching body would allow. As she burst into the now brightly lit foyer, she discovered it to be buzzing with a crowd of people, the murmur of whispering voices all around.

Pushing herself through the tide of people, Lydia forced her way to the front in order to try and see what was happening.

Kelly was currently stood by the front door, looking pale and morose as she talked to a policeman in full uniform. The man appeared to be writing notes, and Lydia could only assume he was taking her statement. This did not look good!

Over on the other side of the foyer, at the top of the old wooden staircase, several paramedics came into view.

They slowly began to descend the stairs carrying a stretcher! It was completely covered with a cloth, unmissable in their tight grip.

Lydia felt sick as they slowly reached the bottom of the stairs. They then lowered the wheels to the ground, and continued to push the stretcher towards the front door as quickly as they could. In fact, the men were in such a rush to remove the apparent body, that they failed to secure it properly. Just as the men were marching past Lydia, a lifeless arm fell freely from beneath the material, almost as if it was reaching out with sinister intent to grab Lydia. The arm flopped downwards lifelessly and limp, right in front of her eyes, the shock almost causing her to recoil and scream!

One of the paramedics acted quickly, raising the arm back up, and placing it below the sheet and out of sight with expert precision. The paramedic then flashed Lydia an apologetic look as they continued on their way out of the Hall, and into the darkness beyond.

Lydia was now feeling even more nauseated and sombre. She then caught sight of Kate in the crowd, and they both worked their way quickly towards each other.

"Oh Lydia! Where have you been? You weren't in your room, I was so worried!" Kate explained, her eyes stained red and her face damp with shed tears.

"Kate, what is it? What has happened?" Lydia demanded to know, grabbing the other woman by the shoulders desperately to steady her.

"It was so horrible! I can't believe he's gone! I can't believe it!" Kate continued to sob hysterically.

"Who's gone? Who was that they took away? Please, Kate, you have to tell me? Who has died?" Lydia begged, unwilling to be kept in the dark any longer.

"It's Bryan . . . he's dead!" Kate finally said, voice barely above a whisper, before she was falling into Lydia's shoulder and sobbing uncontrollably.

Lydia couldn't move! She couldn't speak! She could barely breathe! All she could do was stand still and hold her friend whilst they cried. She felt numb. No, she felt dead!

CHAPTER 10
Aftermath

"I can't believe he's gone!" Kate stated blankly, staring into her cup of tea as if the contents alone could explain all the world's mysteries. "Bryan was here yesterday, and now he's gone!" she said in a daze.

Lydia was currently hosting the other woman within her apartment. It seemed a feeble attempt to comfort her friend with a breakfast of tea and toast, but neither of them had an appetite. Kate's tea was slowly turning cold within her trembling hands.

Lydia sighed deeply as she took her place in her favourite armchair. The night before had left her with bruises, and a headache that still refused to reside. She wanted nothing more than to get some sleep, and to slip away into a peaceful dream of happier times gone by. But, after finding Kate in the crowd the night before, distressed and lost, she had felt obliged to comfort and take care of her friend.

"Can I get you anything? More tea . . . maybe a blanket? Why don't you try a slice of toast, you need to keep your strength up!" Lydia offered, attempting to break the other woman from her looping thoughts and words.

"He's not the first you know," Kate spoke, her voice breaking the words slightly.

"Not the first what?" Lydia questioned with uncertainty.

"Not the first resident to die whilst I've been here," Kate said dispassionately, finally taking the first sip of her now tepid tea, and pursing her lips in distaste, "but he's the first one for you isn't he? You've never seen us lose someone before," she said, her tone suggesting the question did not need an answer.

"Last night . . ." Lydia began, her words catching in her throat momentarily, "last night was a shock to all of us. Bryan was a good man and he will be greatly missed."

"I wonder if anyone will say that about me when I go?" Kate questioned, her tone gloomy and cynical.

"You can't think that way," Lydia replied.

"Why not?" the other woman questioned, her eyes now studying her cup once more, "when I decided to move here, my old neighbour couldn't understand why.

She told me it would be like moving into a funeral parlour. 'God's waiting room' she called it. I brushed her comments aside, convincing myself that nobody really dies in a place like this. I told myself, it would be like living in a luxurious hotel where everybody lives forever. I was only fooling myself. I'm not saying that I would rather be somewhere else. Where would I even go? I have no real family. This is as good as it gets for me," Kate declared, sorrowfully. "I'm sorry for being such a pain Lydia, you shouldn't have to put up with me being all melancholy. It's just . . . losing Bryan so suddenly has hit a nerve," she added, her shoulders slumping in defeat.

"You don't have to explain yourself to me, I understand. I've spent most of my life working with people that are bereaved, and after losing my husband . . ." Lydia tailed off, unable to finish the thought, "there is no right or wrong way of dealing with this. Everyone grieves in their own way. All we can do is try to support each other, because that's what friends do. So, I'm here for you, alright? Like it or not you're stuck with me!" she announced, attempting a small smile to accentuate her point.

"Good, because you're stuck with me too!" Kate replied and actually returned the smile. "You still haven't told me what it was you did for a living," Kate added expectantly.

"Now isn't the time," Lydia told her gently, "just drink your cold tea!"

***

Bryan's death had come as a big shock to everyone. The atmosphere following the event was extremely sombre, with the entire Hall seemingly mourning the loss. The residents were near silent all day long, there was no sound of the television blaring in the lounge, or of laughter coming from the conservatory. In fact, the hallways were eerily quiet, as if someone had sneaked in during the night and stolen everybody else away. Lydia felt like she had been left all alone in this big old house. If it hadn't been for the crooked, stooping figures that she had witnessed wandering around, or the occasional echoed clicking of Kelly's shoes sounding from down the halls, then she truly could have believed that she had been abandoned.

It was a couple of weeks later that Lydia attended Bryan's funeral. It was a very small ceremony at the crematorium, with only a few people in attendance as Bryan had no family.

Mitch kindly drove both Lydia and Kate to the occasion, where Kelly gracefully performed a fitting eulogy. Yet, the ceremony itself felt hollow. Lydia could not stop thinking, that for a man as kindly as Bryan, the funeral did not seem fitting. She wished that they could have given him more, as she sat there with Kate gently sobbing on her shoulder. The coffin slowly disappeared behind the velvet curtain, likened to some kind of sombre magic trick. Lydia looked around the almost empty room, only hoping that when the bell finally tolled for her, there would be more people appearing to pay their respects. It actually made her feel grateful at Robert's funeral, because, as terrible and gut wrenching as the day had been, many people had attended to pay their respects. Bryan's service had been brief and over far too quickly.

After the funeral, Mitch drove them back to the Hall, just as the rain was beginning to fall. The sky itself appeared to be crying out in sympathy for their sad loss.

Kate found the loss of Bryan hard to swallow. She had known him for far longer than Lydia had, and they shared a common bond, formed from similar past experiences and losses. A loneliness the likes of which Lydia had never known. Lydia had a family, and even after losing Robert, she still had her daughter Susanna. Kate and Bryan had no close relatives, only each other, and Lydia could only imagine the isolation Kate must now be feeling. Since the funeral she had been making every effort to be there for her friend, bringing meals to her apartment, and making sure she was eating and lending an ear when it was needed. Kate, however, was mostly keeping herself to herself, and Lydia respected that decision.

As for Lydia, the loss had stirred something up within her. At first, she had felt numbed by her recent experiences, and yes, her body ached and her head pounded after her latest run in with the ghostly apparitions. Her nerve endings were still burning with pure fear at the sound of every creak in the night. She was beyond exhausted from countless sleepless nights, as nightmares continued to plague her troubled mind. But, as time was passing, and the days were now turning into weeks, her bruises had faded away and the bad dreams had become less frequent. She was relieved to report that the spirits had not visited her again since that fateful night, and now, Lydia dearly hoped that they were done with her. Bryan's sudden death from his heart attack had shown Lydia once again how fragile mortality was, and she had now become more determined than ever to enjoy the time she had left, however long that may be.

Instead of sitting around and sulking over what she had lost, Lydia decided to make a greater effort to enjoy the time that she had left. This started with her requesting Mitch to take herself and Kate into town more frequently. They would enjoy walks in the park, local coffee shops, the weekly market, and even go to the cinema. It had been on one of these day trips out that Lydia had caught sight of a local travel agency, and an idea began to form inside her head. She began making plans to take her family away on holiday, somewhere exotic. The young man in the travel agent's office was called Alan, his name tag having been helpfully displayed. He had shown Lydia a variety of vacation options, ranging from all over Europe to as far as Australia. Finally, one deal had caught her eye. She was instantly drawn to this decision, as she had often thought of visiting this country, and something in her stomach was telling her that this was the right choice. And, so it was set, Lydia and her close little family would be jet-setting in the new year. A two-week cruise around the Far East including a visit to Vietnam, a country Lydia herself had always wanted to see. She planned to surprise them all with this great news on Christmas Day. It was to be a very special gift for the ones she loved.

Aside from the secret surprise planned for her nearest and dearest, Lydia had also invited them all to her apartment the following Sunday for dinner. After the first time, Lydia had enjoyed the experience so much, that the event had now become a fortnightly occurrence, quickly becoming a tradition. Kate had joined them on a few occasions, and it was a relief to see she was now coming out of her depression. Lydia knew that Kate didn't have any family members around her, but since she had been so kind as to make her feel welcome at the Hall, Lydia had decided that she would try and make Kate feel welcome within her own family.

The other major step forward for Lydia, was that she had recently spoken to Kelly about drawing up her own will. She had never bothered to write one before Robert's death. But now, after what had recently happened to Bryan, the prospect of a sudden and unforeseen end seemed to loom, and if the worst were to happen, Lydia wanted to ensure that Susanna and her family would receive all that they were entitled. She wanted to avoid any loopholes that could possibly result in somebody else stealing her inheritance away from her family!

Lydia had recently met Kelly in the dining room where she had expressed her wishes. Kelly had been surprisingly joyful at the prospect of helping draft and register a will for Lydia, and the two agreed to meet up soon to start the process. The entire exercise appeared straight forward, and felt quite stress free. It left Lydia smiling gratefully throughout the rest of the day.

***

A few days later, fresh excitement was stirring once more within the Hall. Lydia had been taking a walk through the grounds with Kate, when suddenly a rumbling noise grabbed their attention. It was the sound of heavy tyres forcing their way through the gravel on the driveway. By now, Lydia was quite familiar with the sound of Kelly's little Mini as it scuttled around, and the sound of Mitch's white van rumbling along. But, she knew instantly that this new sound belonged to neither of them. Intrigued, the ladies made their way around to the front of the house, crossing the lawn just in time to see a large, bright red four-wheel drive vehicle rolling its way up to the front of the Hall. Lydia could feel her jaw begin to drop as she witnessed Kelly sitting behind the wheel. She was displaying a huge grin on her face, the likes of which Lydia had never seen before, as she drove her brand new expensive-looking car.

Mitch was already waiting in the doorway, his own goofy smile showing clearly, as his wife pulled up in her new 'Chelsea Tractor'. Kelly clambered out from the car, and the two embraced fondly. It was a rare show of affection between the two, and a sight Lydia had never witnessed before. Yet, she could not help herself from smiling along with them.

It was not until the following day that Lydia would find out how Kelly had inherited such an expensive new motor. Apparently, a distant aunt of Kelly's had passed away, leaving her and Mitch a rather generous sum of money. Kelly had excitedly informed everyone about her windfall, and that the amount was enough to buy the new fancy car. She even claimed that there was enough money left over for them to take a relaxing holiday to Las Vegas for Mitch's birthday. A fact she was particularly ecstatic about, and would continue to brag about quite often for weeks to come.

***

Time continued to pass by rapidly, and the leaves were now beginning to fall from the trees as autumn began to settle in. The grounds of the Hall that not long ago were filled with plush green lawns and vibrant flowers, had now turned amber and scarlet with the falling leaves. This set the garden aglow with sunsets of fire, whilst the air was starting to grow colder, and the wind was beginning to bite. Winter was now closing in briskly. Lydia was standing, gazing out of her bedroom window. The sight of Mitch in the distance had grabbed her attention. She had not caught sight of him all day, despite actually wanting to find him, on account of her newly found leak coming from below her kitchen sink. She had searched all the places that he frequently haunted. He had not been in the fields riding his lawnmower as he usually did, nor was he out by the fountain dead-heading the roses. In fact, he hadn't even been out at the front caring for his beloved van. Lydia had previously assumed that Mitch may have taken the day off in favour of visiting the golf course. This was a hobby she had learned that he possessed on one of their frequent trips into town. It was a hobby that her late husband himself had adored. Mitch may have been a man of very few words, but he seemed very passionate about his golfing days, and was always readily open to discuss the subject. In fact, Lydia had never known him to be so chatty, he had even shared his nickname with her. He was known as 'The Duke' to his golfing buddies. They had christened him with this name in the club house. Mitch certainly seemed proud of the title. Apparently, it was an endearment based on him calling the grand Carnation Hall his personal home, and that he liked to wear expensive, smart-looking apparel. It was Kelly's duty to choose his clothing for him, especially when they were visiting the golf club together for parties and special events. He certainly was an individual with elevated delusions of grandeur! Lydia found all of this information extremely interesting, and since then had felt a stronger, more friendlier bond with the broad man. But, if Mitch had left to go playing golf today, then why were all of the Miller's vehicles still standing in the driveway?

Well, now the mystery had an answer. With the setting sun slowly beginning to fade into gloom, Lydia spied out into the gardens and could see the lone bulking figure of a man walking across the field. He was carrying what appeared to be a shovel, and was looking around indecisively, as if searching for something in the twilight. Lydia watched on curiously, unseen from below as the darkness within her apartment shielded her from onlooking eyes. It took several minutes, but Mitch finally stopped patrolling around. He stood in a clear spot, a fair distance away from any of the other many garden features. He then raised his shovel up into the air, and with some force, slammed it down into the soft ground, scooping the earth away in the process. This action was repeated over and over. Mitch was digging a hole for something, but what? Lydia could only find one reason for Mitch to be digging a hole. Lydia felt her stomach drop as her mind filled in the blanks. Mitch was getting ready to plant a new piece of his artwork! A brand new statue would soon be joining the ranks.

***

That same night, Lydia had yet another nightmare, and this one was more vivid than any previous. Within her deep slumber, Lydia could see the Hall in front of her, the rain billowing down upon its roof with savage force. She found herself standing outside on the driveway, with gravel digging painfully into her bare feet from beneath, her nightdress soaked through, and her skin unnaturally cold. Her body felt numb, and she did not know why she was there, or why she would have wandered out in the middle of the night. A flash of lightning drew her attention back to the Hall with its sudden illumination. The Hall then fell into complete darkness. No light was creeping through any of the windows, and the building seemed as though it had long been abandoned.

Suddenly, realising she was shivering against the cold, Lydia forced herself to try and move. Each step felt sluggish and disembodied, as she slowly walked towards the front door. Lydia knew that the door would be unlocked upon meeting. She pushed it open, its hinges groaning audibly with a piercing screech as it went, making Lydia cringe.

She continued into the Hall, the space now looking quite foreign to her. The once bright and spotless foyer was now dark and dismal, with cobwebs netting their way around the room, and every surface covered in a deep coat of dust. But, the most drastic change of all was the stone statue now occupying the entrance hall. The statue was imitating a beautiful standing woman. Her long thin gown was bustling out around her, long locks of hair reaching down past her shoulders, and her expression placid as she gazed down into her upturned palms. The statue was quite beautiful, yet haunting, there was no doubt!

The frightful loud noise of the door slamming behind her caused Lydia to leap with shock. She momentarily turned her attention away from the statue, just to check that she was still alone. Then, moments later, her gaze returned to the petrified woman in the centre of the room, only to witness that it had changed shape! The arms of the woman were now lying limp at her sides, and her stare was locked directly onto Lydia with burning intensity. Another flash of lightning from outside illuminated the statue, casting its shadow onto the back wall in a sinister giant echo of itself.

Lydia could feel the fear begin to embrace her once more. She knew this was just a dream, of that she had no doubt, yet everything about this statue set her nerves alight. Then, against her control, and in a way only possible in a nightmare, Lydia felt herself take a step forward. She edged her way closer to the statue as it watched her with hideous intent! She tried to struggle, she tried to pull back, fighting desperately against the invisible chains that bound her. She was being dragged forwards against her will, powerless to intervene. She felt a lump swelling within her throat. She willed herself to wake up, pleading with her subconscious to release her from this nightmare, but she was unable to awaken! She was now trapped in this dark world of shadows formed within her own mind.

Lydia almost screamed as she watched her own hand helplessly reach out to touch the statue. She tried to resist with everything she had, but she was unable to deny her fingertips making contact with the statue's exterior. Lydia anticipated the pending icy touch. Yet, at first, nothing happened! The statue did not move. No monster jumped from the shadows in order to attack her, and the building didn't crumble down around her. Lydia was transfixed in disbelief. She almost smiled with relief as the tension began to drain away from her. She just stood there, staring into the statue's eyes with solace, whilst another bolt of lighting struck the building, lighting up its face once more.

As the thunder rolled, Lydia momentarily turned away, and as her gaze was cast elsewhere, the statue struck! It proceeded to wrap its cold and lifeless fingers around Lydia's shoulder, pinning her in place. On this occasion Lydia could not contain her yell of terror, and she spun her head around in order to see the creature that now held her. The statue had once more changed! It was now looming over her, its face distorted with malice and pain, as if it were silently screaming out at Lydia, its eyes glaring viciously! Now, even more desperate to escape the paranormal grasp, Lydia pulled and twisted her way to freedom from the statue's hold, only to throw herself sideways onto the floor of the foyer, landing hard on her hands and knees. With panic rising in her veins, Lydia scurried away from the statue, only allowing herself a quick glance back to ensure that she wasn't being pursued. She wasn't being followed, the statue was completely still, reaching out for her from within its stone casing.

Lydia took the opportunity to find her feet, and once more compelled herself to awaken. It did no good as she was unable to escape the dream.

Feeling frustrated, Lydia glared back at the statue, and noticed something different about its posture. The other hand, the one that had not tried to grab her, was stretched out and pointing directly to the hallway. The very same hallway that Elizabeth's ghost had been pointing her down, and the same hallway where the dismembered man had attacked her outside Kelly's office.

What was going on? Why was Lydia constantly being led towards the office door? Even in her dreams, the door seemed to beckon her, tempting her to uncover the secrets that lie within.

Now, with newly formed determination, Lydia marched herself down the hallway. Legs numbed with each step, reminding her once more that she was dreaming. The hallway seemed very different here than it did in reality. It seemed more elongated and distant, as if with each step she took forward it was moving further away from her. It seemed to be stretching, keeping her further and further away from her destination. Frustration was causing her legs to run, keeping up a pace that would have been impossible outside the dream. It was like running on a treadmill, legs pumping as she tried to close the distance, but to no avail. For a moment, Lydia thought she would be stuck in this state forever, eternally reaching for something she could never catch. Closing her eyes, Lydia was about to accept defeat, when she felt her hand grasp against something cold and metal, a door handle! She gave it a firm yank, but the door refused to budge. Even from within her sleep it was locked, preventing her from entering, keeping her shut out! She pounded her palm against the wooden surface in annoyance, letting the door feel her growing frustration.

Another flash of light and rumble of thunder sent shivers running down her spine. The feeling of dread, and of eyes watching from the dark plotting to harm her had returned. She gulped down the lump forming in her throat, and stepped away from the door. Her eyes tentatively turned, looking down the hallway towards the foyer. She was reluctant to look, yet she knew that she had no choice! The statute seemed to have vanished! She made her way towards the foyer to confirm its disappearance. There was no trace of its existence, just an empty space where it had once stood! Lydia nearly whimpered against the tension in the air. She wished once more to will herself awake and end this nightmare, but her subconscious had other plans for her.

The sound of something crashing echoed down the hallway, far louder than the recent thunder. The office door then suddenly and violently swung itself open! A stream of bright white light was bleeding from within and stole Lydia's vision. She was blinded by the light as a pair of hands encased in cold stone reached out towards her, wrapping themselves around her neck! The hands were starting to squeeze more tightly, stealing Lydia's air and beginning to crush her throat. She couldn't breath, her lungs were burning and her eyes were watering as she struggled within the perilous grip of death! For a moment Lydia believed she was going to die, having her life choked away by her own imagination! It was only as the horror began to slow down, and the blinding light start to fade away, that Lydia could now see the face of the statue more clearly. It was looming over her, its eyes were glowing with fury, wearing a sinister grin that consumed its face as it continued to choke her! Suddenly, the whole world turned black!

Lydia suddenly woke up feeling startled and sat herself upright in her bed, sweat was now smothering her skin. Her feverish temperature was now slowly returning to normal, and she was feeling a little nauseous and disoriented. Her limbs were still shaking from the exertion, and her throat was still feeling tight from the imaginary force that brutally assaulted her. Outside her window the darkness prevailed, with barely any light able to find its way in. The clock on her bedside table helpfully informed her that the time was now twenty-three minutes past four in the morning. It was far too early to start the new day. Lydia knew that she would not be getting any more sleep tonight, and instead, an idea began to form in her mind. A seed had now been planted, and it was time to help it grow.

Lydia had been a medium for many years, in fact, long enough to know that not every dream was 'just' a dream! She had, during her lifetime met people who had based their entire careers around interpreting dreams and messages from beyond! She was now becoming tired and weary of this mystery and the spirits that were continually eluding her. She decided it was finally time to have trust in her own instincts! It was obvious that the spirits, whatever or whoever they may be, were not prepared to let her live in peace, so she decided that she would follow their instruction, and follow the path that they were leading her down. She knew her first step would be to try and investigate inside Kelly's office!

***

It was still early morning when Lydia emerged from her apartment. She now felt somewhat revitalised after taking a hot shower and putting on a fresh set of clothes.

Time was now dragging on as the rain continued to pour, last night's dream still lingering at the back of her mind. She was now sitting at the back of the empty conservatory, watching droplets of water splash and dribble down the surface of the windows. She was keeping a watchful and cautious eye on the nearest statue sitting outside in the rain. Her fingers were drumming against the side of her teacup, whilst she waited impatiently for Kate to make an appearance. Her friend finally showed up some time after ten o'clock, herself looking slightly baffled to find Lydia waiting for her.

"You're keen!" Kate stated, "eager to discuss the works of the 'The Brontë Sisters' with me?" she added, jokingly.

"I need your help!" Lydia said.

"Okay?" Kate replied, suddenly concerned, "is everything alright?"

"I need to tell you something, and you are probably going to think that I've gone completely mad! But, please hear me out," Lydia said, her eyes determined as she waited for Kate to sit down.

"Okay, this sounds interesting. You're not secretly a spy are you?" Kate joked, but seeing the serious look on Lydia's face made her pause, before sinking into the chair across from the other woman. "You can talk to me, I promise! Whatever it is, you can tell me," Kate replied softly.

"You've been asking what I do for a living ever since I moved here. I've been avoiding the subject since I wasn't sure how you would take it," Lydia began, "well, the truth is, I'm a medium!" she stated.

"I'm assuming you aren't talking about dress size?" Kate questioned curiously, almost breaking into a smile which she held back.

"No . . . I communicate with the dead!" Lydia explained calmly.

Kate paused, looking for a moment like she was about to laugh. But, after a second she could clearly see that Lydia was not making a joke. The serious stare and the tired, determined look in her eyes gave the truth away. Kate swallowed, looking both intrigued and uncomfortable as the realisation set in. "You're serious?" she asked.

"Yes!" Lydia responded. Now looking at her lap with disappointment.

"And you do this for a living?" Kate quizzed, her curious streak growing.

"I used to, before I came here," came the reply.

"Kelly told us that you were an author. So these books you've had published, they were about . . ." Kate paused, searching for a fitting word before continuing, "erm . . . this sort of stuff?"

"Yes," Lydia acknowledged, seeming more and more defeated.

"Can I read them?" Kate questioned in a burst of intrigue, causing Lydia to sit up and stare at her, "what? I'm open minded," Kate replied, smiling kindly, "so can I?"

Lydia sighed in relief, leaning back in her chair as the tension left her shoulders. "Sure. If you like. I'll even sign a copy for you," she added merrily.

"I look forward to it. Now, are you going to tell me what's going on? Why did you suddenly decide to share this? I'm not stupid! You haven't seemed yourself for a while now. Ever since . . . since Bryan died!" Kate commented, looking hurt by the words alone.

"If I tell you, you have to promise to keep this between us. Nobody else can know, at least until I get to the bottom of this. Understand?" Lydia instructed.

"Want me to cross my heart or something?" Kate teased, but again the serious look in Lydia's eye deterred her, "okay, I promise! I won't say a word to another living soul."

Lydia nodded slightly, seemingly content with the response. She leant forwards and Kate followed, bringing the two women closer together and turning the conversation more private. "I've been visited by a spirit who I think used to live in my apartment," Lydia whispered.

"A spirit?" Kate questioned shocked, "you mean, like a ghost?"

"Yes!" Lydia agreed.

"Why? What does it want? Is it here now?" Kate demanded to know, sounding concerned as she nervously looked around, checking to see if they were being watched.

"No, it's not here! I've only seen her a couple of times. I think she's somehow connected to the statues. I went out and touched one, and that same night she showed up at my door!" Lydia stated, voice sounding strained. "I don't know why, but each time she has appeared, she has been trying to lead me towards Kelly's office!" she informed quietly.

"Did 'it' . . . sorry, did 'she' tell you what she wanted?" Kate asked.

"No . . . the dead can't speak," Lydia said in a monotone.

"Oh! My mistake then. Couldn't have handed her a note pad or something?" Kate quipped, causing Lydia to give an unamused stare. "Sorry," Kate apologised, "what you are telling me is odd though. What do you think she could want from you? Any idea?"

"I think she may want me to help her move on. I just have no idea how to do that. The spirits I've worked with all wanted to send a message, or comfort a loved one before they could be at peace, but this feels different. I don't know how to explain it," Lydia informed.

"When you say 'move on', do you mean heaven?" Kate enquired.

"I don't really know. All I know is that it's another place, and once spirits go there they can never return. Personally I'm an atheist, but I guess a lot of people, mainly optimists like my husband, like to think of it as heaven," Lydia attempted to explain.

"I'm an atheist too, but sometimes I wish I wasn't," Kate said solemnly.

"I know what you mean," Lydia replied, and the two widowed women shared a moment.

"So what are we going to do about your ghost? What's the plan Velma?" Kate winked, her sense of humour revived.

"My granddaughter loves those cartoons," Lydia smiled to herself fondly, before returning to the matter at hand. "I think I need to take a look inside Kelly's office. The spirit keeps leading me there, so there must be a reason!" Lydia nodded to herself, satisfied that was the right way to continue.

"And how are you going to do that? It's not like Kelly will take kindly to you snooping through her things. She's very private," Kate pointed out.

"Actually, that's where I was hoping you would come in," Lydia informed. Kate raised an eyebrow at her, looking puzzled. "Don't worry, I have a plan," Lydia stated. The two women leaning in closer again as hushed words began to fall, "here's what I need you to do . . ."

CHAPTER 11

Where There Is A Will, There Is A Way

The plan to get inside Kelly's office was a simple one. Lydia had requested Kate's help and her friend had eagerly agreed.

Kate's role was to request that Mitch take her into town for a shopping morning, an excursion that was frequently taken by the pair. But this time, Kate was also to enlist the help of Kelly, requesting that the younger woman aid her during a trip to the bank, as Kate had recently experienced some trouble using her new debit card. This situation would render the Hall free from the Millers, at least for a few hours, and it would give Lydia the chance to investigate Kelly's office.

The day before, Lydia had stood by whilst Kate had told Kelly of her plight, about how she had been unable to get her debit card to work in the cash machine, and that she was uncertain about entering the bank and asking their young staff for help. Lydia had been impressed as she listened to Kate tell her tale, her friend spinning a yarn and putting on a very convincing act of vulnerability. Kelly grew more and more sympathetic towards Kate, and Lydia could have almost laughed as Kate managed to keep up her act.

Kate was one of the strongest and most confident people Lydia had ever met, yet her ability to play the weak and wounded old woman was incredibly convincing. Lydia could have almost fallen for it herself if she didn't know any better.

It had taken a little convincing, but eventually Kelly had agreed to accompany Kate and Mitch into town the following day, promising to visit the bank and help sort out the defective debit card problem.

The groundwork for Lydia's idea was finally complete, and it was now time to put her plan into action. Lydia was waiting quite impatiently, sitting near to the window in the communal lounge. She had chosen her perch very carefully, as from where she was sat, she could clearly see out into the foyer. When Kate and her entourage were due to exit the Hall, Lydia would also be able to peek out of the window, and observe the party setting out on their journey. She patiently waited, occasionally throwing glances towards the glaring television in the room, pretending to pay some interest upon the morning news, just in case anybody questioned her as to what she was doing. Luckily, it wasn't long before her ears tuned into some familiar muffled voices, as they made their journey down the hallway.

After a minute or so later, she could then hear the sound of car doors slamming, accompanied by the crunching of gravel under heavy tyres as the car pulled away. A flash of red paint caught Lydia's eye as it rolled off towards the large iron gates at the end of the driveway, and with that they were gone!

Lydia forced herself to sit still for a few more seconds, as she did not want to arouse any possible suspicions, or attract any unwanted attention. She waited until the news report on the television had ended, before she stood up from her seat, and, as calmly as possible made her way out of the lounge. She made her way into the foyer, and slipped through the reception area without being noticed.

With anticipation brewing, Lydia hurried down the hallway heading for Kelly's office, her feet almost stumbling over each other in haste. She was both excited and nervous all in one breath. The truth was, Lydia had no idea what she may find within, but she knew there must be something that the spirit of Elizabeth wanted her to see. In all her years as a medium, Lydia had witnessed many reasons why spirits failed to move on. In most cases, it was because of a loved one, the spirit not wanting to leave their living relatives to face the cruel world alone. In other cases, the spirits still believed that they had unfinished business with the living. Perhaps it was a message they wanted to send, or an injustice that they needed to expose, one that they were trying to amend. It seemed to Lydia, that this was possibly the reason why Elizabeth was being kept there. She theorised, that since Elizabeth had once lived in Carnation Hall, then maybe she had misplaced something, a piece of jewellery perhaps left in the office. Maybe she wanted it to be found and returned to her family. Once this task was completed, her spirit could finally rest. Lydia could not honestly think of any other reason why she was being led down this path, though this theory did not actually explain the presence of the dismembered man, an incident that Lydia was desperately trying to forget. That particular encounter had left such a stain on her, that she feared she would never be rid of the memory of his horrifying form.

Pushing those thoughts aside for now, Lydia stopped short in the hallway, carefully glancing around to ensure she was not being watched from afar. Pausing briefly to drown the butterflies in her stomach, she gently wrapped her hand around the metal handle of the office door, almost laughing in disbelief when it slipped down under her weight and the door gave way. Without any further hesitation, Lydia forcefully pushed the door open, her prize was now, at last, almost within her grasp!

The office door quickly swung inwards with such haste and vigour that it groaned on its hinges. Lydia stepped forwards after it, quickly entering the room. Her elation dropped instantly as she saw Kelly sitting behind her desk! Kelly was staring directly at Lydia with a wide-eyed expression on her face, looking utterly baffled, as Lydia forcefully entered her office seemingly coming from nowhere! The look on Lydia's ageing face was priceless, as she stared at Kelly in confusion and shock!

Lydia didn't know what to do! She had made the stupid mistake of assuming that Kelly had left the Hall along with her husband and Kate. She now recalled not actually hearing the distinct sound of Kelly's stilettos clipping across the floor of the foyer. Lydia could have kicked herself for her naivety, and now she had been caught red-handed attempting to assault the other woman's privacy! Feeling her heart begin to race, Lydia knew she would have to think fast, very fast, as she watched Kelly's expression change from pure shock to annoyance!

"Can I help you, Lydia?" Kelly questioned, her eyes still wide, but her tone stern with mild irritation.

"I thought you were going into town with Kate, but I erm . . . wasn't quite sure," Lydia heard herself stutter out.

"That was the plan, but luckily for you I'm running a little late," Kelly replied.

"But I saw your car leave and I wasn't sure if you were driving!" Lydia stated, somewhat baffled to be suddenly thrust into this awkward situation.

"Yes . . . Mitch took it. I have a few errands of my own to run this morning, so I will be following on shortly in the Mini. Anyway, what do you want Lydia?" Kelly asked, increasingly impatient.

"I . . . erm . . . I . . ." Lydia stuttered, desperately searching her mind for an excuse for being there, until a thought suddenly hit her! "I wanted to talk to you about my will," Lydia spat out, the words coming too fast, but

Kelly luckily didn't seem to notice. Instead, her expression started to change, going from irritation to one of enthusiasm in a matter of seconds.

"Well I must say, I'm glad you've put more thought into this. You know it's very important for people at your time of life to have their affairs in order," Kelly said, relaxing more into her chair as a bright smile warmed her features.

"I know that you're right. It's just the whole process still feels a little complex to me. I was just wondering if you had any of the forms around that I could take a look at?" Lydia asked calmly, secretly impressed at her own quick thinking.

"Oh, don't you worry about that. It's really not very hard, and I'll be here to help you every step of the way. You have nothing to worry about," Kelly grinned kindly, "I think I do happen to have a few example forms lying around here somewhere, which you are very welcome to look over," she informed. "Now, where did I put them? Bear with me," Kelly added, as she began to root around her desk drawers and through the stacks of papers within.

With Kelly temporarily distracted, Lydia took the opportunity to glance around the office. She noticed that the room was actually quite scarce. There was a main wooden desk in the middle of the room behind which Kelly was perched, whilst a large flat screen computer monitor occupied most of the surface space. At the back of the room was a large window overlooking the garden, filling the bland room with light. The left wall housed a large bookshelf filled with files and such, as well as what appeared to be several photographs of Kelly and Mitch with different tropical backdrops. Along the wall to the right stood two old grey metallic filing cabinets, above which yet another large portrait of Kelly and Mitch, this time happily embracing one another was hanging from the wall. All in all, the mysterious office was pretty anticlimactic after Lydia had waited so long to look within. It suddenly dawned on Lydia that she could be entirely wrong, and that there may be nothing in there that a spirit could want, and perhaps she was simply losing her mind!

It was only then, as the sunlight from the window caught against the surface of the large portrait, that Lydia noticed the glass was actually cracked. It displayed a 'spider's web' effect crawling all over the picture of the smiling couple, fragmenting their faces into distortion.

"What happened to your picture?" Lydia enquired, gesturing towards the portrait, when Kelly glanced her way.

"Oh, that! It fell down in the night several weeks ago. Must have been a faulty hook or something, I just keep forgetting to buy a new frame," Kelly replied absent-mindedly, as she stood up from behind her desk and paced towards one of the filing cabinets, continuing to search.

After hearing Kelly's admission about the portrait, thoughts began moving inside Lydia's head. A realisation was forming. If the picture had fallen down several weeks ago, then that could have been the night she had followed the spirit here. She recalled hearing banging, and a crash coming from the other side of the locked office door. There was now no doubt in Lydia's mind, Elizabeth had been in here, and she herself had caused the picture to fall, presumably to grasp Lydia's attention. There must be something in the office that Lydia was supposed to see!

Taking the opportunity whilst Kelly's back was turned, Lydia glanced back at the door. She could see that the lock was a simple catch, indicating that it could only be unlocked with a key from the outside, unless the catch was unhooked from the inside. Carefully keeping her stare locked on Kelly, Lydia leant across and flicked the catch back as quickly, and as quietly as she could, hoping the action would prevent the door from locking the next time it was closed. Lydia managed to complete the task just in time, as Kelly then turned herself around, a couple of files sitting perfectly within her manicured hands.

"Here we go!" Kelly held them out proudly, "take these with you and give them a good read. They should help you get a sense of what we need to do. Take a few days, and then we can begin the process. If you have any questions I will be back later this afternoon, but for now, I must get going!" Kelly informed, grabbing her handbag from the floor beside the desk. She then herded Lydia out of the office door, shuffling along after the older woman.

Lydia held her breath as she watched Kelly grab the door handle, pulling it tightly shut, before marching off down the hallway towards the foyer. Kelly kept Lydia close by as they moved away from the office. Lydia felt endlessly relieved that Kelly had failed to check that the door had been properly locked. Now, all she had to do was hope that setting the catch had worked! And, as she now waited for Kelly to drive away, she knew she could then enter the office and investigate matters further.

***

Lydia had never felt so impatient in all her life. She waited nervously in the shadows of the upper landing for Kelly to leave. Kelly eventually grabbed her car keys and coat, and she made her way out to her car. She then drove away and out through the iron gates. Even now, after Kelly had been gone a minute or so, Lydia still refused to rush in. Instead, she allowed several minutes to pass, just to be absolutely sure that Kelly would not make a surprise return, having possibly forgotten some item of importance. She also didn't want to appear suspicious to her fellow housemates as they wandered around the hall.

Finally, Lydia decided it was time to enter the office, and as quickly, and as quietly as a woman of her stature was able, she sneaked back down the hallway heading for the office. Upon arrival, her hand once again found the handle, and with a gentle push this time, it granted her entry! Sighing with relief, she stepped into the room, quietly pushing the door shut behind her, so as to hide her actions from any potential passers-by.

 At first, Lydia was unsure where to begin searching. She had no idea what she was actually looking for. Without much of a plan, she began to rifle through the drawers in the desk, hoping to find a clue, but all she found was a few items of stationary and some blank printing paper. Feeling a little disheartened, she slumped herself down into the office chair, her eyes now scanning the bookcase looking for anything noteworthy. Everything appeared pretty standard, so once again her eyes searched the room, until finally, they closed in on the shattered glass of the portrait hanging above the filing cabinets. It suddenly occurred to Lydia, that when this picture fell previously, it must have landed on top of the filing cabinet. Could it have just been a coincidence, or was it a clue left by Elizabeth? Curiously, Lydia stood up and walked around the desk to stand before the portrait. Feeling intrigued, she was compelled to begin pulling open the drawers of the filing cabinet, taking note of the contents within. She found each drawer filled with papers and files of all different kinds. Kelly had arranged all of the papers very neatly, with items such as bills, various receipts and other records all carefully filed away. After rummaging through several of the drawers, Lydia failed to come across anything unusual. That was, until something interesting caught her eye. In the top drawer of the cabinet, arranged in neat alphabetical lines were a series of named files. Lydia randomly pulled one free, and discovered it was the last will and testament of a man named *'Colin Lancaster'*. Lydia did not recognise the name, and she naturally assumed that the man must have been a past resident of the Hall, someone who was no longer around. Lydia hastily returned the will to its resting place and then proceeded to check another file.

After a few moments, it was clear to Lydia that all of these files were the wills of residents at the Hall. At first, nothing seemed out of the ordinary as she searched through more of the files. It was then, with a sudden burst of adrenaline, that Lydia pulled out a file displaying the name *'Elizabeth Holland'*. Was this it? Did Elizabeth's ghost want Lydia to find her will? Lydia found herself flicking through the papers displayed before her, she couldn't work out any reason within herself, why a restless spirit would want to show her this file. Then, at the bottom of one of the pages, something very intriguing grasped her attention, it was the names of the main beneficiaries of the will. They were clearly marked as *'Kelly Samantha Miller & Mitchell William Miller'*. Lydia was somewhat confused. She recalled Kelly telling her that she and Elizabeth had been good friends. But, for this woman, who supposedly had been a successful artist, to leave her entire fortune to Kelly and Mitch, just felt odd somehow. Obviously, Lydia had never met Elizabeth, at least not in life, so she could hardly say she knew the woman or her relationship with the Hall's manager. Yet, she could not fight the slowly building feeling of dread within herself. Confused, and unsure of what to do, Lydia returned Elizabeth's file to the drawer, but her intuition that something more sinister was going on refused to let her just walk away! Instead, she began searching through more files, pulling names out at random. After several minutes, Lydia had viewed a number of files, and to her dismay she discovered that many of them had Kelly and Mitch registered as the sole beneficiaries! Among them was a copy of Bryan's will! Lydia was now beginning to feel a little unwell. She knew it was plausible that all of these people, now deceased, had left their entire estates to Kelly and Mitch. Perhaps it was in gratitude for all the wonderful care they had received whilst residing at Carnation Hall. She also knew that many of the residents, past and present had no living relatives. Yet, something about this felt very wrong! Perhaps it was her heightened senses that were sending out a warning, or maybe it was just common sense, but whatever it was, Lydia just knew something sinister was lurking beneath the covers of this situation.

Suddenly feeling the urge to run, Lydia turned around to leave, half hoping that she was once again in a dream. But, before she could walk away, a name on another file caught her attention! *'Katherine Donovan'*, the file read. Lydia could feel her heart drop as she pulled it loose and turned the pages. She could almost cry when she witnessed Kelly and Mitch's names decorating Kate's will. Now, Lydia knew something was deeply wrong! Kate had told her first hand that she was leaving everything she owned to her nephew Gary, so how could Kelly and Mitch now be marked down as the sole beneficiaries? This made no sense! Lydia felt like breaking down, the realisation of her discovery cutting inside her like a deep wound.

She knew she had to talk straight away with Kate about this. Maybe it was just an error, and everything could be sorted out. But, even Lydia knew she was deluding herself with that thought. She realised that she may now be in this situation way over her head, and she knew that she must leave the office quickly before Kelly returned. Lydia had become very fearful of what Kelly might be capable of if she were to be found out. Hurriedly, she placed Kate's will back into the filing cabinet and shut the drawer. She then scanned the room one last time to ensure that everything was in place, and swiftly left the office, not forgetting to drop the catch on the way out. Kelly would never know that she had been in there! Lydia kept telling herself this repeatedly as she headed back to her room, her mind reeling over the day's sickening discovery!

The more she thought about it, the worse she felt! What she had discovered could not simply be dismissed as a coincidence or an innocent mistake. This was a crime! And, Kelly was using her position of trust and reliance to steal money from the residents, cheating their families out of their rightful inheritance. Lydia had no doubt that everything now made sense, with the exotic holidays and expensive new car. How else could that couple be affording all of those luxuries? However, it was only as she was walking down the hallway to her apartment, the paintings once birthed by Elizabeth Holland hanging proudly on the walls, that a new and even more sinister thought began to form. What if the residents, whose money Kelly and Mitch had been stealing, had not actually died from natural causes! Lydia's mind immediately jumped to Bryan. He had been perfectly well and healthy, yet just a few hours after she had last seen him, his heart had suddenly stopped and he was gone! All this happening just a few weeks after Kelly herself had helped him write his will. Then, immediately after the man's death, Kelly comes rolling along driving a brand new four-wheel drive vehicle! What if Kelly had done something to him? In fact, the sensation now crawling up Lydia's spine told her that this was indeed what had happened to her friend, yet how could she prove it?

Lydia felt like she was going to be sick! She felt even more certain as she reached her apartment door, letting herself inside and locking it securely behind her. She made it to her bathroom, just in time to release the entire contents of her stomach into the toilet, continuing to retch violently until her body accepted it was finally empty!

Leaning back against the cool tiled wall felt pleasant against her heated skin. The sweat covering her forehead was causing her hair to plaster itself against her hot brow. Lydia sighed, feeling older and more exhausted than she had ever felt before. She just didn't know what to do! What she had just uncovered was slowly bringing the safe and peaceful world she had built up around herself crashing down, and with every breath, she could feel it crushing her under its weight. She wanted to shout! she wanted to scream! But most of all she wanted to cry! She wanted to cry for all those poor people who had been wronged by their supposed caretakers. They obviously had no idea of the danger that they were facing! And, most of all, she wanted to cry for herself, because since Robert had died, Carnation Hall had become the closest thing to home that she had felt for a long time. Now, and almost in the blink of an eye, it was all gone! She now felt that she would never be able to feel that way again. Instead, she now felt cold and hollow inside.

Lydia couldn't hold back the tears any more and they began to flood down her face. Her breath was quickening in her chest, and it wasn't until the air became harder to find, that she realised she was hyperventilating. Lydia was having a panic attack! Her heart began pounding violently in her chest and her eyes were watering through the terror of not being able to breathe. The last thing Lydia recalled before darkness overtook her, was wondering if this was how Elizabeth had felt as she died!

***

Lydia woke up and found herself lying on the bathroom floor. Her neck was sore from the uncomfortable position she had taken to, yet another part of her silently thanked the invention of underfloor heating, as it had stopped the cold from seeping into her old bones.

Pushing herself up, her mind still groggy, she stumbled her way out from the bathroom and into her living room, using the furniture for support. She was taken back by the sight of twilight setting in outside her window, the sky was a dark blue, tinged with red as the setting sun sank away out of view.

Lydia had no idea how much time had passed since she fell asleep, or fainted, which seemed the more likely. But, it was now approaching night time, and that meant Susanna would be home. Lydia felt an overwhelming urge to call her daughter. She had to tell somebody about what she had discovered, and there was nobody else on this earth that Lydia trusted more. Without even realising, she was already reaching for her phone, grasping out in desperation to type in the numbers, just so the sound of a familiar voice could soothe her troubled mind.

The phone rang for a few moments, and Lydia feared it would not be answered. So much so, that she could not contain her gasp of relief upon hearing her daughter's voice.

"Hello? Mum? Are you okay?" Susanna's voice met her ears, sounding somewhere between concerned and confused from the out of routine call.

"I need to tell you something!" Lydia blurted out, deciding to skip pleasantries as the stress overwhelmed her.

"Mum, what's wrong? Are you okay?" Susanna's voice was all worry now.

"Please, this is going to sound mad, but you've got to believe me!" Lydia stated, almost whispering into the receiver, just in case someone was outside her room waiting for her to tattle.

"What is it? What's wrong? Tell me!" the younger woman demanded, "has something happened?"

"There's something bad happening here at the Hall! Something very bad!" Lydia stumbled over her words, "I think Kelly is stealing money from the residents, and that's not even the worst of it!" she exclaimed!

"Wait! What do you mean mum? Stealing what? How?" Susanna sounded confused again.

"Kelly! She's taking their money!" Lydia whispered, glancing nervously at her front door, paranoia beginning to drown her.

"Taking it how? I've met Kelly, she wouldn't go around stealing cash out of people's pockets!" Susanna said in bewilderment. Lydia could almost see her shaking her head in disbelief.

"No! She's changing their wills and then taking it . . . after they die!" Lydia tried to explain.

"What! How do you know any of this? Do you have any proof? This all sounds pretty wild." Susanna asked dubiously.

"I've seen it, it's in her office. I've seen the wills! They have Kelly and Mitch down as the beneficiaries," Lydia stated.

"And that instantly makes them criminals?" Susanna said bluntly, "mum, you've told me yourself, there are a lot of lonely old people living there. You know better than most about all the kind things they do for people. Is it that far beyond belief, that some of those people might want to show their appreciation by leaving Kelly a thank-you gift when they pass on?" she tried to rationalise.

"No! I'm not saying that! But the spirits . . ." Lydia began.

"The spirits!" Susanna exclaimed, sounding frustrated now.

"Yes, they were trying to show me. They kept leading me to Kelly's office. They wanted me to see!" Lydia told, her voice pleading Susanna to understand.

"Oh, mum. Don't start that again!" Susanna groaned down the phone, "ghosts are not real! When will you accept that? I'm honestly too tired right now to listen to your ghost stories. I know they've made you a lot of money over the years, but none of it is real! You can't keep filling your head with these fantasies. It's not fair on you, and it isn't fair on us! This isn't healthy, and you have no idea what your delusions have been doing to me and

Jess. I found her reading your book not too long ago, and now she hardly sleeps any more. When she does she has nightmares! I don't know what to do!" Susanna stated, her tone filled with exasperation, making her sound older and more exhausted than she had any right to be.

Lydia felt her chest tighten at Susanna's words. She had always known that her daughter was a disbeliever in her abilities, but she had not expected to be dismissed so easily, or so bluntly by her only child. She could understand her daughter's distress, yet Lydia was still in such a panic about her own situation, that she could hardly take in what Susanna had to say.

"Susanna, please!" Lydia said, begging to be heard, "please listen to me. There is something very wrong going on here!" she said desperately. Susanna sighed again.

"You're just being paranoid mum! I suppose it's natural living in that big old place, and being surrounded by sickly old folk. I get it, I do! Losing one of your neighbours suddenly is a shock and must be a horrible thing to witness. But, that doesn't mean that something sinister is actually going on. People dying suddenly in their twilight years isn't that unusual. Just like . . ." Susanna paused, her tongue stopping the words, whilst she decided whether to speak them or not. She continued, "well, just like Robert. Okay? These things happen and they are tragic and unpredictable, but they are not suspicious! People die all the time and I'm sorry, but that's just the way it is! And, as for these apparent wills, it genuinely doesn't surprise me that these people have left gifts for Kelly and her husband, especially if they didn't have any family around them any more. I'm not trying to dismiss you, I'm not, but please just think for a moment. Are you sure it isn't possible that you're overreacting?" Susanna questioned, trying to sound sympathetic.

Lydia took a deep breath. What Susanna had said did make sense. There was a part of her that agreed with Susanna. Perhaps she had overreacted, and the circumstances were possibly not as bad as she was making out. Yet, she knew deep down that something very sinister was going on at Carnation Hall!

Now, knowing that she would not be getting any help from her daughter, Lydia realised that she would have to figure this one out alone. She was now wishing that she had taken Kate's will with her when she left the office, she could have then shown it to both Kate and Susanna. She could have shown them the evidence they needed to believe her claim. But, she hadn't done that, and now the familiar feeling of doubt was beginning to well up within her. Without physical proof, there was a possibility of doubt and misrecollection. It was possible that Lydia could have been wrong about all of this. And, in a way, Lydia truly hoped that she was wrong. She wanted to be mistaken, she wanted her life to return to the normal bliss of ignorance. But, she couldn't let this go, even if she wanted to. Her heart wouldn't let her!

"Look, mum. If you're really that worried, why don't you come and stay with us for a while? You know you're always welcome here. Just say the word and I'll come and get you right now," Susanna offered. She sounded soft and remorseful, as if she felt she knew she had crossed a line with her mother and now regretted it.

"No. You're right! I'm probably just letting my imagination run away with me. I'll be fine love," Lydia replied, simultaneously rejecting the offer. "I've kept you long enough. Don't let me keep you from your dinner. I'll talk to you tomorrow . . . goodnight," Lydia said, rushing over her words before hanging up. She suddenly felt exhausted and eager to spend more time alone with her thoughts, away from her doubting daughter.

Lydia had forced herself to eat a small sandwich before turning in for an early night. But, not before she checked three times that her apartment door was securely locked! She then pushed the waist high dresser that resided in her entranceway, right up against the front door, barricading herself against any potential intruders. She told herself that she just had to make it through until the morning. Then, she would find a way to finally expose Kelly and her antics, however malevolent they could be. She owed it to Bryan, she owed it to Elizabeth, and most of all, she owed it to herself. She certainly wasn't going to let this go, no matter what!

***

"You okay, Susie?" Christian questioned, as he watched his wife move back into the dining room. She had a bewildered look upon her pretty face. "Your mum okay?" he asked, slightly concerned.

"That was very strange!" Susanna declared, flopping down into her chair at the dining table, apparently exhausted.

"Care to elaborate on that?" Christian requested, almost amused by his wife's baffled face.

"I've just got off the phone with mum," Susanna paused to take a sip from her wine glass, seemingly to calm her nerves, "she suddenly seems convinced that the organisers at the Hall are actually criminal masterminds! Unbelievable, right?" she exclaimed, looking at her husband for agreement.

"What do you mean?" Christian asked, pushing for more information. His face flooded with curiosity.

"Oh, she's got it in her head that Kelly and her husband are changing people's wills, and then making off with all their money. How insane is that?" Susanna informed, almost chuckling the words.

"Why would she possibly think something like that?" Christian enquired.

"She says that a ghost told her about it, and then she apparently found some wills in Kelly's office naming

Kelly and Mitch as the sole beneficiaries," Susanna now sounded exasperated with the tale, "she even told me that she thinks some of the residents' deaths might not have been from natural causes, and she even thinks that Kelly had something to do with that!" Susanna swallowed down more wine in response. "I love my mother, but that wild imagination of hers doesn't half make it hard sometimes," she added. She then turned to her husband, expecting him to look as bewildered as she was, but Christian didn't say anything. Instead, his brow was furrowed in deep thought, and they both ended up eating the rest of their dinner in relative silence.

Once they had finished eating, Christian headed upstairs, he took a shower and got ready to go to work. He kissed his wife goodbye at the door as part of his usual routine, and then began his drive to the hospital. Christian was currently working the graveyard shift at the local hospital. He was the chief pathologist, and since Susanna had mentioned her mother's claims, the words had resonated in his mind and had jogged his memory about something from the past. He had overseen the autopsies of many elderly people, and could vaguely recall one of his staff voicing some concerns about a certain case about a year ago. The body in question had been that of an elderly woman, she had apparently died from drowning following a sudden aneurysm. Yet, during the autopsy, a trace of an unknown substance had been observed in her blood sample. Given the patient's age and condition, the aneurysm seemed the most likely cause of death, and the finding was pretty much ignored. The case was then just filed away into the archives. However, what truly had Christian's memory racing, was remembering the note he had read from the paramedics attending the incident. The body had been collected from none other than Carnation Hall. At the time he had thought nothing of it, as old people passed away regularly, and subsequently ended up on his slab in the morgue. But, for whatever reason, this particular case had stuck with him somewhat!

Christian had known Lydia for a long time, ever since he had first met Susanna during his teenage years. Lydia's so called sixth sense had always been a touchy subject for his wife, having apparently caused her much grief and concern during her childhood. But, Christian himself had always held more faith in it. He had seen first hand some of the people she had helped, and after working most of his life in a morgue, he would be lying if he said he hadn't seen some strange things happen that defied explanation. So, whilst Susanna may be a sceptic, Christian was quietly a believer.

When he arrived at work that night, Christian immediately spoke to a member of staff at the morgue. He requested that all files relating to patients from Carnation Hall be sent to his office. The receptionist had looked both confused and somewhat irritated by his request, but had agreed without complaint. She didn't wish to displease the chief in any way, least of all with insubordination. Though she had warned him, it may take quite a few days for her to search through all the files in the hospital archives.

Later that night, with his graveyard shift well under way, Christian was sat alone in his office thinking to himself. An uneasy feeling settled itself into the pit of his stomach. At first, he had mistaken it for the first signs of heartburn, caused by his wife's cooking no doubt, but he later placed it as the feeling of dread! He didn't know how, but he felt deep down that something terrible was about to happen, and that his family could quite possibly be right in the middle of the impending storm!

CHAPTER 12

The Fall

Kelly and Mitch returned from their trip out with Kate at around five in the afternoon. Kelly had left Mitch to carry in her shopping bags, which he did obediently, and then took them into the kitchen for unpacking. Kate had also wandered off since returning, she had hurried away with an excuse about having some frozen food to put away, the words falling from her lips as she rushed up the stairs. Kelly thought little of the old woman's erratic behaviour, as Kate was starting to act a little more senile in her old age. Kelly had made this assumption following their arrival at the bank earlier, their journey proving to be pointless, as Kate's supposedly faulty debit card decided to perform perfectly. This fact had irritated Kelly greatly, but she managed to maintain her composure, without the other woman viewing her foul mood.

Still steaming from her wasted trip, Kelly had decided to head straight to her office the moment her heels hit the wooden floors inside the Hall. She was intent on basking in a little peace within the sanctuary of her private room, before being forced to slave away in front of the stove in order to cook Mitch's dinner.

Kelly entered her office without delay, intent on spending the next hour or so sat in front of her computer. Her mind was set on browsing the internet and possibly purchasing some more designer handbags. However, once she flopped down into the chair behind her desk, a strange feeling began to well up within her. The small stack of papers that were sitting on the desk were left in a perfectly square pile, with just one exception. A single document lay at a slightly different angle, causing it to protrude slightly out from the rest of the stack. It was a small detail, almost invisible really, but to Kelly, it stood out sharply against the usual neatness of the rest of her desk. She knew it was possible that she herself had overlooked placing the document back correctly, after shuffling through the pile earlier that day. But, for Kelly, the unsettled feeling continued to grow and she could not ignore its presence, or pass it off as insignificant. Suddenly riled, Kelly shot up from her chair, pacing across the room searching for any other inconsistencies that may surround her. With clinical precision, she started searching through her filing cabinets, and it wasn't long before she discovered what she feared most. The drawer that contained the wills had been disrupted! Kelly was always extremely precise with her filing system, to a point it was purely obsessive! There was no possibility that this mistake could have been made by her own hands. Placed before her in the drawer, a single file instantly caught her eye, it was totally misplaced, and out of order from the rest. The sight of this lonely muddled file was enough to make Kelly's temper begin to boil!

"Mitch!" Kelly called, her voice echoing almost comically down the hallway as she waited impatiently for her husband. Her foot was tapping away under the desk as she waited, frustration flowing from her in waves and thickening the air. If anyone had been dozing in the communal lounge, then they surely now would have been awakened violently by her outburst.

It took a few moments, but just as Kelly was about to shout out again, Mitch suddenly appeared in the doorway. His expression apparent with confusion, and perhaps, with just a hint of worry in his eyes.

"Yes?" Mitch questioned sheepishly, lingering in the doorway with no clear intention of moving.

"Come in here!" Kelly ordered, her voice coldly calm, "shut the door behind you!" she added swiftly.

Mitch did as he was told, kicking the door closed behind him, now looking like a trapped animal, as he stood before his wife awaiting her instruction.

"Sit!" Kelly ordered. Mitch dropped into a chair in the corner of the office, almost before the word had even left her lips. She looked mildly pleased at his obedience. "Now!" Kelly stated, leaning forwards in her chair to catch his eye, hands pressed together beneath her chin elegantly. "Have you been in this office without my permission?" she questioned, the words gentle, but the look in her eye told another tale.

"What? Me . . . no I haven't!" Mitch replied quickly, looking worried.

"Are you sure? Hmm . . ." she leered at him.

"No! Why would I?" Mitch asked.

"I don't know what goes on in that funny little head of yours, do I? Now . . . last chance! Are you positive you've not been in this office without my permission? Can you promise me that you haven't been in here rummaging through my files?" Kelly questioned again, her eyes almost burning as she waited surprisingly and patiently for his reply.

"No! I swear to you, I haven't been anywhere near here!" Mitch answered, his voice pleading innocence.

"Shit!" Kelly suddenly yelled, her arm swiping at her desk sending all manner of stationery flying from its surface and onto the floor.

"What's wrong?" Mitch asked quietly, clearly looking upset that his wife was distressed. He stood up, trying to decide whether to approach her or keep his distance.

"This is what I was afraid of!" Kelly declared, leaning back in her chair, apparently exhausted.

"Afraid of what?" Mitch asked again.

"Somebody has been in here! And, if it wasn't you, then it must have been one of them!" Kelly mumbled angrily.

"One of them?" Mitch looked confused.

"Yes! One of the residents. Some nosy bastard has been going through my things!" she sounded furious as the words left her mouth.

"But who? Why?" Mitch asked.

"I don't know! Otherwise I'd be out there asking them instead of talking to you!" Kelly yelled again, glaring at him menacingly. Mitch was glad he hadn't approached. A moment passed before she collapsed back into her chair, and Mitch felt relieved. "Look! Just keep an eye out. If you see anyone acting oddly, come and let me know immediately and I'll handle it. This may just blow over. It's unlikely that anybody would realise what they were looking at, they aren't the smartest bunch. But, on the off chance any trouble arises, we have to be ready to contain it!" Kelly explained, sounding clinical and rehearsed.

"Contain it . . . how?" Mitch asked, looking concerned.

"Like I said, I'll handle it!" Kelly declared, in a tone that confirmed the conversation was over. She waved him away with her hand, and he left eagerly leaving Kelly alone with her thoughts.

***

The very next morning, Lydia had risen around five o'clock, having almost had no sleep at all. She hurriedly got herself ready, and stepped out of her apartment and out into the hallway. It was a trip in the dark she had taken several times before, but this time she wasn't being summoned and led by a supernatural being. Instead, she had set herself her own mission to complete. Lydia took quiet careful steps along the wooden panelled floor, somehow terrified she would be discovered skulking around in the dark. She was half convinced that a spirit would suddenly appear behind her to inflict unrelenting fear, or that the sound of Kelly's heels clicking down the hallway would meet her ears, signifying her approach. Luckily though, despite her anxiety, Lydia arrived at her destination undisturbed by a soul . . . living or dead!

Lydia had visited Kate's apartment many times before, but never like this. The gentle rapping of her fingers against the wooden door echoed progressively down the hallway in the quiet of the early hours. Kate did not respond, so Lydia tried again, more forceful this time, yet desperately hoping nobody else would be alerted. It took her a few minutes of increasingly loud knocking, but eventually Kate's apartment door opened with a click of the lock, revealing a dishevelled and very tired-looking Kate standing before her.

"Lydia? I thought I could hear knocking. What's going on?" Kate asked through a sleep-filled haze.

"We need to talk!" Lydia whispered, her tone serious.

"Oh . . . am I in trouble?" Kate asked teasingly, yet unable to take in the serious atmosphere surrounding them. Lydia ignored her, and instead forcefully let herself into the other woman's apartment, brushing past her friend to do so. "Would you like to come in?" Kate said sarcastically as she shut the door, "I'm guessing you have a good reason to be disturbing my beauty sleep?"

"I got inside Kelly's office!" Lydia told.

"Okay. Good! Did you finally put that ghost of yours to rest?" Kate questioned, stifling a yawn, "you look terrible by the way," Kate added, noticing the dark circles under the other woman's eyes and the paleness of her skin. Kate was now somewhat concerned with the situation at hand.

"I found something very disturbing!" Lydia spoke in hushed tones, her eyes looking around the room nervously, ensuring they were truly alone.

"What do you mean? What's happened?" Kate questioned, her face paling at the look of distress Lydia appeared to be in.

"It's Kelly, she's changed your will! She's changed them all!" Lydia whispered hoarsely, her throat dry and raw from sobbing.

"I don't understand," Kate replied, her tone blank, as if she was unable to process the news and her head tilting to accentuate the point.

"Listen to me Kate! The will you made with Kelly has been changed! Kelly's made herself the main beneficiary, so when you die she will get everything and your nephew Gary will get nothing! Do you understand what I'm telling you?" Lydia questioned softly, now trying to guide her friend further into the apartment, and down onto the sofa in fear that she may become faint when the words finally sank in.

"Changed my will, but that's illegal!" Kate responded, sounding distant in thought.

"I don't think Kelly really cares about the rules here!" Lydia muttered to herself kneeling down before her friend. She took another quick glance around the room, watching her own back with a pinch of paranoia. "Look! Whatever is going on here, it's bad. Kelly can't be trusted and we need to put a stop to what she's doing!" Lydia stated, attempting to rally the other woman.

"Are you sure you've got this right? There has to be some mistake? Kelly wouldn't do this to me. She takes care of us here. We wouldn't have a home without her," Kate sounded immensely saddened as she spoke.

"Look, if you don't believe me, then get Kelly to show you your will. It's been changed, I've seen it with my own eyes," Lydia returned, feeling stronger and more determined now out of necessity. If no one would believe her at her word, then some proof should do it for her.

"Okay. I'll do that. I need to see it for myself," Kate said, sounding as if she was speaking only to herself, while she ringed her hands nervously in her lap, "it's not that I don't trust you Lydia, it's just that seeing it for myself will eliminate any doubt," Kate spoke again, now looking apologetically into Lydia's eyes.

"It's okay, I get it," Lydia replied, attempting to keep her tone calm and neutral, "but you need to be careful, Kelly is dangerous and you can't trust anything she says. Promise me you'll be careful around her. I have a feeling this may be more than just a fraud claim," she informed, though deciding to keep the true extent of her thoughts a secret for now. Kate was already distressed, and making her fear more would not help her case.

"I promise!" Kate replied, "I promise I'll be careful, thank you Lydia."

***

For the rest of the day Lydia had been too frightened to leave her apartment. She was suspicious of Kelly discovering her deed, and this plagued Lydia. She had visions of Mitch waiting menacingly out in the hallway, ready to strike her down in retaliation. None of this was true of course, and deep down she knew it was impossible for Kelly or Mitch to find out what she had done. Even if they did have their suspicions, they would never be stupid enough to threaten the operation that they had going on at the Hall. Nevertheless, Lydia decided to keep herself hidden away, somewhat safe behind the lock on her door.

At some point during the afternoon, Lydia finally gave in to her sleep deprivation. She drifted away sat in her cosy armchair, as she listened to the wind gently ruffling the trees outside and to the distant sound of birds chirping. Hours soon passed as Lydia's exhausted body and troubled mind found the rest they desperately needed, undisturbed by the plaguing dreams of ghosts and figures stalking the hallways of her vivid imagination. The sun was now setting and the night was drawing in as Lydia slept. The gentle wind that brushed its way through the trees had now turned into harsh blusters, making the branches shiver and cower in its wake. But, even this could not stir Lydia from her deep slumber. It seemed nothing would disturb her. That was, until a commotion out in the hallway found its way to her ears. The sound was subtle at first, just the raised voice of a woman throwing demands, yet the retort became louder, and soon an amplitude of harsh shouted words filled the air, rousing Lydia from her much needed sleep.

As soon as she heard the shouting, Lydia jumped to her feet in alarm! Her sleep-filled body almost unable to keep up with her hurried movement, and a head rush nearly took her down to the carpeted floor. She soon found her footing though, as adrenaline began to run its course. With tentative, yet hasty steps, Lydia rushed to her apartment door, laying an ear against its surface as she listened with all her might, straining for sound.

"Why - Show – Liar," were the only words Lydia was able to catch clearly through the wooden door, both voices being too far away to infiltrate the room.

Nervously, Lydia reached for the lock, clicking the bolt open as quietly as possible, whilst she listened to more of the muffled conversation.

"I - Told - Stop - Shut!" another broken sentence filtered through just as Lydia was about to open her apartment door and expose herself to whatever awaited outside. The apartment door opened, and she was hit fully by the noise of the scuffle. Two people, clearly both women, were locked in a bitter and angry debate! Their shouting echoing loudly for all close enough to hear. It was only as Lydia stepped out into the hallway, keeping her back pressed against the wall in an attempt to make her presence go as unnoticed as possible, that she recognised the owners of the two voices. Her stomach sank into a pit!

"If there's nothing to see then why won't you show it to me? It's mine to do with as I please, and if I want to see it or even destroy it, then that's my god-damned right!" Kate yelled loudly. Although Lydia could not see her friend directly from this position, she could just imagine the rage on her face from her words alone.

"I told you to shut up and mind your own business!" Kelly snapped back like a viper, her tone dripping with venom.

"Why . . . what are you hiding? Come on admit it!" Kate edged, determination and accusation fuelling her voice.

"Don't be so stupid!" Kelly called back.

"Oh really? So if that's the case, why won't you just show me my own damn will? You have a copy sitting in your office and we all know it! Go fetch it!" Kate bellowed.

"You insolent little bitch! Do you enjoy snooping your nose into business that doesn't concern you? Hmm, I'll make you regret it, mark my words!" Kelly hissed.

"Regret what? Wanting to see my own will? It's hardly an outrageous request, and the only reason you won't go and get it right now and show it to me, is because you've obviously got something to hide. Admit it! You're a dirty fraud! You've been lying to us all from day one, going around pretending you're all noble and saintly, when in reality you're nothing but a dirty lying little thief! I'm going to make sure everyone knows what you're doing! You're not going to get away with what you've done!" Kate threatened menacingly. With the way Kelly suddenly froze, Lydia thought she had won the argument, and maybe Kelly would now confess and end this nightmare!

But then, time seemed to slow down, and in a hushed and whispered tone, words went through the air that Lydia was unable to catch. A scream then followed, the kind of scream you only hear in your nightmares. An echoed gasp of pure terror radiating into reality via sound. The noise echoed violently for a few seconds until it was followed by the most sickening sound Lydia had ever heard. It was a wet crunching thud that hung dully in the air. Complete and utter silence followed and Lydia felt as if she couldn't breathe. As she advanced a little further, she stumbled as the realisation of what had just happened burrowed itself into her mind. A small bowl containing pretty pink pot pourri met Lydia's fleeting hand, causing it to fall from its home upon the hallway sideboard. It created a deafeningly loud crash as it hit the floor due to the pure silence of the hallway. The sudden noise caused Kelly to step back and shoot her head around, catching Lydia's horrified and pale face staring straight at her from down the hallway. A mix of fury and sick satisfaction was plastered across the younger woman's face, as their eyes met for the first time. Lydia found herself torn, as in part she wished to run, escape from this house of horrors and never look back. The rational side of her mind reminded her of the thundering noise just moments before, and she was left nauseated at realising what must have caused it, now understanding that without caution she herself could suffer the same destiny.

Suddenly to her left, she heard the creak of an apartment door being edged open, a wrinkled old face of a resident was poking out, clearly investigating the ruckus. This was followed by another door opening at the opposite end of the hallway, and the gradual appearance of further witnesses. Lydia found her courage knowing she was now temporarily safe from any wrath. She threw herself towards the spot where Kelly was standing just moments ago at the top of the old wooden staircase. Then, gripping hold of the banister, her knuckles white under her tight grip, she forced herself to peer down and confirm the suspicion in her mind. She was unable to hold back the gasp of horror and despair at what she then saw.

Lying on the foyer floor at the very bottom of the staircase was Kate. Her previously frail, yet elegant frame now lay in disarray. A halo of dark red blood began to flood out around the woman's body, originating at her head, and spreading out along her back. It resembled an exhibit of sinister looking artwork. Kate's left leg was bent back at an unnatural angle, and Lydia nearly vomited once more as she saw a jagged piece of bone sticking prominently out from the skin, looking like sharp teeth pointing from the gruesome wound. But, by far the worst part of this grisly display was the way Kate was lying, her eyes wide open and staring in a terrified manner at the ceiling. Her face looked as if she were about to rise up and wonder what had happened, but the grey tone of her skin and the lack of movement from her chest informed Lydia that it was already far too late! Kate was dead, and this harrowing scene was her swansong!

At first, Lydia thought she would faint from the shock of what she saw. Her knees grew weak, and bile was burning in her throat as she looked upon the awful gory mess that had once been her best friend. The air became thick once more, and before she could stop herself, Lydia stumbled away, falling back against the landing wall. Her hand was pressed tightly against her chest as she attempted to control her sporadic breathing, while a faint buzzing of white noise rose in her ears. Lydia couldn't stand, she could hardly move and she feared that she was falling into a catatonic state from the shock. Perhaps, she would now be the next person to die alongside Kate, then Kelly would no longer have either woman to worry about. Lydia almost laughed to herself at the gallows humour! But, that thought triggered something else, a realisation that if she herself were gone, nobody would be around to stop Kelly hurting anyone else!

Suddenly, feeling the hairs on the back of her neck stand up, Lydia looked away, searching the increasingly large crowd that had gathered to investigate the commotion. But, Kelly was no longer in sight. She had slipped away like the reptile she was, leaving the hoard of pensioners to gasp and gawk down at the bloody scene below.

A loud buzzing began to overtake Lydia's mind, one that she recognised as a migraine filtering into her head. Lydia could still not force herself to move, she could not speak and she could not scream. All she was capable of doing was sitting on the hallway floor, her head in her hands as she sobbed in pure anguish and terror!

Clearly, Kelly had made her escape down the staircase in order to call an ambulance for the latest dearly departed, and to then get herself ready for her finest act of all.

The police arrived along with the paramedics, but it had been clear to all that there was nothing anyone could have done to save the elderly woman. Kelly played out her usual routine as she spoke to the young policeman. She was silver tongued as ever, whilst she relayed to him the events that led to this unfortunate accident. Apparently, Kate had been harassing Kelly for some time over a missing earring. Clearly the old dear had mislaid it when she was out and about, and wouldn't accept that it hadn't been stolen. That simple lie excused the argument the residents had heard from within their apartments. Then, as Kate had been following Kelly up the stairs, the older woman had simply missed a step in her haste, falling down backwards and arriving at the grim outcome they had all witnessed. The policeman ate every word of her lies, lapping them up like a dying man finding water in the desert. There seemed no reason to believe otherwise, and nobody spoke out, even if they had disagreed.

Many of the residents were briefly questioned by the police officers, but for the most part the stories matched up, and what more could you ask from a group of dementia-riddled pensioners. Kelly was smart, far smarter than anybody could have given her credit for. She knew all the right things to say and when to say them. It was an Oscar-worthy performance, Lydia figured, watching the woman lie with more ease than most people could breathe with. Kelly had even forged a plan that would prevent Lydia, her only potential witness, from speaking out against her once the shock had worn off.

As the police questioned the other residents, Kelly made her way over to one of the paramedics. She had whispered something into his ear, and with a nod of understanding the two of them made their way upstairs, the man then hovering over Lydia's cowering form. He spoke to her kindly, but she was too shaken to listen to what he was saying. After a moment trying to find her voice and trying to push him away, a needle suddenly found its way into her forearm, and the whole world began to tilt and fade around her.

"Don't worry, love, you'll be alright. You've had quite a nasty shock tonight! I've given you something to help you sleep," the paramedic told Lydia kindly, his tone soft and understanding, though 'she' didn't see it that way! She tried to fight the sedative, but it was no use. Lydia suddenly found herself being pulled to her feet and dragged along the hallway towards her own apartment. She knew she was going to pass out, it was inevitable! What made things worse was that she found Kelly suddenly standing at her side, helping guide her into her apartment and then dropping her onto the comfy bed. The paramedic swiftly left as the sedative set in, but Kelly remained, only for a second longer, just long enough to whisper into Lydia's ear.

"Forget everything you think you saw tonight! It was an accident, just a silly little accident! They happen all the time, and we wouldn't want one to happen to you next would we?" Kelly hissed. Lydia's vision now began swimming and her world vanished into nothingness. "I'll be keeping my eye on you!" and with that Kelly slammed the door. She had work to do!

CHAPTER 13

Stalemate

"We have a problem!" Kelly said, suddenly into the darkness. Her and Mitch were currently lying side by side in bed, the lights all out as they tried to find sleep after the eventful day. The ambulance had long since gone, and the police had packed up and left the Hall. Kelly felt confident that the police officers were none the wiser to the crime that had just been committed. Kate's fall had convincingly been passed off as an accident, and nobody would waste any more time or effort looking into the frail old woman's demise. Of this, Kelly was certain, after all, she had ridden a similar storm before, yet she could not rest too easily. Not this time, as something was stirring in the back of her mind, something telling her that her troubles were not over yet, and that she would probably have some more cleaning up to do!

"What do you mean 'we' have a problem?" Mitch asked, mumbling the words into his pillow, "the nosy old bag's dead now! So, what's the problem?"

"Use your head for once will you!" Kelly hissed angrily, her voice so close to his ear that a shiver went down his spine waking him up further, "Kate wasn't the one who was in my office!"

"But wasn't she the one who came to talk to you about her will? Wasn't she the one accusing you of changing it? It had to be her!" Mitch replied, clearly confused.

"I thought so too. The crazy old bitch barged into my office before chasing me up the stairs. She started running her mouth off, she nearly blew our secret," Kelly agreed, "but you see, whoever went into the office did so whilst we weren't around. We both went into town with Kate the other day. We were gone hours, and now that I think about it more, Kate was acting a bit strange whilst we were out. It was as though she was trying to keep me there for some reason. No! It wasn't her, but she was covering for somebody, I'm now sure of it," Kelly explained.

"I hadn't thought of that," Mitch admitted.

"Of course you hadn't! Thinking isn't your strong point!" Kelly rolled her eyes in the dark.

"So what are you going to do?" Mitch questioned.

"Well my love, we are going to track down the little snitch and find out how much they know. Until then, we can't risk any of this getting out. Nobody is allowed to leave!" Kelly stated, pondering over the predicament.

"What do you want me to do?" Mitch asked reluctantly.

"Lock the gates!" Kelly informed.

"Nobody leaves!" Mitch echoed, nodding his head in understanding.

"The snitch will be revealed soon enough. Until then, we have another problem to deal with," Kelly announced.

"What?" Mitch gasped.

"Lydia Jones! She was creeping around the hallway when Kate had her unfortunate accident. There's a chance she saw what really happened," said Kelly. Mitch felt himself go pale, and worry was now brewing in his stomach as he listened to his wife talk. "Don't worry, I've handled her for now. I made one of the paramedic's sedate her, should keep her quiet for a while. I'll assess the situation more in the morning," Kelly explained, rolling away from her husband as she attempted to find sleep, "whatever she thinks she saw, I'll convince her that it's wise to forget. If not, well she'll only have herself to blame for the consequences."

***

Lydia spent the night drifting in and out of consciousness, with images constantly flashing through her mind as she was sleeping. Horrifying scenes of Kate's disfigured body lying lifeless at the bottom of the stairs, and visions of her friend all drenched in blood, watching her as she slept. She was restless and groaning in her sleep as the nightmares continued. Lydia's waking moments were spent fearing Kelly's probable retaliation, and what future fate would be awaiting her.

At some point, Lydia's drug filled mind registered the apparition of light flooding her bedroom, yet she was unable to move, or even fully open her eyes to acknowledge its presence. Whatever the paramedic had injected her with was strong, and its only purpose was to keep her trapped and restrained in her bed. At one point, Lydia even thought that she had seen Kelly's face looming over her, lips moving, but no words were heard. The image soon faded, and Lydia couldn't actually recall if it had been real or not, or just another fragment of a nightmare echoing across her distressed brain.

It was several hours later when the fog finally cleared, enough for some order to return to Lydia's mind. It was as if somebody had just suddenly pulled back a curtain shielding her mind from the light, and now she could finally think clearly again.

As she lay on top of her duvet on the bed, the first thing Lydia noticed when she awoke was the sunlight creeping through her window. Her limbs felt numb and heavy as she attempted to push herself up, firstly onto her forearms, and then sluggishly sitting herself up.

The Hall was deadly silent. There was no faint sound of the television downstairs, or of shunted footsteps coming from the hallway, not even the sound of birds chirping outside. It took a few more moments for her sluggish limbs to comply with her foggy mind. But eventually, Lydia was able to find her feet and stumble slowly towards her bedroom window. She paused as she saw the grey clouds bellowing above, and the coating of fresh frost across the field below. It was true, winter was finally here, and by the look of the sky above, snow could begin to fall at any moment.

Looking out at the scenery, a statue below met her eye and a flood of emotion overcame Lydia. Hitting her like a tidal wave, she was unable to hold back, as tears began to well up in her eyes and run down her ageing face. She fell to her knees, one hand gripping desperately at the curtain. Choking sobs began to work their way out of her throat, wrecking her entire body as realisation set in once more. Kate was dead! Lydia had seen the body herself, and as much as she wished it had all been just another nightmare, the truth was that it was all real! Kate had fallen down the stairs and her frail body had broken on impact! Kate had always seemed so strong, but to then suddenly see her looking so fragile, was just too unbearable for Lydia to think about. She would never see her friend again! They would never go out for lunch together, or spend countless hours in the conservatory talking about life and adventures of the past. It was all over, and now Lydia felt more alone than ever, and all because of a stupid accident. Was it an accident? Lydia's mind helpfully provided that thought, with the image of Kelly standing at the top of the stairs. She recalls Kelly's emotionless face meeting with her own immediately after Kate had fallen, landing with such a heavy thud. Lydia had never seen anybody look so indifferent to a situation. The calmness that Kelly displayed didn't quite fit the circumstance they had both found themselves to be in. From the look on Kelly's face, you would think that she was simply looking down at a swatted fly, and not the lifeless body of a woman she knew well, and supposedly cared for. Sure, she had carefully sculpted her emotions later, skilfully playing the injured party for the authorities, crying fake tears onto Mitch's shoulder as Kate's body was being taken away. But, during that first moment after Kate had fallen, when it was just Kelly and Lydia alone in the hallway, there appeared to be no emotion at all in Kelly's eyes. No shock, no sadness, and above all, no regret! They weren't the normal reactions of a person who had just witnessed the death of another human being, especially with the event happening right before their eyes. To Lydia, these actions were those of a psychopath!

When Lydia had first witnessed the altered wills in Kelly's office, she had been struck with the thought that maybe something more sinister than simple theft was going on. But, after her brief chat with her daughter, she forced those thoughts away. Now, after what she had witnessed last night, those thoughts were coming back to her with full force. Lydia was now convinced that Kate had not fallen, but she had been deliberately pushed! Either it was an act of pure rage, or a premeditated plan, designed to stop Kate from asking any more questions about things she wasn't supposed to know.

Lydia urgently needed to call someone! She needed to contact the police to come and investigate what had been going on at the Hall. They needed to see the evidence in Kelly's office, and expose what the woman was really capable of. Feeling a burst of energy within, Lydia rushed to her feet and headed to the living room where she grabbed hold of the phone and held it to her ear. She hurriedly dialled '999' into the keypad, her fingers appearing blurred. Her heart sank as she was met with silence! Worriedly, she tried dialling again, but there was no response, no dial tone, just silence! A lump formed in Lydia's throat as she placed the phone back down, her fingers feeling along the back looking for the cable. She grabbed the cable and followed its path down towards the wall, only to find that it had been cut! This act was clearly intentional, the threads appearing to have been neatly severed by a pair of pliers or strong scissors. Lydia felt sick now, but she refused to panic. Instead, she began to scour the apartment for her mobile phone. She searched high and low, unable to locate it, despite the fact that it would permanently lay on her bedside table when she was home. She never wavered from this habit, so somebody must have taken it!

Lydia was now sat on the bedroom floor, her hands pulling tightly at her hair in frustration. Tears were slowly cascading down her cheeks due to the pure helplessness that she felt. A thought from the night before returned to her, vaguely recalling seeing Kelly standing above her, watching her as she slept restlessly. This meant that Kelly must have been in her apartment! The other woman must have entered and taken her mobile phone. She then must have cut the landline to isolate Lydia completely! It was now occurring to Lydia how intelligent and thorough Kelly truly was. The other woman clearly didn't trust her, and Lydia no longer had any idea what fate awaited her!

The sound of a car horn disturbed Lydia from her thoughts, and she curiously crawled back towards the window. She secretly hoped it was the police returning to the Hall, and that they had seen through Kelly's act and would now want to arrest her. But, no such luck was going to afford itself to Lydia's plight. She could see a small dark-green car at the end of the driveway. It was angrily blaring its horn, and was positioned directly in front of the old and rusted iron gates. The gates were now closed and locked preventing the vehicle from leaving! Lydia hid behind the curtain, watching patiently as Mitch came into view. His bulking body was trying to jog down the driveway to meet the car near the exit. He reached the driver's side door, leant down and made some dismissive arm gestures. Lydia continued to watch as the car turned around and came back up towards the main house. A small part of Lydia's mind told her that the car belonged to the Johnson couple. They lived just a few doors away from her, but the larger part of her attention was focused on the fact that Mitch had prevented the couple from leaving! Lydia couldn't help thinking that this was all about her. The telephone line had been cut, her mobile phone had gone missing, and the grounds were now on lockdown! Yes, she knew she was now definitely deep in trouble, but she had no idea how she would escape it!

The sun looked like it was preparing to set, when there was a sudden knock on Lydia's door. It sent an ice-cold feeling through her veins! She stood rigid! She couldn't bring herself to move, neither to open the door or cower away. There were several seconds of silence before the knocking returned, but this time it was more forceful!

"Lydia? It's me, Kelly. Are you awake? Hope you're feeling okay?" the voice called gently from the other side of the door, sounding friendly and concerned. *"Damn it!"* Lydia thought. If Kelly was here, she would have no choice but to let her in. If she didn't she would become suspicious, and Lydia didn't need that attention. As of yet, it was unclear to Lydia what Kelly thought Lydia might know. Lydia would have to be smart in this situation. She knew that Kelly mistrusted her, and the feeling was certainly mutual. But, if Lydia played her cards right, she might just be able to shift Kelly's concern away from herself. This might be her only chance of getting out of the Hall, and away from the hellhole she once thought of as home.

Decision made, Lydia forced her muscles into action, stepping stiffly towards her apartment door.

Upon lifting the catch and opening the door, Lydia was met with Kelly's ever cheerful face, grinning down upon her like a Cheshire cat about to catch a mouse.

"I thought for a moment there that you weren't going to let me in," Kelly smiled, but try as she may, it did not reach her eyes. It was only as Kelly stepped forwards, letting herself confidently into the apartment without being invited, that Lydia noticed what the younger woman was carrying with her. A large silver tray containing a teapot and cups, along with a platter displaying a sponge cake, was carefully held in Kelly's grasp. "I thought you might be hungry," Kelly added, noticing Lydia staring at the tray cradled in her arms.

"That's very kind of you," Lydia croaked. It was the first time she had tried to speak since waking up, and it was only now that she realised how dry her throat had become.

"Oh dear! You look awful. Come sit. A hot cup of tea will do you good!" Kelly insisted, laying the tray down on the coffee table. She then helped herself to a perch in Lydia's favourite armchair after pouring them both out a cup.

"Why are you here?" Lydia questioned quietly. She was looking uncomfortable and out of place, as she was forced to sit on the sofa and not in her usual spot. She didn't like sitting there as it felt foreign, she liked it even less that Kelly of all people was taking residence in her seat.

"Well, I thought it best I come and check on you," Kelly answered, sounding somewhat shocked that she was being questioned, "after all, last night was a terrible shock for all of us. But, I'm told that you and Mrs Donovan were rather close. After having seen her like that, it's really no wonder you had a bad turn. I'm only thankful that someone was present to aid you," Kelly said, sounding dramatic in her explanation.

"It was a terrible accident!" Lydia replied, trying to force her voice to stay steady as she did so. She looked down at her lap, so that the other woman wouldn't be able to see the anger in her eyes.

This reply stunned Kelly somewhat, and she was unable to keep herself from raising an eyebrow in surprise, despite her well trained features.

"Yes. A terrible accident!" Kelly echoed, seeming slightly amused, "I only wish there was something I could have done," she added. Lydia almost choked at hearing this. The blatant lies this woman could spit out were almost beyond belief. But, Lydia knew she wouldn't be doing herself any favours by letting her true opinions show, so she swallowed them down with a sip of the bitter and milkless tea.

"I'm sure you did all you could," Lydia forced herself to respond.

"I'm glad you think so," Kelly returned, now sounding far more gleeful than a moment previous, "it's always so sad when we lose a resident here," she added pensively.

"I'm sure it is. I don't envy your position," said Lydia, looking at the younger woman, attempting to seem sympathetic.

"Sadly you get used to it. I've seen so many people pass on from here that I can't even remember all of their names. One day they're here, and the next they're gone. The same thing will probably happen to you one of these days!" Kelly stated. Those words made Lydia's heart clench. Was that a threat or a simple fact? And, of all of those other deaths, how many could Kelly personally be responsible for? Either way, Lydia wanted to ensure that she would not allow Kelly the satisfaction of living on as a free woman. Not after seeing what she had done!

By now, the room began to darken as the clouds were building up in density, casting the entire apartment into a grey gloom. The perfect scene for the grim conversation at hand.

"Looks like it's going to snow!" Lydia remarked after taking a fleeting glance out of the window.

"Would seem that way. Wouldn't surprise me if we lose power again like last year. I despise this weather. Give me a sunny beach any day!" Kelly stated casually, elegantly sipping her tea, "I hate this time of year. First the snow will fall, then the roads will be all icy and dangerous, nobody should be out in that," Kelly continued, thinking out loud.

"Is that why the gate has been locked?" Lydia questioned. Seeing an opportunity into Kelly's motives. It was a faint possibility now that Lydia had overreacted, and that the locking of the gate was not to trap her in, but could have been a legitimate safety precaution until the pending storm had passed. That didn't however explain what had happened to her mobile phone. Lydia knew that if she kept on playing this game efficiently, she could convince Kelly that she was just a clueless old woman, and perhaps her phone privileges may soon be returned.

"What?" Kelly had replied at first, confusion etched onto her face.

"The front gate. I saw Mitch locking it earlier when the Johnson couple were trying to leave for their daily shopping trip. Mitch stopped them going," Lydia explained, "I suppose I don't blame him if the roads are dangerous," She quickly added, trying to appear understanding rather than assuming.

"Oh . . . yes! That's exactly it!" Kelly jumped in instantly, too eager in Lydia's opinion, "there's a lot of old dears here and getting caught out in a snow storm could see any one of them off. We wouldn't want that now, would we? Best to keep the gate closed and locked for now, so I can ensure everyone here is safe. Better safe than sorry as they say," Kelly continued, back to playing her usual caring role. She was a fine actress indeed.

"We're clearly lucky to have you," Lydia replied, grateful that no trace of sarcasm entered her voice. Everyone else might be easily fooled and swayed by Kelly, but Lydia was now officially free of that illusion. Nothing seemed kind or sincere about this woman any more. She wasn't a gentle guardian, but a sickeningly twisted manipulator. How easily Kelly had latched on and presented her feeble excuses only proved Lydia's point. Lydia had been testing Kelly, watching carefully for the small signs and traits that would give her away. It may have been down to her so called 'sixth sense', or maybe just natural good perception, but as Kelly spoke, Lydia could only see the lies in her eyes. It was there, deep down under the false smiles, fake tan and dyed blonde hair. It was hidden so well, that Kelly probably couldn't even sense it herself. But, it was there, and Lydia would never be fooled by this unpleasant harpy of a woman again.

Lydia became aware, as her thoughts tailed off, that Kelly was now staring at her, perhaps attempting to sum the other woman up, as Lydia herself had just done.

"I've read some of your book, by the way," Kelly said suddenly, and Lydia felt a boulder drop in her stomach with the words.

"Oh, really?" Lydia responded, desperately trying to not sound flustered and disinterested. She didn't know if she had succeeded.

"Yes, very interesting! I'd have never taken you for a soothsayer, you've always struck me to be more of a rational thinker, rather than all that Voodoo stuff. Just goes to show, you can't always trust your first impressions," Kelly stated in a pensive manner.

"I couldn't agree more," Lydia replied, before she could stop the words falling from her mouth.

"So, tell me Mrs Jones, is there any truth in what you do, or is it all smoke and mirrors? Don't get me wrong, I won't think any less of you if it's all a sham. Whatever it takes to make money, am I right? Needs must! So, tell me honestly, do the dead really speak to you, or is it all just an act?" Kelly practically purred as she spoke. Lydia couldn't help but feel she was now being cross-examined and assessed, scrutinised like a laboratory rat. But, Lydia wouldn't fall for it, she could see exactly what Kelly was doing, and was confident that she could play the same game too.

"No," Lydia replied, smiling confidently at the other woman.

"So it's not true . . . not even a little?" Kelly pushed, leaning forwards to peer down at her.

"No, the dead don't speak to me," Lydia repeated, grinning quietly to herself, but knowing all too well how good they are at leading the way. She could never have said that of course, or else find herself in deeper trouble. But, merely the satisfaction of knowing she had a step up on Kelly made her feel prideful.

"I'm disappointed in you, Lydia, lying to vulnerable people in order to take their money. Shame on you!" Kelly responded, her tone mocking. How Lydia longed to label the other woman a hypocrite. But, any other words from Lydia right now would surely not improve her situation. She needed a distraction to escape this conversation.

"How about some cake? It looks delicious," Lydia stated, leaning towards the plate in order to quickly change the subject. But, just before she could reach it, Kelly jumped up from her seat and took hold of the tea tray, as if she had been physically thrust to her feet by an unseen force!

"I don't think that's a good idea, do you? I mean, it wouldn't do you any harm to cut back a little. You're not getting any thinner these days!" Kelly suddenly spat out, her voice cold and disapproving as she turned to leave. Before Lydia could grasp what had happened, Kelly was gone, and Lydia could not recall ever feeling so relieved before in all her life.

***

As Kelly stepped outside the apartment, completely unbeknownst to Lydia, Mitch was waiting in the hallway, leaning against the wall as he listened and waited for any sign he might be needed.

"Well! Does she know?" Mitch questioned, falling into pace beside his wife as she marched down the hallway.

"She doesn't know anything, at least not anything important! We'll keep a close eye on her from now on. I still don't trust her," Kelly replied, whispering in case the walls had grown ears, "go back to work, we don't need anybody else getting suspicious around here," Kelly ordered as the pair entered the kitchen. Mitch gave her a confirming nod before scouring off and leaving his wife alone. With a distasteful grimace, Kelly began clearing her tea tray, only stopping for a second to lift the freshly baked sponge cake and drop the entire thing straight into the rubbish bin. She wiped her hands clean, and got on with her day.

Chapter 14

Toxicology

Christian had spent several hours sifting through a large stack of patients' records, all of which were files of patients who had previously been residents at Carnation Hall. The search had revealed an alarming amount of files, more than fifty covering the past twenty years. That in itself wasn't all that surprising to him, as the place was after all a home for the elderly who did tend to have a habit of pushing up daisies on a regular basis!

Yet, there was something about the situation that just felt wrong to Christian. He couldn't shake off the feeling that he had somehow overlooked something. Something fundamental had been missed! Even going through every file with a toothpick, he had not found any obvious irregularities. The most common causes of death had been diagnosed mainly as heart attacks, a few strokes and various types of cancer. Include a few accidents to this list, and you would have pretty much the full story. However, after probing through these files for the best part of the day, Christian had indeed found a few abnormalities. He noticed that quite a number of the reports had included some additional observations by the toxicologist.

The first bundle of case notes that Christian examined were those of a certain Mrs Sheppard. The report stated that she had died on the 18th of May 2003. The official cause of death was due to a fatal stroke, and all the evidence from the autopsy supported this diagnosis. However, the toxicologist who had assisted the pathologist at the time, had in fact discovered small traces of an unknown substance in the woman's blood report. However, these anomalies had been dismissed, mainly due to the overwhelming evidence that the cause of death was a blood clot in the patient's brain.

More notes had also preyed on Christian's mind. One in particular belonged to a man called Thomas Rhodes. He was an elderly man in his early nineties, an old soldier who had clearly gained some serious injuries during his time in active service. The report did not express how he had sustained his wounds, but the extent of his injuries had been quite unmissable. Both of Thomas' legs had been amputated above the knee. Christian himself could recall this man's arrival at the morgue about 18 months ago. In this case, the official cause of death was pulmonary cancer . This was due to him being a life long heavy smoker, this having eventually caught up with him, or so it seemed! What appeared now to be screaming out to Christian in the case notes, was that the 'unknown substance' statement had again reared its head in his blood test results. In fact, this had happened more than once over the two year period he had been attending the hospital for treatment. The nurse who had often cared for old Tom had noted these findings in his file. However, she had put the findings down to the possibility of the patient ingesting something voluntarily, or the fact that at this particular time, he was receiving both chemotherapy and radiotherapy treatment. Mr Rhodes had also been taking many herbal remedies to help relieve his symptoms during this time.

Several more of these irregularities also started to appear in some of the other files, but apparently nothing was either said or done about them at the time. The official causes of death seemed pretty indisputable, and it didn't surprise Christian that none of them were ever investigated further, although the evidence did seem strong enough to warrant further investigation!

Christian's curiosity had now peaked, especially since the latest appearance of the mystery substance. This had appeared only a month or so earlier on the report of a man named Bryan Williams. This case now needed to be looked into more thoroughly, but above all, immediately!

"We've got a new stiff, boss!" was the phrase that roused Christian from his thoughts. A young orderly was standing in the office doorway, disturbing him from his work.

"Have Dr. Khan handle it. I'm busy!" came Christian's reply, not lifting his nose from the page before him.

"I would, sir," the young orderly said apprehensively, yet unwilling to be dismissed, "but I think you should take a look at this one yourself."

"Oh, really? And why is that?" Christian questioned, disinterestedly. He was starting to feel a little annoyed now.

"Well sir, it's because I saw the pick up notes from the paramedics. This woman came from Carnation Hall and I thought that would be of interest to you," the orderly explained, seeming shy as he stood in the doorway.

Christian was up and out of his chair before the young man even had chance to finish his sentence, brushing past him, forcing the younger man to rush after him.

"Thank you for bringing this to my attention!" Christian stated, "now, I need you to do something else for me."

"Yes sir! Whatever you need," the orderly responded, puppy-like in his glee of being praised.

"On my desk there's a report under the name of Mr Bryan Williams. I want you to take it down to toxicology and see if they still have a blood sample from him. I want a complete analysis report of that sample, and I want it on my desk as soon as possible!" Christian stated, "understood?"

"Yes, sir! I'll take it down right away," the eager young man replied, turning to head back towards Christian's office and retrieve the file.

"Good lad!" Christian called after him, continuing his own march towards the examination room, which they had nicknamed 'The Ice Block'. The morgue attendant should already be on duty and waiting for him. Christian did not want to delay this investigation any longer. He now had so many questions, and it was high time he got some answers.

***

The sun was now long gone, itself desperately trying to hide away from this sinister old house of dark intentions. Lydia now found herself trapped within it, but she felt appropriately confident that Kelly had been fooled by her act of playing the clueless and dumb old woman! Despite this, she was still somewhat on edge after being locked in and having her mobile phone mysteriously go missing. This just made the ice in her bones set harder, yet, the sad fact was there was nowhere she could now go, and nobody around she could trust. Lydia was by no means helpless, and as she thought about her situation all the more, it dawned on her that there 'was' somebody she could rely on and trust for guidance, it was just making contact that would be the hard part.

With that, Lydia began rifling through her kitchen drawers, rooting to find any old candles that she owned. She carefully and methodically went about placing and lighting them around the living room of her apartment, before heading back to her bedroom. There was something very specific in this room that she needed. It had made a home above her wardrobe, and had not seen the light of day since Lydia moved in. She reached up and lifted its casing from the top of her wardrobe, carefully wiping the thick layer of dust from its surface. It felt as though she was being reunited with a long lost friend, handling it with the care that was only reserved for the most delicate and priceless of objects. She then carefully unpacked her spirit board from its tattered old box.

After a few moments she felt ready. She turned off the lights in her apartment, plunging the room into a dull amber glow. She then dropped slowly down to her knees on the living room floor. The old board was laid out before her. Its worn, wooden surface still shining in the dim light, even after all its years of loyal service. Despite her nerves and apprehension at the situation she was in, Lydia couldn't help but put on a gentle smile. A month after her arrival at the Hall she had put the board away, fully convinced it would never grace her hands again as she started her new life. But, here it was again, faithful as ever, and at a time she really truly needed it. She was extremely glad of its company.

Taking a deep breath to help steady her nerves, Lydia placed her hands above the board. The index finger from each hand stretching out to gently rest on the heart-shaped planchette, its touch so familiar to her skin.

"Spirits of the past, hear my voice," Lydia began, her tone quiet but firm, "be guided by my voice and come towards me. I wish to speak with you!" the words falling from her lips like it was second nature.

Lydia paused for a moment, waiting and looking around. She was listening for any sign that her call had been heard, either by the living or the dead! Nothing was happening. She took another deep breath, feeling the air sticking to her throat as she did so, before trying once more.

"Spirits of this house, I wish to speak with Elizabeth Holland. If you can hear me Elizabeth, come towards my voice. Speak to me!" Lydia recited, trying to keep her tone steady.

Another few moments passed with Lydia trying several variations of the summoning, but nothing seemed to happen. "Please!" Lydia eventually called out, "I need your help! I followed the path you guided me down, and now I need your help again. Answer my call!" she cried out, her voice filling with anger from her desperation. That's when it happened! To her left side sitting beside her television, a row of candles suddenly and violently blew themselves out. One after another, the wicks were left smouldering in the increasingly dark room, and after a few moments longer they then started to cool. The shock of the extinguishing made Lydia gasp! She let out a small squeak of fright, and as it left her mouth her breath hit the air. It puffed out into a cloud of steam, and a cold shiver ran down Lydia's back as the room began to chill further around her.

Lydia could feel it now. Even if she couldn't see it, she could definitely feel it! A presence was looming over her and surrounded her as she knelt silently on the floor. The air around her felt like static electricity, her lungs filling with the ice-cold vapour, her fingers quickly becoming numb from the severely decreased temperature that the room now possessed! Yet, she refused to move her hands from the planchette.

"Have you come to help me?" Lydia asked the air around her, feeling it shift invisibly at her words. A moment later the planchette moved! It moved so fast and violently racing around the board, that Lydia almost lost her touch on it. But, after working with this board for so many years, Lydia's eyes were well trained in following the glass window of the planchette around the board, no matter how fast it was moving. Finally it settled to a halt, spelling out the word *'Y-E-S'* before her!

"Thank you!" Lydia whispered gratefully, "you've guided me before, so please tell me what I must do. Is there any way I can get out of here?" she questioned quickly. She was fully aware that she sounded like she was panicking, as she attempted to fight the feeling down. She waited for a reply, and then it arrived just a moment later!

'S-T-O-P', the planchette spelt out, moving as forcefully as it had the first time.

"Stop?" Lydia questioned, "stop what? Stop trying to leave? Do you think it's safer for me to just stay here until the snow storm passes?" she didn't even have to wait before the planchette started moving again.

'N-O-T S-A-F-E', the spirit spelt out on the board in record time, 'S-T-O-P T-H-E-M'.

"Okay! But I don't know how! I'm sorry!" Lydia exclaimed, fighting back her tears now, "I don't know what to do!" It was clear the ghost did not agree with this answer, as it took over control of the planchette once more.

'S-T-O-P T-H-E-M', the spirit began continually directing the planchette towards the same letters over and over. The force and speed was such, that Lydia's arms began to ache from the jarring.

"Okay, okay, I get it! Stop!" Lydia cried out. The planchette abruptly froze mid-sentence. "What do you want me to do?" Lydia requested to know, sounding as exhausted as she felt.

'S-T-O-P T-H-E-M', was written once more on the board.

"Stop them how?" she questioned. Everything went still for a moment, and Lydia feared that the connection had now been lost. But, thankfully, the planchette slowly began to move once more.

'C-O-M-E', the spirit replied.

"Come where?" Lydia asked.

'C-O-M-E T-O M-E', the board wrote after a pause.

"What does that mean?" Lydia pleaded to know, "come to you where, Elizabeth?"

'O-U-T-S-I-D-E'.

"You want me to go outside . . . now?" gasped Lydia.

'Y-E-S', the planchette continued to spell.

"Why? What's outside?" Lydia asked, now confused.

'M-E', was the reply, *'C-O-M-E T-O M-E N-O-W'*.

"What do you want me to do? What am I looking for?"

'M-E', the spirit wrote again.

"Okay, how do I find you?" Lydia questioned, knowing that if she wanted help from the ghost, she would have to play along with this game. It wouldn't or couldn't tell her anything more, so she would just have to trust it. She had been guided by Elizabeth's spirit before, so she would just have to have more faith in the spirit. Because, at this point she really didn't have any other choice!

'S-T-A-T-U-E', the planchette wrote out suddenly, Lydia staring at it curiously.

'C-O-M-E T-O M-E', *'F-R-E-E M-E'*. If she didn't know any better, she would have thought the ghost was screaming at her, the words being spelt out in such a violent manner! That's when a thought wormed its way into Lydia's head, and a sinking feeling began to drop in her stomach. She had a strange feeling from the second the spirit had answered her call, that something seemed different. She was becoming familiar with Elizabeth's presence around her, but this wasn't it. Lydia had been so desperate to communicate with Elizabeth, that she had let this uneasy feeling slip by, but now she couldn't hold back!

"You're not Elizabeth, are you?" Lydia asked uneasily, feeling her throat tighten with the anxiety.

'N-O', the spirit replied.

"What do you want?" Lydia practically whispered.

'R-E-V-E-N-G-E', the planchette revealed slowly.

"Who are you?" Lydia demanded to know, her voice hard and determined as she spoke, masking her fear. The planchette began to move, dashing about over the board again. Lydia felt horrified as she watched the letters being revealed.

'M-O-T-H-E-R', the board displayed.

As soon as the board went still, Lydia jumped up from the floor. She grabbed her coat from the back of the door, and rushed down the hallway at a speed unbeknownst of a woman her age. Lydia was now fuelled with pure adrenaline. All this anger and sorrow had suddenly given her strength, and with the final words of the spirit still echoing in her mind, Lydia knew exactly where she needed to go!

***

At the morgue, Christian slowly pulled back the sheet to reveal the corpse beneath. The last thing he expected to see was a face he recognised lying face up on the cold slab before him. This woman, with her thin features and ash-grey hair, had recently joined him and his family for dinner at Lydia's apartment. This was only a couple of weeks ago, yet now, here she was, gracing his morgue with her presence. It was extremely sad to see her like this, stripped of her former glory and dignity. She was now just another cold dead body, awaiting its turn on his table.

"A one Mrs Katherine Donovan," the morgue attendant declared, reading in a monotone voice from a file in her hand. "She was brought in last night. She fell down the stairs apparently. Looks straight forward! Shouldn't take us long," she said, throwing the file back onto her desk dismissively. She then pulled on a pair of latex gloves. Christian did the same, relishing the satisfying snapping sound they made as they consumed his large hands.

The woman was right. The examination didn't take long at all. The cause of death was very easy to determine, and a full internal autopsy was not required. The fact that the back of the woman's skull had been severely fractured due to its collision with the floor, rather gave the game away. And, if the impact alone hadn't done it, the rapid blood loss from the open wound in her leg would have certainly finished off the job. They were indeed ghastly wounds to look at, but by no means the worst that Christian had dealt with over the years! After working here as long as he had, nothing really shocked him any more.

After the examination was complete, Christian began the return trip to his office, but before doing so, he ordered a toxicology report to be carried out on Mrs Donovan. The attendant had argued as to the validity of this investigation, but being the boss had its advantages, and Christian got his own way.

He arrived back at his office to find the door slightly ajar. He curiously pushed it open, revealing a familiar tall thin woman with long raven-black hair sitting across from his desk. She was dressed in a white laboratory coat, and she turned to watch him as he entered the room, clearly awaiting his arrival.

"Hello Vanessa!" Christian greeted as he entered, shutting the door fully behind him. He knew this woman fairly well. She was a promising young doctor working in the toxicology department. They had worked together fairly often during the past year. However, her professional prowess did little to quell the aversion he felt towards her brash and cocky attitude. "And to what do I owe this pleasure?" he asked, looking her over and taking his seat comfortably behind his desk.

"I come bearing gifts," she replied confidently, lifting a black file up from her lap and waving it before him triumphantly, "I've got to say, I'm thankful somebody finally looked into this, although I never expected it to be you! Would have thought it a little too inconsequential for the mighty boss to get involved with," she stated, looking around his office.

"Mind telling me what we are talking about?" Christian asked, leaning back in his chair as the young woman spoke. He had a feeling this was going to be a long night, already irritated by the woman's presence.

"Mr Bryan Williams," Vanessa declared bluntly, "earlier this evening you sent an orderly to my lab, asking questions about the patient and wanting a blood analysis. Correct?" she asked, crossing her arms over her chest, her voice grating against Christians ears.

"I did. However, I didn't expect any results back so soon," Christian replied, rubbing a palm over his forehead to help ward off his ever looming headache.

"Well, you've got me to thank for that!" she grinned arrogantly, "I was the one who first noticed the abnormality in Mr Williams' test results. I brought it to the attention of Dr. Ashworth, but she dismissed me. Said it was probably nothing, and that I should get on with my other work," Vanessa rolled her eyes with apparent distaste for her superior, "you'll be very glad to know that I chose to ignore her advice, and I ran the tests anyway in my spare time! You're very welcome!" she added with a sarcastic smile.

"So these are the results?" Christian questioned, pointing to the file still held in her hand.

"Full analysis!" Vanessa confirmed, handing him over the file, "and, you'll be pleased to know that I have identified our mystery substance!" she told him smugly as he read the file, his eyes flashing all over the page searching for his prize.

"Aconitum?" Christian read out loud, raising an eyebrow in curiosity, as he looked at her for confirmation.

"Yep. No doubt about it!" she replied, nodding to accentuate her point, "Aconitum, Wolfsbane, Monkshood. Whatever you want to call it, it was running around the man's bloodstream."

"Well that's . . ." Christian tailed off, unable to find the words.

"Odd?" Vanessa offered and Christian nodded, "you're telling me! I had to run the damn thing three times before I could believe it myself!" she laughed to herself seemingly in disbelief. "Now, the bigger question is, how the hell did it get inside him?" she asked, looking at him expectantly.

"Would the amount you found be enough to kill him?" Christian asked her bluntly. He was beginning to feel totally perturbed as this puzzle began to unravel before him.

"A dose that size? No! He would have needed to ingest a larger amount for it to be the direct cause of death. And, if he had done that, there is no way that it could have been overlooked in the test results," she explained, leaning down over the desk to examine her own notes.

"So, in your personal opinion, what would the size of the dose that you found do to his body? Would it have had any effect at all?" Christian questioned, now leaning forwards.

"Of course it would! It's one of the most fatal toxins in nature!" Vanessa declared, before taking a breath to think, "a dose that size would take a few hours to work its way around the body, then we would be talking about extreme metabolic stress. We would be looking at a list of possible effects, with everything from acute gastroenteritis to impediment of motor functions. It's hard to say what the individual outcome would be, as there are too many variables," she explained calmly.

"What was the official cause of death again?" Christian questioned, hands resting under his chin as he was deep in thought now.

"Myocardial infarction," Vanessa replied, her voice going quiet, as her own thoughts were following the same path that Christian's must be taking.

"Could that have been caused by the Aconitum in his blood?" Christian requested to know, eyes glassy and unseeing, as the feeling of bile rose in his throat.

"In theory, yes! If the patient had a pre-existing condition or defect, then the toxin could have exacerbated the condition," Vanessa informed. She was looking at Christian now, taking note of his increasingly pale complexion, and the beads of sweat beginning to form upon his brow. "But this could all just be a coincidence," she continued, "there's no real evidence to say otherwise, and coincidences do happen on occasion," Vanessa declared, trying to lighten her tone and dismiss the tension in the room.

"You're right!" Christian agreed, his voice hard and determined as he spoke, "coincidences do happen! But, I'm pressed to believe that all these other cases are coincidences too." He then stood up, pushing a large pile of files towards her forcefully. "These are all former residents of Carnation Hall," he declared. A few files fell on the floor at her feet, the papers spilling out where they landed. Vanessa fumbled to pick them up.

"Where did you get these?" she questioned breathlessly. She looked over a document she had retrieved from the ground, seemingly shocked to see her mystery substance appear on yet another report.

"I've found eleven of them so far, and those are just the ones we've picked up on! Eleven corpses, all with that same chemical in their veins at the time of death, and all delivered from the same place. Still think this is a coincidence?" Christian asked her bluntly as he slipped out of his lab coat, throwing it off into the corner inattentively.

"Oh my god!" Vanessa croaked, seemingly in shock as she scanned multiple papers and files. She looked up at him, eyes sunken in as realisation dawned on her firmly. "Where are you going?" she questioned, as she watched Christian grabbing his leather jacket from the back of his chair, and shrugging it onto his shoulders.

"I have to go! Call the police and tell them to get to Carnation Hall! You'll find the address in those files," Christian ordered, kneeling down beside Vanessa and forcing her to catch his eye as he spoke, "can you do this for me?" he asked her gently. There was a moment of silence as Vanessa fought through her shock and was able to recover her voice.

"Yes boss!" she replied obediently, with just a hint of sarcasm on her lips.

"Thank you!" he told her, turning to leave.

"But wait!" Vanessa called out, "where are you going?" she demanded to know.

"You can tell the police I will meet them at Carnation Hall," Christian declared, and with that he marched from the room. His only thought now was getting to Lydia as fast as possible and putting an end to this conspiracy.

***

After fleeing her apartment, Lydia now found herself outside in the grounds of the Hall. By now, the snow had been falling for quite a few hours, and every visible surface was covered in a thickening blanket of white dust, a beautiful sight to behold. The way the dark stone of the statues contrasted against the freshly falling snow, gave the Hall and gardens a haunting beauty that Lydia feared she would never forget. But, now was not the time to admire poetic beauty, or dwell on tragedy! Lydia had a purpose to being there, and she was determined to see this through!

Escaping the Hall had thankfully been remarkably easy. With the bad weather and the impending notion of a power outage, all the residents had been locked away in their apartments, holding up against the cold weather with whatever personal comforts suited them best.

As for Kelly, Lydia had thankfully avoided the vile woman's presence. But, the telltale sound of classical music coming from the kitchen met Lydia's ears as she entered the main foyer. This music warned her of Kelly's most likely location, and she was now able to slip out of the front door, undetected by all.

Outside, the cold air was biting viciously at Lydia's exposed skin, as she trudged her way down the path. The sound of fresh snow could be heard crunching loudly below her feet, sounding suspiciously like footsteps following her as she walked. This added to her paranoia, and forced her to continually look back over her shoulder into the darkness. Despite all this, Lydia was not turning back. She knew exactly where she was heading for, even with the falling snow veiling her way. But, Lydia knew her surroundings far too well for it to deter her. She was heading slowly across the field, carefully scanning the surrounding statues as she passed their petrified forms. There was only one statue that interested her now. It was a statue she had only ever cared to admire from a distance.

It took several minutes for Lydia to reach her destination. The cold and the snow was slowing her pace down to a crawl, but soon enough she arrived at where she needed to be, directly in front of 'the' statue. This one was far older than any other she had encountered at the Hall. Its surface now was mostly covered with snow, covering a much more haggard and worn exterior beneath. A clear sign it had spent years, maybe even decades fighting against the elements. In comparison to the other statues, this one appeared plain and rather unremarkable. It was a much simpler design compared to the more extravagant works that had been added more recently. The design was of an angel, its wings outstretched as it stood looking sorrowful and resigned, its face down turned with a look of mourning. The angel's forlorn features had long since worn away, and part of its left wing had broken off, being left crumbled on the ground at its side. It was a sad sight to behold, and unlike the rest of the statues in the grounds, this one appeared unwanted and unloved. It had even been placed in the far reaches of the garden, as far away from prying eyes as possible, or so it seemed. There were no flowers around its base, just overgrown grass and weeds poking out from beneath the snow. This was a stark contrast to the heavily pruned and cared for flowerbeds surrounding the other statues.

But, it wasn't the sorry looking state of the statue, or its lack of maintenance that Lydia had come to see. What caught her eye all those months ago, was the fact that this sculpture had a plaque on its concrete base. It was the first thing she had noticed about this particular statue. It was a feature that none of the other statues possessed. The plaque itself had deteriorated almost beyond recognition, its edges appearing sharp and dangerous to the touch. But, the engraving was still clearly visible! Just one word had been carved upon the metal, and it was 'that' word that had led Lydia back to it now!

The word *'MOTHER'* was engraved on the plaque. A shiver ran down Lydia's spine, as she recalled the spirit upstairs violently manipulating the spirit board, demanding her to come to this very spot. She hoped she was doing the right thing heeding its call.

Knowing what she must do, Lydia stood within reaching distance of the statue. She held her head up high, trying to express a tenacity that she actually barely felt. Her hand was shaking violently, as she reached out and bridged the gap between her own flesh and the cold stone of the statue.

'F-R-E-E M-E', the spirit had told her, spilling out the letters boldly across the board. Lydia now understood the meaning of those words.

It now felt like an age had passed since Lydia first reached out and touched Elizabeth's statue, releasing her from her stone prison, and beginning this whole adventure of betrayal and treachery. How she longed to turn back time, and go back to remove the knowledge that she now possessed. She just wanted to live out her days in ignorant bliss, as was the original plan when relocating to Carnation Hall. But now, that was just a fool's thought. If she were to ignore the ongoing corruption at the Hall, she felt that she herself would be left with a stain on her very soul, blackening it, and leaving her just as much to blame for this corruption of justice as Kelly must surely be!

With a final, and longing thought as to how things could have been in her life, Lydia pressed her hand forward, placing her palm flat against the statue's chest. Her breathing was in spasm, as the feeling of an arctic chill set in against her body, her veins running cold as her blood grew frigid within her. It was a ghastly invasive feeling. Almost as if someone was trying to pull the very life out from within her, and taking it as their own. But, Lydia had felt this tortuous feeling before, and she knew that she could withstand it, even though every fibre of her being was screaming to pull away in retreat.

Respite finally came a few moments later, and Lydia let out a sigh of relief when the feeling began to fade from her bones. Yet, the air surrounding her was left feeling dense and pulsating with energy, making her chest ache as she tried to inhale. It took a few more seconds before Lydia found the strength to finally retract her hand, and as she did so, she witnessed a shimmering light beyond her fingertips.

Slowly, a spectral hand began to emerge from within the statue. Its long skeletal fingers burst forth from the stone angel's chest, extending out towards Lydia, as if trying to grasp her fingers in its own. Lydia stumbled back, fearing it would try to pull her in, to become a companion in its own fossilised cell. As she moved away, her numb legs crumbled beneath her, and she found herself lying back against the hard cold ground. She barely had a sparing thought of gratitude towards the snow for cushioning her fall, as she looked up to view the horrifying display now unfolding before her eyes.

The spirit's hand continued to reach out from within the statue, making its way towards Lydia, its arm now free of the concrete confines of its statuesque tomb. Its translucent skin looked insubstantial, as it attempted to take form. Soon, a second hand emerged to join its brethren, reaching up to take hold of the statue's shoulder as it attempted to drag itself forward. The force of this act made the stone statue itself shudder, causing the snow to fall from its shoulders, and forcing the birth of a heinous creature. A head now began to emerge, tilting downwards, with long thinning hair shielding its face from view. As the spectre pulled itself forth into this new plane of existence, it proceeded to materialize further, falling free of the statue like a slithering snake, and slipping its way to its feet.

The spirit was now towering above Lydia, still flickering dangerously in the half light. She could see the full extent of its ghostly appearance. The woman was tall and skeletally thin, her bones protruding out from every angle, giving a sharp appearance to her joints and structures. Her face looked so gaunt, that it looked as though her entire skull was on display beneath. She appeared sickly and half-starved. Her hair was patchy and thin, with only a few long tangled strands remaining. But, what was standing out as the most prominent feature was the head, permanently tilted towards the shoulder. Large patches of bruise-like marks were covering her skin, pulsating black and purple against the paleness of the ethereal body. Her neck was clearly broken, and appeared to be snapped out of place. It was just hanging there loose and limp in its own lonely, and eternal purgatory.

The spectre stepped forward towards Lydia. She instantly shimmied backwards in the snow, instinctively wanting as much distance between herself and this creature as possible. Even its motion was stiff, like a moving mannequin, its limbs popping and jumping out of place as it attempted to walk. The creature's gaze met her own! Its ice-blue eyes almost glowing against the white snowfall. For a moment, Lydia thought the spectre was poised to attack her. The way its eyes violently glared into her soul, it seemed enraged and prepared to lash out as it moved towards her. But, just as suddenly as it had appeared, it vanished! The spirit moved past her, flitting itself away across the garden, its feet not once leaving any footprints as it moved through the snow.

Lydia watched it travel, intrigued as to where it was heading and why. The spirit suddenly stopped! It stood stationary, waiting impatiently, its body still jerking uncontrollably in the dark.

Lydia realised that she was supposed to follow the spirit. Like an obedient pet on a leash, she had no choice! Lydia clambered to her feet as quickly as she was able, and began stumbling after the spirit. It appeared satisfied with her obedience and continued on its journey. It was leading her once more down a 'rabbit hole' and into the unknown.

The deep snow was making it hard for Lydia to walk, but soon enough she appeared to have arrived at her destination. The spirit stopped in its tracks! Its spine-like finger stretched out, and pointed into the distance away from her. Lydia's eyes followed its direction, and Mitch's work shed came into view.

"You want me to go there?" Lydia asked the spirit, her voice hoarse due to her sore throat.

The spirit stared at Lydia, unable to answer by nodding its head, but the gesture was clearly an instruction to proceed. Her destination could only be the work shed. She would have no choice but to visit this old building if she had any further intentions of finally unlocking the mystery!

Lydia stood still for a moment, the serenity of the Hall's grounds disguising the atrocities that had been committed upon this land. From her position, standing in the snow covered field amidst the trees, Lydia could see more statues laid out around her. Solid stone figures, standing forever vigilant in the carefully manicured grounds of the Hall. It occurred to Lydia with fleeting despair, that each of these statues here, out in the cold, could also be victims of Kelly's iniquitous and wicked reign! Each and every one of these statues could contain a disembodied spirit, filled with fury at the injustices thrust upon them, whilst trapped within their concrete shrines. With this thought, the embers of an idea began to rekindle in Lydia's mind as she leered at these motionless statues standing before her. Their appearance was that of an army, paralysed concrete soldiers waiting in their ranks for their orders!

Stepping forward to trudge once more through the snowy grounds, realisation presented itself to Lydia. If it had only taken a simple touch of her skin against the statue to awaken Elizabeth from her tomb, perhaps, all that was needed to summon and free the other spirits trapped within the statues would be a similar action. She now quickened her step as the cold air sent chills through her body. Lydia was no longer marching directly towards the shed, instead, she was heading towards the other statues. Her mind was fixed on touching and reviving as many spirits as she possibly could. She shuffled through the snow, meandering and zigzagging around the gardens. Each time she approached a statue, Lydia would stretch out her arms, looking as if she was about to embrace the statue, before pressing the palm of her hand briefly down upon its rough, cold surface. Each statue she touched sent icy tingles through her skin, racing up through her nerves, and into her arms. It was a sensation that verged on the painful, but never quite registering as such.

Lydia continued through the gardens, winding and racing towards the work shed, still gazing, and laying her hands upon every statue she encountered! After brushing against several more statues, she found herself standing in the silhouette of the work shed, its menacing structure looming over her like a mighty beast! A lump formed in her throat as the dread began to pool in her stomach. This was it! It was now time to prove her valour, and unlock the final pieces of this puzzle laid out before her. Now, all that remained was for Lydia to take a few steps forward, and enter the building!

***

Kelly had spent most of the evening obsessively cleaning her kitchen. The last few days had taken its toll on her, and she had been left feeling tense and stressed. For most women, that might have been an invitation to open a bottle of wine and relax in a hot bath. But not for Kelly, she had to keep her head and remain calm, no matter what! This place would disintegrate without her, and all her plans along with it! So, here she was, rubber gloves pulled up to her elbows, vigorously scrubbing her oven clean. The melodic sound of a classical piano concerto soothed her ears whilst she carried out her tasks.

She was aware that Mitch was standing right behind her. He was watching the football match on his smartphone. By the sound of his grunts, mumblings and curses, it was clear his beloved team were losing the game. In the old days they had made a habit of watching the football together, but those days had long since gone. Football just didn't interest Kelly these days, in fact very little did! She was now far more interested in lying on an exotic beach somewhere, sipping a cocktail. All that really mattered to her now was keeping up her appearances, and ensuring that she would live the life she felt was due to her. It annoyed her beyond compare that Mitch didn't share her passion. Sure, he was as obedient as a gun dog, fetching and playing his role, but he had no real passion or drive for anything more in life. His life mainly consisted of playing golf and tending to his beloved gardens. This lack of initiative was extremely irritating, to the point she couldn't help but roll her eyes at the thought. Even just watching him sitting there whilst she was working, was really getting on her nerves!

"Mitch!" Kelly exclaimed suddenly! Her hand firmly placed on her hip, as she turned to glare at him.

"Yes, my dear?" her oaf of a husband replied, not even looking up from his screen.

"Take the rubbish out!" Kelly ordered.

"At half-time, love," Mitch said innocently, still not looking at her. Totally fixated on the game.

"No! Not at half-time . . . now!" Kelly stated sternly.

"But . . ." Mitch stuttered, finally looking at her, his eyes pleading.

"Now!" Kelly reaffirmed her orders, her voice sounding dangerous, and Mitch knew he would not get another warning! Slumping his shoulders in exasperation, he stood up from his chair and skulked across the kitchen to do as he was told.

A minute later, Mitch was standing by the back door, a bin bag in each hand, as he used his back to push open the door. The chill from outside hit him like a brick wall, and he began to wish he was wearing more than just his woollen jumper. He somewhat begrudgingly worked his way around to the back of the house, his destination being the set of large dustbins. As he approached the bins, something in the distance caught his eye. A glint of light flickered, appearing to be emanating from around his work shed. He could see a lone figure trying to push open the door, and seemingly trying to break in!

He only then realised that he had earlier forgotten to lock the door in his haste to get out of the snow. *"Kelly was not going to like this!"* he thought, *"she was really not going to like this!"*

CHAPTER 15

The Queen Of More

When Kelly was just a young girl, many decades before arriving at Carnation Hall, it would have been inconceivable that she could grow up to be the perpetrator of any such heinous crimes. Yet, sometimes fate can work in such mysterious ways, that it takes only one incident, or even just a single unwarranted action to forever stain a person's soul!

During her childhood, Kelly had been raised single handedly by her mother Lilian. They had never held a close relationship, despite Kelly's best efforts to the contrary. She had, nevertheless been raised into a somewhat privileged lifestyle, living in a comfortable terraced house, not too far from Kelly's school. They owned a modest family car, and were also able to afford several short holidays each year. You see, Kelly's mother, Lilian, had suffered a workplace accident several years earlier. It was a simple slip on a wet floor, but had caused serious damage to her leg, leaving her with a permanent limp. At the time of the accident she was working for a high-powered company in the city, and she subsequently received quite a substantial compensation payment, which indeed had been very generous. Her physical condition resulted in Lilian requiring the constant assistance of a cane to aid her walking. She had never been a warm woman, Kelly's father abandoning them both shortly after Kelly's birth. This apparently was the catalyst forming the rift between the two women. Her father's departure had seemingly left an everlasting wound upon Lilian, and she had in turn taken to silently and subtly blaming her daughter for his desertion. As Kelly grew, she would rarely ever receive any affection from her mother, the woman always being extremely distant and undemonstrative. That wasn't to say that Lilian was in any way abusive towards her daughter. Kelly was in fact always well kept, she was well clothed and the pantry was always well stocked with quality foodstuffs at her disposal. As a child, the only thing that Kelly really lacked was endearment. She had spent her life attempting to impress and befriend her mother, but all her attempts were to be proven futile. It became blatantly apparent that Lilian was incapable of showing Kelly any love and devotion. And, as a result, Kelly became intent on leaving that frigid place she reluctantly called home at her earliest possible convenience.

As the years followed, Kelly went on to complete high school achieving exceptionally high grades. She then attended university where she later graduated with an honours degree in botany. Somewhere along her journey through high school, Kelly had acquired a profound fascination for growing plants. She would be fascinated to watch small insignificant and dull-looking seeds grow and bloom, developing into bright and beautiful flowers. These processes captivated her mind, and in a way reminded Kelly of herself, waiting in the dark for her special time to break free and blossom. Her love of plants had unknowingly led her down the path of botany and mycology. This passion, along with her degree in botany would surely bring along an array of career prospects for her future.

However, soon after Kelly had graduated from university, she had been forced to turn down her first serious job offer from a well known and renowned pharmaceuticals company. Her mother's health had suddenly deteriorated, taking a dramatic downward turn. She had been stricken by an acute case of pneumonia, further aggravated by Lilian's relentless chain-smoking, at one point almost taking her life. Following a course of intense medical treatment, she began to make a slow and steady recovery, but her illness had left her severely weakened. Lilian was now unable to fend and look after herself, and being the stubborn woman that she was, she had instantly refused all offers of home nursing and care whilst she was recovering. As a result, Kelly had no choice but to return back home and become a full-time carer for her mother.

Luckily her infirmity did not linger for too long, and Lilian began to slowly recover. But, by this time, Kelly's employment opportunities were beginning to dwindle away. The pharmaceutical company had already filled the vacancy previously reserved for her, and despite sending out numerous applications to other companies, Kelly hadn't received a response from any of them.

This brief event during Lilian's illness had done nothing to heal the relationship between herself and Kelly. If anything, it had ruptured it even further, Kelly growing ever more resentful for the loss of her career, and blaming her mother for robbing her of her future. Whilst Lilian, even in her weakened state, still felt profound bitterness towards her daughter's good health and youthfulness. She was resentful that Kelly still had her entire life ahead of her, whilst Lilian herself was now declining steadily with old age.

After many months, Lilian had recovered sufficient strength to be able to now care for herself, and Kelly was finally free to break away from her shackled existence. She did so, and with little hesitation she promptly reapplied for similar positions of employment. However, this proved to be a pointless endeavour, and after countless rejections, she found herself resorting to waitressing in a local patisserie. It was only intended to be temporary work, for maybe just a few weeks, waiting until something more suitable came along, but a year went by and her situation hadn't changed! Kelly was a fast learner, and whilst working in the patisserie she had gained a talent for baking fancy pastries and elaborate cakes. This earned her a degree of fame and notoriety with the regular patrons, and some well-earned praise from the owners. She was extremely popular with the customers, and had actually encountered her first serious boyfriend after serving him her celebrated and quite delicious home-made apple pie. That relationship though did not last very long, Kelly soon growing bored with his tedious habits, one of which was to actually go out in the evenings with his friends rather than spend time with her! Kelly promptly terminated that relationship, and shortly afterwards a better option presented itself, this time in the form of a good-looking boy working at the local florist shop.

Eventually, Kelly moved on from the patisserie, now putting her new found culinary skills to use with another catering company. A few more years then passed, with Kelly continuing to climb up the ranks of success, until eventually she became the manager! It was here that she was destined to meet her future husband. You see, Mitch worked as a van driver, delivering ready-made meals to the elderly, and to those who could no longer cook for themselves. The two of them had met purely by chance when the company that Mitch was working for, suddenly decided to change their supplier. They had fortunately chosen Kelly's catering firm as their new business partner, so from then on Kelly and Mitch would see each other practically every single day. Mitch fell for Kelly almost immediately when they first met, due mostly to her strong presence and gentle good looks, although he was far too shy and reserved to say anything to her. On the other hand, Kelly actually took quite some time to warm towards her future husband. Mitch had never been particularly good-looking, or even talkative, but he was quiet and obedient whilst they were together, and Kelly liked those qualities. It had been the first time in her life that somebody had ever really listened to her, or done as she had suggested things be done. It also helped the fact that he had a fairly well-paid job. It was one Friday night after they had both finished work that Kelly asked Mitch to go out on a dinner date. It would be his treat of course, as she was a lady and would surely not be expected to pay. Mitch, without hesitation jumped at the chance of going on a date with Kelly, and so the rest became history. After a short engagement of just a few months they were married, purchasing their first home, and planning to live a long and happy life together. Or, so it was supposed to be. But, fate clearly had other plans for this couple!

***

Kelly was now in her thirties, and one day whilst she was at work she received a call that would forever stain her life. It was from a hospital claiming to be looking after her mother. Apparently, Lilian had suffered a sudden and debilitating stroke, leaving her blind in one eye and partially paralysed. She was now going to need constant care. Claiming that she no longer had any funds to feed herself, and seemingly with no other options, Lilian ended up moving in to live with Kelly and Mitch.

Lilian had always been a cold and distant woman, but with age and her illness, she had now grown even more bitter and conceited. The stroke had affected her emotionally and physically, causing one side of her already wrinkled face to droop. She was now blind in one eye, and had also lost complete use of one of her long skinny legs. Clumps of her brittle white hair had become detached from her head, leaving large patches of her scalp on full display, only accentuating the sorry state of the feeble old woman. Thin and frail, Lilian was now spending her days glaring at the television, whilst Kelly was forced to cut back her hours at work, handing over her managerial position begrudgingly to a younger woman, and now having to spend each and every day caring for her decrepit mother.

A burning anger began to form within Kelly for the woman who raised her. Anger at the deprivation she had to experience due to her mother's constant needs and attention-seeking. Kelly now had to feed her and bathe her, even clean her backside, and be on hand twenty-four hours a day, just on the off chance she would be needed by this callous and bitter old hag. Whilst all this time, Lilian would be sat in her chair, slurring her words, complaining about what a disappointment her daughter was to her. The two women were growing to despise each other, but Kelly didn't let it show, preferring instead to disguise and conceal her true feelings. On the outside she would smile and speak kindly, but internally she was burning with resentment for being forced into this infernal predicament.

Mitch was able to escape most of the drama, as he was working all hours, and could thus avoid the hellhole of a house that he now resided in. Kelly, however, was unable to escape, she couldn't even take a quick trip to the local supermarket without her mother throwing a fit and calling her a disgrace.

Eventually, Kelly was forced to give up her job altogether. Her mother could no longer be left alone, as she would hobble herself out of her wheelchair and wander dangerously around the house. She had fallen several times in the past and injured herself, so Kelly had no choice but to stay and watch over her mother, whilst Mitch picked up some extra shifts at work to support them all.

Over the next few years, Kelly and Mitch's home became a virtual prison! Kelly was the guard and Lilian was the sole inmate, or perhaps it could possibly be the other way around! The two women would spend all day locked within the same walls, with nothing but their own company all day until Mitch would return from work late in the evening. Each day would pass the same as the one before, with Kelly cooking, cleaning and caring for her mother. The house was quiet apart from the blaring sound of Lilian's television, or the squeal of the wheels from her wheelchair as it passed along the hallway above.

Whenever Kelly afforded herself some free time, she would care for her precious plants. The town house held a modest garden where a small greenhouse featured prominently. Within this glass palace, Kelly would feel most at home. The rest of the main house felt quite alien to her, as if it had been invaded and terraformed against her will. But, within her greenhouse she could relax and feel at home. The garden was inaccessible to Lilian, as she was unable to descend the stairs and reach the ground floor without any assistance, much less navigate the narrow kitchen doorway strapped into her bulky wheelchair. Kelly was safe out there in the garden, safe from her mother's criticism and demands The greenhouse itself was a paradise for Kelly's ambitious mind, filled with rare and expensive plants that she herself had nurtured and grown. Her selection of rare orchids was the diamond in her collection, combined with a compilation of wild-growing herbs that she had accumulated and used regularly in her cooking.

Lilian's eventual demise had been a profound turning point in Kelly's life. The event itself had occurred quite suddenly and with no prewarning. It all started on a very wet winter's morning, lashings of water pelting continuously against the windows of the house. The noise was echoing violently around the hallway, shrouded in gloom due to the thick cloud cover outside. The weather forecast showed no signs of improvement throughout the day.

As usual, at the start of the day, Kelly entered her mother's bedroom, intent on waking her with a tray in hand and her breakfast ready to serve. Lilian was already awake, sitting upright in her bed as she watched her daughter enter. She scowled at Kelly, the expression being visible on the one side of her lip that could move, whilst the other side lay hanging in a permanent droop.

"What muck have you brought me now?" Lilian spat, the words muffled by her unresponsive muscles as she spoke. But, Kelly was long accustomed to making sense of her mother's slurring, though any other possible witness would not have been so able.

"It's time for your breakfast mother. I've made you fresh porridge this morning," Kelly replied, doing her best to mould her tone into something resembling friendly, although the result was more dismissive than kind.

"I don't like porridge!" Lilian slurred once more, "I've always hated porridge. You know I hate porridge! Why would you bring me something you know I hate? You're trying to poison me, aren't you?" she shouted, looking at Kelly in disgust as her daughter set the tray down beside the bed.

"Don't start, mother!" she sighed, "you had porridge last week and you said you liked it. Don't be difficult now!" Kelly returned, silently groaning in detest at her mother's ungrateful attitude.

"No I did not! You're lying! I'd never eat that filth, and you know it! The only one being difficult here is you! You never bring me anything I like!" Lilian said, turning her face away like an insolent child, as Kelly attempted to spoon feed her mother the oats from the bowl, "get that disgusting slop away from me!" Lilian slurred aggressively, angrily lashing out with her one working arm, sending the spoon and its contents messily crashing to the floor.

"Why the hell did you do that?" Kelly bellowed, suddenly furious, "you know I'm going to have to clean that up now, when it's your mess!" The younger woman stood up angrily, throwing the bowl none too carefully onto the bedside table in her anger.

"How dare you speak to me that way, after all I've done for you. You ungrateful little bitch!" Lilian spat, the words falling in mumbles from the side of her mouth.

"Done for 'me'! What on earth have you ever done for me?" Kelly demanded to know, standing tall in her heels before the frail bed-ridden woman.

"I raised you, gave you life, and this is how you repay me, by keeping me trapped here, feeding me your scraps and leaving me to fend for myself for hours on end. Your father would be so ashamed of you if he could see you now!" Lilian bit back bitterly.

"Are you delusional? You stay here for free while me and Mitch cater to your every whim! You eat better than we do, and I'm around every second of every day to serve you like your own personal housemaid!" Kelly snapped back, leaning over her mother intimidatingly, "and, as for my father, don't you dare try and put that on me. If he left, then it was because of you! You only ever cared about yourself and he knew that. He obviously couldn't stand to be around a stony-hearted harlot like you a second longer!" The force of Kelly's words had Lilian cowering back into her pillow, with a look of outrage on her wrinkled and drooping face.

"Don't you insult me!" Lilian slurred angrily.

"I'm not insulting you mother, I'm describing you!" Kelly said, her tone as cold as ice, "if you don't want to eat the porridge I made for you, then fine, go hungry, I don't care! Perhaps you'll be feeling more accommodating come dinner time." And with that, Kelly stormed from the room, taking the breakfast tray with her and leaving her mother alone to wallow in her own bitter juices.

Kelly had retreated to her kitchen after that encounter. To an outside viewer, it may have looked like a nasty confrontation had just taken place, but at this point Kelly was more than adjusted to it. Those bitter discussions with her mother would occur regularly since the stroke, and they had been growing more frequent during recent months. Kelly couldn't decide if it was just because of mental illness setting into her mother's mind, or just a side effect of ageing that was making Lilian antagonise her so. Either way, Kelly didn't care any more! She had never had a good relationship with her mother, and now, since the stroke, Kelly was just biding her time until the old woman was gone, then she herself could return to her own life.

The rest of that morning would pass in a blur, as Kelly devoted her time to working on Mitch's accounts whilst sitting at the kitchen table. She made a point of not going back upstairs to check her mother's well-being, as a punishment for the defiance she had experienced at breakfast. It wasn't until late afternoon that Kelly would hear the distinct sound of wheels squeaking along the upstairs hallway. It was clear that Lilian had tired of sulking alone, and since Kelly had refused to go and offer her some assistance, the older woman was now showing further insubordination.

Although the stroke had taken away the use of half her limbs, Lilian had realised long ago that she was still more than capable of moving about with her remaining functional arm and leg. It would take some time and a considerable amount of effort, but Lilian was able to drag her limp half out of her bed, and push herself around the upstairs hallway in her wheelchair using just her remaining arm. The procedure was strenuous and exhausting, and often left Lilian with dark bruises and agonisingly painful joints. On the rare occasions that Lilian would make these efforts, Kelly actually found herself struggling to sympathise with her mother's plight, and felt it to be just another annoyance she had to contend with.

"Kelly!" Lilian suddenly called, her voice echoing as it travelled down the stairs. Kelly felt herself bristle in response to the voice. She was unsure what was special about today compared to the countless other days this situation had occurred, but something about the way her mother summoned her made her veins boil with rage. Perhaps Lilian had finally pushed her daughter too far, or Kelly's patience was now running too thin. But, whatever it was, the situation had caused Kelly to finally reach the end of her tether.

Without any hesitation, Kelly rose to her feet, the chair she was sitting upon shrieking painfully against the floor as she stood. And, taking confident broad steps, She stepped out from the kitchen and into the entrance hall to greet the sight she had already expected to see. Lilian was perched in her wheelchair high up on the landing, her good arm gripped firmly to the rail overlooking the foyer below. She pulled herself closer in an effort to peer down over the barrier, whilst her paralysed arm hung loosely at her side like a dead weight. Her old face displayed a mixture of worry, annoyance and curiosity as she watched and waited for Kelly to appear in her line of sight.

"What do you want now mother?" Kelly questioned, her arms crossed against her chest as she stood impatiently at the bottom of the staircase.

"I'm hungry!" Lilian stated bluntly, as she leered at her daughter's defiant stance.

"Is that it?" Kelly questioned dismissively, "well you know where the kitchen is, and seeing as you don't like anything I make for you, I suggest you come and cook something for yourself!" she added coldly, glaring at the old woman, and almost smiling to herself when Lilian's face fell at her words.

At the top of the staircase, Lilian mumbled something, but the slurring from her drooping mouth, and the distance between the two women made the words impossible to decipher.

"I didn't catch that, care to repeat it?" Kelly remarked unkindly.

"I can't get down!" Lilian repeated her previous words, but this time with increased volume. The look on her decrepit face was a mix of outrage and sorrow, as she was forced to repeat her sentence, much to Kelly's delight.

"You can't get down? Hmm . . . what a pity! If only there was someone here who could help you," Kelly replied, unwavering in her stance at the bottom of the staircase.

"Stop being so childish and come and help me!" Lilian demanded, her patience all but gone, with desperation littering her enraged voice.

"I'm being childish? Who was the one throwing their breakfast all over the bedroom like a two-year-old?" Kelly demanded to know.

"Stop this! Come and help me back into bed and bring me some food!" Lilian ordered stubbornly.

"Really? You're not even going to say please?" Kelly huffed, almost laughing in disbelief.

"You're pathetic!" Lilian spat.

"No, mother! You're the pathetic one! Look at you, you can't even stand on your own two feet. You sound like a drunken sailor, and not a soul on this earth gives a damn about you! Hell, you can't even handle a set of stairs. You truly are pitiful!" Kelly hissed, as she watched her mother's angry and defeated glare fall upon her.

Nevertheless, Kelly took a step forward and slowly started to ascend the staircase. She was convinced she had defeated her mother for the moment, and that the verbal assault was over for the day. However, when Kelly arrived at the top of the staircase, it became clear that wasn't the case! To her right, her mother was sat immediately in front of her still holding on to the rail.

"You think me pitiful?" Lilian said angrily, once her daughter had reached her side, "well, save your pity. I don't need you or anybody else to cater for me. I can look after myself, just as I've always done!" she continued, beginning to slowly lift herself free from the wheelchair. She was now clinging on with her able left hand in order to stand upright, as her useless paralysed leg dragged itself behind her.

Kelly could do nothing but watch as her mother found her feet. The younger woman felt a wave of admiration, mixed with the usual aversion she felt for her mother as she stood. Kelly said nothing, simply remaining still as she watched the decrepit woman limp towards her, using the banister as a crutch to aid her movements.

"You act like you own me! Just because you believe yourself to be better than me! Well you're not better than me and you never will be! You were a bastard child. Your father left because he was embarrassed by your existence. He didn't want you! He begged me to give you up after your birth, but I stupidly refused. If I had listened to him, then maybe I could have been happy! But I was naive, I felt sorry for you and look what that gained me. Nothing! I lost the man I loved and gained a trollop for a daughter. You're a disgrace to me, and there isn't a day goes by that I don't wish you had never been born!" Lilian ranted, her face turning red as the words fell from her barely responsive lips.

"Screw you!" Kelly hissed, a look of disgust overtaking her face as she looked down upon her mother's frail and infirm form.

The sound of skin striking skin could then be heard, echoing alongside the sound of the falling rain as it reverberated along the hallway. Lilian had momentarily released herself from the railing, she then lunged forwards and swiftly struck Kelly across the face with the back of her able hand. The two women were now almost nose to nose standing directly at the top of the staircase. The stinging slap reddened Kelly's cheek, making it stand out sharply against the rest of her pale skin. The sudden pain came as a shock to Kelly, catching her by surprise, and causing her to freeze momentarily as she grasped at her still stinging face. What happened next was almost as if she had been possessed. Without thinking, and without hesitation, Kelly lashed out at her mother. Possibly in retaliation, or maybe just from an overflow of rage and emotion she could feel rushing violently through her body. In one brief and swift movement, Kelly had grasped her mother firmly by the shoulder, and with uncontrolled and sinister joy, she thrust the old woman away from her towards the descending staircase.

It seemed as though time had slowed down as Lilian began to fall. Lilian's frail form was no match against Kelly's forceful thrust, and her remaining useful leg instantly lost its footing and collapsed beneath her! With no chance of grabbing hold of the banister, Lilian began to descend, the air rushing up to meet her as she fell. Her eyes momentarily locked with Kelly's, wide open and fearful as realisation set in. She continued to plummet down the staircase, with only a few pain-filled grunts escaping from her throat. As her frail body connected with the hard and unforgiving steps of the stairs, it wasn't long before Lilian was lying motionless at the bottom! A loud dull thud could be heard, accompanied by a sickening and crunching snap! An eerie silence then followed, engulfing the house. The only sound now being the ever pouring rain tapping against the window pane in its persistent assault, and the steady rhythm of blood flowing past Kelly's ears.

For a moment Kelly was frozen and unable to move! She was stood alone at the top of the staircase, completely paralysed by shock and fear as she looked down with horror-filled eyes. From where she stood, she could see her mother's prone form lying far beneath her, making no sound and unmoving! It took several seconds before Kelly was able to force her own body to move, and with extreme caution she slowly descended the stairs, keeping her eyes firmly fixed on her mother every step of the way. Once she reached the bottom stair, it was clear that Lilian would not be rising to meet her!

As Kelly examined her mother's condition, Lilian appeared eerily peaceful from where she was lying, face up on the ground. There was no blood, no grizzly open wounds or agonising shouts, only silence and an unmoving form. Kelly could have assumed that her mother was merely sleeping, if it hadn't been for the fact that her neck was lying at an unnatural angle. A fragment of her neck vertebrae was protruding from below the layers of her skin, jutting out sharply below the jawline. Bruises were already starting to form and steadily darkening by the second. Ruptured blood vessels were leaking profusely below the skin's surface, turning the flesh a putrid array of red, purple and black, standing out sharply against the sickly pale white of the rest of her body.

With her expression completely blank, realisation hadn't quite sank in deeply enough for understanding to accompany, as Kelly knelt down at her mother's side. With vigilant eyes she examined Lilian's chest, searching for any signs of movement. She placed her hand directly in front of Lilian's face, poised to catch any lingering breath. Nothing came, no air was expelled or raised in the woman's breath. She had seemingly died on impact, her neck having twisted and snapped as she crashed down upon the floor! Kelly didn't move. She sat beside her mother for several minutes until her mind finally caught up with her eyes. Lilian was dead, lying like a broken doll at the bottom of the stairs! Her mother was gone, and Kelly had killed her! Despite the tragedy, Kelly was unable to force herself to cry. She felt nothing for the corpse that lay upon the floor. The rift between the two women had burrowed itself so deep, that no emotion other than hatred could escape its depths. Yet, her thoughts inadvertently shifted to concern. She had killed her mother! Accident or not, she had inflicted the fatal push and now she would have to face the consequences of her actions. That was, unless she could convince the authorities otherwise. What sense would it make for Kelly, an innocent woman and victim of her own mother's abuse, to be sentenced for what was essentially a blameless accident. Lilian's fate was due to her own error, Kelly had committed no crime, unimpeachable in her actions. She had spent years caring for her witch of a mother, the best years of her life stolen away by the thankless bitch. Kelly would not allow Lilian to ruin her life further from here, and with this decided, and her determination renewed, Kelly found her feet.

The first step in her plan was to perfect her appearance. She raced to the bathroom and proceeded to apply a thick coating of foundation, helping to disguise the reddened blow from Lilian's hand that still marked her cheek. A ruffle of her hands disturbed her perfectly positioned hair, offering a more dishevelled and untidy look. Finally, a bottle of menthol mouthwash caught her sight and Kelly wasted no time in putting it to good use. She filled the cap with the mint scented liquid, but instead of raising it to her mouth as one would expect, Kelly had in fact lifted it to meet her eye. She tilted her head back to the desired angle, and tipped the menthol solution directly onto her open eyeball. The liquid caused the sensitive organ to sting severely, a constant burning that made Kelly hiss through her teeth as she endured the assault. But, the discomfort had been well worth it, as the results of her unorthodox applications were infallible. Her eye now stood out bright and red, shining feverishly in the bright light of the bathroom. Tears were now flooding out in a constant stream down her face. As she wiped her fake tears proudly away, she took a moment to compose herself, before repeating the act once more upon the other eye.

Several minutes later and now looking perfectly dishevelled, Kelly made the emergency phone call to the authorities. She forced her voice to stay low and quake as she spoke to the dispatcher, requesting an ambulance to visit her address immediately. The tale she spun to the paramedics who arrived at her door was a simple one. Kelly had learned long ago that the best told lies should never vary far from the truth, and with that thought firmly fixed in her mind, she proceeded to tell the two men, both dressed in bright yellow and green, about the calamitous events that had just befallen her.

She informed them how she had earlier been working in her kitchen, listening to the radio whilst she slaved away over her husband's business accounts. She had assumed that her mother had been sleeping peacefully in her room upstairs, completely content as far as Kelly had been aware. However, it seemed that Lilian must have awoken and began to wander the halls. This was a habit Lilian often acted out with obstinacy, and total disregard for her own safety. In the past, Lilian had been caught several times wandering around the house, and even been left in need of medical attention after tripping and injuring herself. Kelly was fully aware that this fact could be backed up by her mother's medical records, and would certainly add further to the credibility of her own deceitful tale.

She went on to tell how she had been disturbed by a sudden loud sounding thud, and had emerged from the kitchen to find her mother lying crumpled at the bottom of the staircase. Her mother was motionless and wasn't breathing. Neither paramedic made any further enquiry into Kelly's version of the events. They had simply bagged up the body of the elderly woman and left the building, only pausing for a brief moment to pay their condolences to the seemingly distraught Kelly.

Kelly would later tell the policeman who arrived at her door the very same fable, and despite her trepidation, the man had not interrogated her in the slightest. He had believed her story without any hesitation, and Kelly was elated at the result. It seems that elderly and frail people are continually being involved in unfortunate accidents, and such occurrences are very common. So much so, that even the authorities did not feel the need to scrutinise such events in great detail. Kelly thought it was comical how willing everybody had been to accept her version of the accident. Even Mitch did not question her story, not that he would have had the courage to cross question his own wife, even if he did possess some doubt. If only the rest of the world would now be so willing to accept her conclusions as well.

A few weeks then passed, with Kelly filling the time organising her mother's funeral, and tending to her greenhouse in blissful peace for once.

Then one day, a letter arrived through the letterbox. Its markings looked official, and it was addressed directly to Kelly herself. Upon opening the letter, she could see that it had been sent from a lawyer in the city. Or, to be more specific, her late mother's lawyer. What happened next came as a great shock to both Kelly and Mitch, as the letter contained a copy of Lilian's will. The will itself from the outside looked innocent enough, mostly lawyer jargon, but what intrigued Kelly the most was the beneficiary. As her only child, Kelly had assumed she would inherit the total of her mother's feeble possessions. But, what Kelly discovered upon reading the will was that not only was she the sole beneficiary, but that her mother's estate was far from feeble. It turned out that Lilian had lied about her financial well-being. The old woman was far from desolate, and in reality had accumulated the sum of around eighty thousand pounds, stored away in various bank accounts. Kelly was in total disbelief with this news. Her mother had claimed to be so poor that she couldn't afford a home-care nurse, or even pay her various hospital bills. Yet, with her available funds, Lilian could have afforded to stay at any number of the finest care homes, and not have needed to scrounge from her daughter. Kelly felt betrayed following this discovery. She had spent years caring for her mother like a personal slave, having given up her own career on two separate occasions, and having lost a multitude of friends in the process. Kelly had spent years practically alone and isolated thanks to her mother's lies, and that infuriated her beyond compare. Yet, the new found influx of cash into her bank account helped to ease the pain somewhat. Kelly now only wished the funds had come to her much sooner!

***

It wasn't long before Lilian's money was all but gone, Kelly and Mitch having squandered their inheritance on lavish holidays, luxury new cars, and many other fancy indulgences that they could have easily lived without. In all that time, Kelly had not taken to finding work, leaving Mitch as the only breadwinner, whilst she spent her days socialising or tending to her beloved greenhouse. But, now that the money was dwindling, Kelly realised that she had no choice but to return to work once more. It was during her time searching for employment that she first discovered Carnation Hall. The establishment was operating as an assisted living complex, fully renovated from a grand old Georgian manor house. It was designed to contain individual apartments, with the aim of offering the over fifty-fives both independence and support. The

Hall was actually owned by a large consortium of businesses from within the city. The firm was advertising the position of manager at Carnation Hall, and Kelly didn't hesitate in forwarding her application for the position. Several interviews later, and thanks to her glowing background in both catering and home care, Kelly was offered the managerial position, which she readily accepted.

Soon, Kelly and Mitch had their own private apartment within the grand Hall. They sold their house, and Kelly allowed Mitch to use the remainder of her mother's funds to purchase tools and equipment for his new found hobby. You see, Mitch always had a flair for model making, especially creating fine plaster figures cast from moulds. He took great pleasure in buying various moulds and creating ornate concrete figures that he would position carefully around his garden at the back of their home. But now, having such a vast workspace within the grounds of Carnation Hall, Kelly had finally agreed to allow him to expand his hobby, and provided him with the equipment to create much larger and more grandiose figures. As part of their agreement, Mitch had to leave his previous job, and Kelly promptly hired him as her personal handyman and grounds keeper at the Hall. It was a position Mitch was elated to accept, and one in which he took great pride.

Unbeknownst to Kelly, Mitch had never actually held much resentment towards Lilian. Instead, Mitch felt nothing but gratitude for the large sum of money they had both inherited from his mother-in-law. He didn't really know what he had done to deserve it! He was just thankful for the various gifts and joys that they had been able to bestow upon themselves with the funds. So, Mitch set about installing his new statue-making equipment inside the the old coach house which was only a short walk behind the main Hall. With unparalleled determination, Mitch turned the unwanted building into his own personal work shed. Over the next several weeks Mitch would devote every second of his free time into working on a special surprise for his beloved wife, a unique and special stone statue. He wanted to reward her for all the hard work she had done to find them a new home, and provide him with a job that he adored.

The evening before Mitch was planning to mix the concrete to fill his chosen mould, an idea came into his head. He knew that Kelly had always had a difficult relationship with her mother, and the subject of what to do with Lilian's ashes had been a matter of concern since the funeral. Kelly did not want her mother's ashes in their home. She did not want to look upon the urn each day as if it were a decoration, yet she could equally not bring herself to dispose of the ashes in the dustbin. So, whilst his new cement mixer was working away, blending the various ingredients, Mitch decided to add Lilian's ashes to the mix before pouring it into the mould.

It took several days for the mix to fully harden, before Mitch could remove the mould and unveil his new creation. During this time he had carefully prepared an area of the garden where he was planning to place his ornate masterpiece. He had chosen the location with extreme care, placing it quite far from the main house in a secluded corner. This was so that it would not be so imposing upon Kelly as she went about her day. However, it would not be too far away if she ever wished to visit her mother and pay her respects.

It was a beautiful sunny autumn day when Mitch finally decided to unveil his new creation to his wife. The grounds of the Hall were seemingly painted in an array of amber's and beige as the falling leaves settled on the fields, blowing gently in the crisp chill of the morning breeze. Kelly had been reluctant to leave the comfort of the warm Georgian house, not wanting to step outside and sully her expensive heels on the muddy ground. But, with some insistence from Mitch, and the lure of a surprise special gift, she readily conceded. Mitch held her hand proudly as he led her down the garden path, the sound of her heels clicking like castanets on the uneven paving stones, before turning silent as they stepped onto the soft grass in unity.

At first, Kelly had looked pleased as her eyes fell over the statue Mitch presented to her. Its form was of a tall angel, graceful and proud in its motionless stance, looking down upon the ground veiled in eternal sorrow. A vast assortment of colourful flowers lay around the base of the statue. Various roses of red, white and yellow added a needed splash of colour to this bland section of the garden. Mitch felt quite pleased with himself as Kelly was admiring his work. She was even starting to congratulate him on his wonderful craftsmanship, when something suddenly caught her eye! The smile instantly fell from her lips, her eyes turning cold, and any previous kind words she may have shared became a distant memory as she read the shimmering metal plaque fixed to the base of the statue.

"Mother?" Kelly questioned, her tone deadly serious, and her eyes burning red with barely contained rage.

"Yes. I made it for you, in honour of Lilian," Mitch replied smiling, clearly oblivious to the aggravated look his wife was throwing his way, "you kept saying that you still didn't know what to do with her ashes, so I mixed them in with the cement. I thought it would be the perfect memorial for her," Mitch continued. It was only now as he looked to catch Kelly's reaction did his own smile fade. "Is something wrong?" he questioned looking concerned.

"Are you really that bloody stupid?" Kelly questioned, her jaw slack in disbelief at her husband's words.

"I . . ." was all Mitch managed to stutter out. His face flooded with confusion as his eyes glanced around wildly, as if the correct answer would suddenly appear somewhere in the grass around him.

Instead of waiting for him to find his words, Kelly turned around sharply on her heels and paced across the grass a few steps. Her destination was a nearby tree, at the base of which lay a shovel that Mitch had left after using it to dig the flowerbed. Kelly picked up the shovel as soon as she could reach it, she then tossed it over in her hands to get a feel for its weight, before returning to the statue.

Mitch felt horror run through his veins as he watched his wife return, potential weapon in her hands. He could only stand back and watch in disbelief, as Kelly raised the shovel up above her head, and then proceeded to pelt it down with all her strength upon one of the angel's wings. An instant crack formed in the concrete directly where the bevelled metal edge of the spade had struck the statue. Kelly repeated the action, swinging the shovel down several more times. A huff of exertion accompanied each blow, until finally the stone wing was severed from the body of the statue, falling to the floor with a heavy thud. Kelly remained still for a moment, panting rapidly to steady her breathing as she admired her handy work. Mitch could feel the tears welling up in his eyes, as he tried to absorb the destruction his wife had just inflicted upon his beloved creation. Watching her vandalise his prized artwork had caused Mitch's heart to ache, and for the first and only time in his life, Mitch felt aversion for the woman he had married. Mitch sank to the damp ground on his knees in defeat as he struggled to swallow his feelings down.

Kelly barely even spared Mitch a glance, before dropping the shovel to the ground dismissively, where it landed softly in the grass. She never once looked back as she marched towards the path and up to the house, leaving Mitch to wallow all alone as he sat mourning the remains of his first and finest statue.

The couple would never again speak of the events that occurred that day. Kelly would never again return to visit her mother's statue, and Mitch would never again build any statues without Kelly's explicit consent.

***

It was around that same time, whilst Kelly and Mitch were still encased in their honeymoon period at Carnation Hall, that Mitch's father suddenly passed away. The man had suffered for many years with heart problems, so his tragic demise had not come as a great surprise. However, the event did leave Mitch's mother, Peggy, a widow. After her husband's death, Peggy decided she no longer wanted to live alone in the large house she had previously shared with Mitch's father, and since she was a woman of modest wealth, a move to Carnation Hall now seemed an attractive option.

In only a few short months, Kelly found herself in the same familiar situation as before, but this time she was now caring for her mother-in-law! The only difference this time was that Peggy would not keep herself confined to her own personal space. The elderly woman felt that she was entitled to special treatment and privileges, especially as her daughter-in-law was the manager of the Hall. One such issue being that the other residents were obliged to pay a fee to dine in the restaurant, but not Peggy. She would saunter into the dining room waiting and expecting to be served practically every lunchtime, with no intention of offering to pay anything! In the evenings, she would invite herself to join Kelly and Mitch for dinner within their private quarters, and then proceed to sit with the couple all evening, watching the television or chatting casually, but never allowing the couple an ounce of privacy. Even during the days, Peggy would shadow Kelly around the Hall as she went about her duties, passing comment on Kelly's actions, stating how she herself could complete the task more efficiently, or criticising her technique. All in all, this constant loitering and lack of peace and solitude was beginning to wear Kelly's patience down to a very thin edge! Peggy's persistent presence was really getting on Kelly's nerves, and it was grating against her mental state like sandpaper against glass. It did not help the fact that Peggy had never really liked Kelly, the two women having never seen eye to eye. Peggy had always felt that Kelly was never good enough for her son, and Kelly found her mother-in-law too elitist with her overbearing attitude and impossibly high standards. But neither woman would admit their true feelings to the other, and as a result, distaste was allowed to brew and grow deeply beneath the surface, whilst fake smiles adorned the exterior.

Peggy had been living at the Hall for almost a year, before the day arrived when Kelly would finally snap! What it was that caused her to do so nobody could say, but it was the result of being dominated by a matriarchal figure for far too long. Kelly had always had a loose wire that was destined to snap if the right pressure was applied, no matter the cause. She had finally reached the end of her tether, and the following events would be a catalyst for untold horrors!

In the past, and even after their move to the Hall, Kelly had never let her passion for botany fade. Instead, she had nurtured and perfected her skills quite privately. Her latest fascination was acquiring and nursing rare herbaceous plants, more specifically ones that contained toxins. Kelly had gained a sadistic thrill from growing potentially deadly flowers and plants, knowing she potentially had the power of life and death over all those around her. The diamond in Kelly's small collection was the wild Wolfsbane she had harvested whilst on a hiking holiday. The plant was said to be highly toxic and Kelly thought that the plant was all the more beautiful for it. For a time, Kelly had shared the work shed with Mitch, keeping her plants safe within its stone cladded walls. Mitch had never once complained about the arrangement, as long as Kelly, his 'queen' was happy, then so was he!

The final straw for Kelly, and the event that would derail her sanity forever, occurred on a seemingly quiet summer's day. Kelly was alone in the kitchen, quietly ironing some of Mitch's golfing shirts, when the idea suddenly struck her! It hit her hard like a blow to the head, seemingly from nowhere! Peggy had been following her around and irritating Kelly for almost a whole week! Nothing she did was right, and Kelly was left feeling increasingly dejected. She just wanted Peggy to go away! The rest of the residents she could handle, with their petty problems and their never ending lists of medical concerns they insisted on sharing. But, Peggy had hit another level!

She was always in Kelly's face and degrading her while she worked. The woman had to be stopped, and Kelly finally realised how she could make that happen . . . permanently!

By the end of the day Kelly had already set her plan into motion. She had taken some of the dried Wolfsbane root which she kept in Mitch's work shed, and added a pinch to her cake batter mix whilst she was baking. A few short hours later, Kelly was making her way up to Peggy's apartment with a freshly baked tray of half a dozen cupcakes, all elegantly decorated with white fondant and pretty little edible yellow flowers. A gentle smile graced Kelly's face as she marched on, the destination of her mother-in-law's door now in view, only serving to broaden her glee even further.

Standing before Peggy's apartment door, Kelly softly knocked upon the polished wooden surface, her knuckles repeating the action twice before the door opened.

"Kelly! What are you doing here?" Peggy questioned, sounding tired and stifling a yawn as she spoke. It seemed Kelly had disturbed her from her afternoon nap.

"I was doing some baking in the kitchen just now, and I thought you might fancy some cake," Kelly smiled broadly in reply, her teeth shining almost menacingly in the dull light of the hallway, as if she were a predator stalking its prey.

"That's not like you. I usually have to come down and scour your kitchen if I want a treat!" Peggy replied, eyeing Kelly suspiciously.

"The truth is, you and I have always had our differences, and I'd very much like to put an end to that!" Kelly replied, sounding as sincere as she was able.

"You want us to become friends?" Peggy asked, looking both confused and humorous.

"Something like that," Kelly told the other woman, still smiling.

The conversation did not last much longer, and soon enough Kelly was retreating down the hallway, the sound of her own heels echoing as she walked, her arms feeling much lighter without the weight of carrying the tray.

Nobody would see Peggy for the rest of that day. The evening came and went without her presence being made in any of her usual haunts. She didn't join the other residents in the communal lounge for a game of checkers, nor did she invade upon Kelly and Mitch's dinner that night. Her room was quiet, without a peep from either the television or her radio. For once, all was peaceful at Carnation Hall until the sun rose high in the sky the following day. With still no sign of Peggy roaming around the Hall by the afternoon, Kelly finally decided it was time to check on her darling mother-in-law. In all honesty, Kelly was apprehensive about what she may find within Peggy's apartment. Would the woman be long dead? Or, would she be clinging to life like an injured feline lying at the side of the road? Or, perhaps there had been no effect at all, and Peggy had simply become suddenly antisocial? Whatever the result, Kelly almost felt an echo of regret for her actions. Well, not necessarily for her actions, as she herself would never regret anything that she had done. She merely felt more concern for the possible consequences that may be awaiting her!

Regardless of this, she entered the apartment without hesitation. Once inside, the atmosphere was deathly quiet, the only sound being the echoes of Kelly's own breath reaching her ears. Peggy's living space was laid out like all the other apartments within Carnation Hall. The main door opened out into a small entryway, which in turn split into two further doorways. She could see that both of the internal doors were shut tight, concealing all that was hidden within. Kelly had chosen to investigate the bedroom first, half expecting to find Peggy lying on her bed, perhaps a vomit-stained pillow at her side, and a glazed look in the old woman's yellowing eyes. But, a swift tug at the door revealed the bedroom to be completely empty. A similar gesture revealed the bathroom to also be vacant. That only left one possibility. The living room loomed like an imposing beast, and Kelly held her breath as she opened the door and slowly entered, stealing herself against the horrors that may soon meet her eyes. However, the living room displayed nothing sinister upon first inspection. A completely silent room, bathed in warm summer light, the atmosphere being surprisingly pleasant. The only real foreboding observation was that she could see tufts of light-grey hair protruding from the top of the armchair near the window. The chair was turned away from Kelly, so she would have to walk around the furniture to view the figure more closely. However, Kelly held no doubt even before seeing the figure's face that this was indeed Peggy!

When she spotted the old woman sitting in the chair, Kelly was momentarily convinced she was merely sleeping. Peggy was slumped back in her armchair, eyes closed peacefully as if her mind was consumed by wistful dreams. However, a closer inspection of the old woman unveiled the full true story. Her chest did not expand with breath, nor did her lips part to expel air. Peggy had expired, very peacefully it would seem, whilst she slept watching the sunset.

Kelly cunningly slipped from the room after her discovery. Not even a single pang of guilt plagued her conscience following her actions. There was no regret! Peggy had annoyed Kelly to no end, and now she was gone, Kelly's problem was solved! Now, all that remained was to cover up her involvement and pray that her actions were not discovered.

Kelly promptly called the emergency services to report the death, and this was punctuated by the muffled sobs escaping Mitch. The normally reserved and unsentimental man could not restrain his grief once Kelly told him about his mother's sudden demise. Kelly just rolled her eyes at his sorrow whilst she spoke down the phone. His constant sobbing was now starting to irritate her, and she yearned to slap his face in the hope that it would bring her some silence. But, Kelly didn't act upon her desires, and despite the tremble in her fist, she hung up the phone and left the kitchen without incident. There was always work to do at Carnation Hall, and if Kelly didn't do it, then nothing would ever get done!

The paramedics arrived an hour or so later to collect Peggy, and carted her corpse off to the nearest morgue. At this point, Mitch had finally stopped sobbing as they both watched the ambulance roll away. With Peggy finally out of her hair, Kelly turned and retired to her bedroom, and before long she was enjoying the most peaceful night's sleep she could ever recall.

The weeks came and went, and there were no signs that her treachery would be revealed. Peggy's death was concluded to be cardiorespiratory failure. The death certificate even declared it as natural causes, a fact that had Kelly rolling with laughter upon reading the document in the privacy of her own bedroom. Yet, being the good wife that she was, Kelly dutifully arranged the funeral for her mother-in-law. She ordered flowers, arranged the music and reserved a venue for a small wake. Kelly did everything right, everything that was expected of her. She played her part and she played it well! Now she just had to wait for the riches that would be her reward once Peggy's will had been read.

On the day the will finally arrived, Kelly carefully read it over several times, each time the words turning to ash in her mouth. Her face was pale and gaunt as she read the will in shock and disbelief. The formalities of the document were standard and conventional. But, after reading a little further, the words were now beginning to turn into an instrument of torture, as inside the document where Kelly and Mitch's names were supposed to be printed as the sole beneficiaries, she could read only the name of another! *'Angelina Miller'* was the name printed in bold upon the line marked beneficiary. Mitch's little sister was now Peggy's main heir! The will told that Angelina was to inherit seventy-five percent of Peggy's estate, whilst further down the page it was claimed that Mitch would inherit the meagre twenty-five percent that remained. The shockingly unfair split was beyond Kelly's comprehension, but what really boiled her blood was what was highlighted under the 'exceptions' clause. Kelly's name had been expediently marked, barring her from ever claiming any part of Peggy's estate. Even in the case of Mitch's death and Kelly's own widowhood, she would not be permitted to inherit her husband's pathetic share, and the entire amount would go to Angelina. This news sent Kelly into a fit of rage that resulted in various smashed pots, and the will itself being torn into shreds, before her temper finally simmered down!

The amount of money they would now inherit would not be enough to soothe Kelly's ambitions or satisfy her visions of grandeur. The humble fund would pay for little more than a couple of holidays, and possibly pay off the finance owing upon her car. It would take time for her to accept the situation as it was. The unfairness of the will caused a deep pain within Kelly, and it was a wound that would take an eternity to heal. But, over time, the pain would fade away and the injury would eventually heal.

Bitterness would always remain, as would Kelly's eternal quest for more! The situation was wretched and unfair, and there was nothing that Kelly could do to change it. However, there were other ways to get what she wanted. Carnation Hall was full of elderly people. Elderly folk with riches they no longer needed, and with undeserving relatives living far away. Nobody would miss these people once they were gone, of that Kelly was sure. Nobody came to visit, nobody would call on the phone, and most were lucky if they received so much as a Christmas card from their so-called families. Kelly was the one who cared for the people under the Hall's roof. She was the one who spent time with them and tended to all of their needs, far more than their own families ever did. So, why should she not be the one to benefit from their demise? These people were old and they were destined to die! Who cared if Kelly gave one of them a gentle push off the mortal coil every once in a while. Their money was Kelly's, whether the residents knew it or not, she was the only one who deserved it! Kelly would take what was rightfully hers, no matter the cost to anybody else. Besides, getting away with murder was surprisingly easy, especially when you were an innocent looking middle aged woman thought to have a heart of gold!

CHAPTER 16

The Work Shed

Lydia had never been up close to the work shed before. She had only ever seen it at a distance until today. There had never been any need or interest to investigate this building. But, now that she was stood outside, it appeared very different. The building was larger than Lydia had expected, being constructed of stone with an old slate roof. A large wooden door stood at its centre, and Lydia could see a stream of light seeping through the cracks from within. Lydia pressed her ear against the wood, straining to listen for any sound, but she could hear nothing! There was a dead silence within, but that didn't necessarily mean that the old shack was unoccupied! Lydia had to make a choice, she could either take her chances and return to the main house until the snow storm passed, hoping that nobody would see her or question where she had been. Or, she could carry out the wishes of the spirit and enter the work shed, fully aware that the intentions of the ghost may have been to lead her into some sort of trap!

But, the numbness in her fingers quickly helped her with the decision, and she hastily turned the handle, pushing against the shed door with her shoulder. Surprisingly, the door slowly opened, groaning and creaking from the old hinges as it arced its way into the workspace. Luckily for Lydia, the previous inhabitant had left the building unlocked.

Inside, the space appeared exactly as Lydia had expected, filled from floor to ceiling with various tools and machinery, mostly covered with a healthy layer of dust. The light Lydia could see from outside was emanating from a single central light bulb, gently swaying in the breeze as it hung from the main wooden beam.

As quietly as she could, Lydia skulked around the room having no idea what she was supposed to be looking for, or even if she was truly alone!

The work shed contained Mitch's tractor, sitting spotlessly clean and proud in front of a pair of metal doors at the far end of the building, waiting to be released upon the fields when needed. Mitch's vast array of tools were carefully arranged on the walls and workbenches all around the work shed. Lydia could see several very large moulds strewn about the place, with bags of sand and cement stacked up against the wall. These must be the materials that Mitch uses to make his statues. An industrial looking cement mixer sat in the corner immediately to her right, whilst various chains on pulleys were hanging from the ceiling beams, probably used to help raise Mitch's creations. All in all, the place looked pretty cluttered, and to Lydia, very uninviting.

As she made her way towards the back of the work shed, taking a closer look at one of the workbenches, she discovered a wooden hatch down on the floor. She had accidentally caught her foot on the wooden edge of the hatch, and a dull thud echoed around the room in accompaniment. The sound surprised Lydia, her head turning around like a shot looking for any advancing and potential threat, but none arrived! She found herself staring intently down at the square wooden hatch. The dull light made it almost impossible to see it against the dark stone surface of the floor.

She knelt down to try and get a better view, as now she wasn't able to hold back her growing curiosity. With tension growing within, she felt her fingers run along the edges of the wooden board, searching for anything she could use to find a grip. She looped her fingers down the side of one of the edges, and gathered as much force as she could muster to shift the panel, her brittle old finger nails threatening to break from its weight. With a grunt of exertion, she managed to lift the panel and shimmy it back and away, revealing a wooden ladder below her, dropping down into the dark black hole of the unknown!

"Hello?" Lydia whispered into the pit, not expecting to hear any reply, but poised to run if she did.

No sound came to meet her! She slid forwards on her hands and knees, not caring about the thick dust marring her clothes. She had no choice now but to descend into the hole. It was impossible for her to walk away, and if she was going to find any evidence to use against Kelly, the odds were that it would be found within this mysterious pit below!

Lydia braced herself and blindly attempted to place her foot on the first rung of the ladder. She couldn't see anything, not even her own hands before her face. She took each step down the ladder incredibly slowly, relying on feel alone to find each step. She had a tight grip with both hands on the sides of the ladder to prevent a fall if her foot slipped!

Lydia knew when she had finally reached the ground, as the echo from each footfall on the wooden ladder suddenly turned into a clap of sole meeting stone.

She then reached out blindly into the darkness, her fingers managing to grasp a long cord, and with an experimental tug she was relieved to discover that she had found the light switch.

The lights came on, and for a moment she was blinded by their power, forcing her to cover her eyes until they could adjust. The room was being lit by several small fluorescent lights scattered around the area, filling the room with a blue clinical light and illuminating a rather long and prominent workbench.

What was this place that she now found herself in? Lydia questioned herself. The air was thick with the stench of dampness and soil, making the place feel like a large open grave. The long wooden workbench was currently bare, but it was the large shelf above it that drew Lydia's attention. Along its surface lay several small ornate pots of various shapes and sizes. Lydia stepped closer and noticed a small metal cabinet fixed to the wall at the far end of the shelf. It looked fortified and uninviting. Lydia couldn't resist the urge to pull open the door to find out what was within.

The inside was surprisingly bare, with just a few very small glass bottles sitting upon the middle shelf. There were no labels to express their contents, only a small hand-written note saying *'DO NOT TOUCH!'* placed upon one of the tiny bottles. This was all that Lydia needed to know that the contents were hazardous! A box full of disposable latex gloves sat at their side deterring Lydia even further. She knew that whatever was in those bottles was most likely going to be extremely dangerous, and she knew better than to touch anything!

Beneath this hatch, more mysteries were now starting to reveal themselves to Lydia. But, the most unnerving items were the actual vases themselves on the shelf. At first, Lydia didn't know what to make of them, and it took a few moments of closer inspection for her to even realise what they truly were. She carefully picked up one of the vases and turned it over in her hands, looking for any insight into its purpose. Initially, she assumed it was just another one of Mitch's creations. If the man enjoyed fabricating statues so much, then perhaps he also enjoyed fashioning pots and vases. As Lydia turned one pot over, she noticed a small inscription amidst the plain decor, and squinting in the dull light, she attempted to read the words imprinted upon its surface. The inscription read:

'Margaret Brigshaw'
'Rest In Peace'

It was an urn! She was so taken back by this discovery, that the pot immediately slipped from her grip and fell to the floor, smashing loudly into the ground! Now, with the urn lying broken on the floor, cracked and shattered into pieces at her feet, Lydia instantly raised her hands up against her face. She felt shame and remorse, as she had never intended to perform such a disrespectful act with somebody's remains. Looking around anxiously, she searched for anything she could use to collect the contents of the urn, and ensure they remained together. Looking down at the mess she had caused, Lydia came to an odd realisation. Upon the floor were only pieces of broken urn and nothing else! There weren't any ashes or dust spilt across the ground, just splinters of pottery and flecks of paint. The urn was completely empty!

Now, confused beyond belief, Lydia stepped over the broken pot, turning back towards the shelf. She grabbed hold of the nearest urn and gripped it tightly as she pulled the lid free. This pot was also completely empty, not even the corpse of a spider lay within it! Lydia repeated the action several more times, vigorously yanking the tops from the other urns revealing them also to be empty receptacles! It didn't take long before realisation began to bloom within Lydia's mind. It was all starting to make sense to her now! The building materials, the urns, the statues, the spirits! Lydia felt nauseated as she realised what was going on here. She now understood, she understood it all, and the realisation was vile!

Kelly wasn't just manipulating the wills from these people, she was specifically targeting the weak and the old. She was preying upon the most lonely and vulnerable residents at Carnation Hall, knowing full well that she could easily convince them to fashion a new will under her guidance. Once she had their signatures written down, then their usefulness to her would be at an end, and so would their lives! The majority of these individuals had no family or close relations, so their ashes would have been returned to Carnation Hall. Kelly had once told Lydia in passing that some of the past resident's ashes had been spread around the gardens, but it now seemed that she was not telling the whole truth! The victim's ashes were not being released over the fields, or anywhere else for that matter! Instead, it seemed that Mitch had himself been collecting the ashes from the crematorium, and it didn't take a genius to realise what his intentions for those ashes had been. All his building materials were there, sand, cement, and all the tools necessary to construct his beloved statues. Lydia could never look upon the statues with such innocence ever again. At first, she thought that the spirits had attached themselves to the statues because of their appreciation for the memorials, but now her mind had changed. Mitch had been incorporating the ashes of the victims in with the mix he used to form his statues, and that's why the spirits remained here! They weren't attracted to the statues, they were actually trapped within them! Their unearthly souls forever tied and chained to the statues, as their ashes lay entombed within the cold hard structures. The spirits had been left alone, fearful and angry for such a long time, unable to break free and move on. Their mortal endings had been extremely traumatic, leaving them with a strong will to obtain justice against those who had done them wrong. That is why Lydia herself had been singled out by these spirits! Being a powerful psychic, she had been drawn to their calling, and by giving them just a touch of her life force, they had finally been able to step free from their stony crypts! This had led her down a path of discovery, and perhaps their only chance of salvation. She now felt indebted to them, and knew it was her duty to put these benevolent spirits to rest, even if it was the last thing she would ever do!

Lydia had to call the police! She had found the evidence she needed, and now all she had to do was expose it to the world. Her own phone was not an option, and any attempt to find it would probably expose her. To add to this, she had no doubt in her mind that Kelly was capable of murder! Her close friend Kate had already paid the price for that discovery, and Lydia would never forgive herself for her own naivety.

The only plan Lydia could now form was to find her way back inside the Hall, and convince the other residents to aid her in calling the police. She was prepared to fake a heart attack if that would assist in calling for help! But for now, getting back inside the Hall was a challenge in itself, before trying to convince her neighbours to call the police.

Feeling a flood of adrenaline begin to course its way through her veins, Lydia turned to leave. She started to climb out of this subterranean hell pit, moving swiftly at what seemed to her to be record speed, feeling lighter than she had done in a long time.

Once she had climbed out and was free from the hatch, she headed straight for the main door to escape! The thought of doing the right thing, and putting an end to Kelly and Mitch's schemes, fuelled her with determination as she headed for the exit. This was the first time since Kate had died that Lydia had felt any hope. Hope that this nightmare could now be at an end, and hope that she would survive this place and all its hidden horrors.

Her special gift had helped liberate the spirits that had become trapped, and hopefully would help preserve the lives of the other people still living within the Hall. Lydia felt hope that everything would finally be put right once again.

But, these wishful thoughts abruptly came to an end, her hope wilting and dying in her chest as quickly as it had grown. Because, as she reached the door, she could see that her path was blocked! Directly ahead, standing in the doorway was the bulking and gloomy figure of Mitch himself! His eyes were set cold in the pale light, and the tightness of his jaw gave away his silent rage.

Lydia almost cried as she stepped back, her entire body overshadowed by the statuesque man looming over her. There was no way out now! She could run but she couldn't hide, and escaping seemed virtually impossible! Mitch physically outmatched her in every way, she would stand no chance trying to get past him! It was over, and she knew the thought to be true! The waves of anger emanating from Mitch confirmed her thoughts. He had the strength to snap her neck in one move, and drag her body outside to watch her expire in the cold. Whatever he was planning to do to her, one thing was certain, her quest had failed! The spirits, the residents, herself, everyone. She felt she had failed them all.

Mitch stepped forward towards her, his fists clenched in rage as he watched her with a piercing gaze.

"You're not supposed to be here!" Mitch bellowed, his voice shaking the work shed from within. And, with one swift motion, his huge hand lashed out and caught Lydia across the face, knocking her to the ground with immense force! Now, lying on her side, Lydia instinctively curled herself into a protective ball, her knees pressed up against her chest. She could taste the copper sting of blood in her mouth as her lip swelled and split from the blow. She was left rigid with fear as the man towering above her advanced once more! She was terrified! She stood no chance against him! With seemingly nothing left to give, she couldn't hold back her sobs that were escaping her chest. Tears began to flow from her eyes as she watched Mitch standing over her. His giant boots were just inches from her face, and she knew just one step would be all it required to end her! She let herself cry as she was overwhelmed with fear! The blood rush in her ears was drowning out the world as she closed her eyes, possibly for the last time! Her sobs echoing around the work shed as she wept uncontrollably!

Somewhere in the far distance, what seemed like church bells were ringing out into the night, signalling that the eleventh hour had come. Somehow, the sound found its way to Lydia's cowering form, and as the chimes fell, Lydia couldn't help but think that the sound was for her! *"For whom the bell tolls,"* she thought, tears still flowing freely as she now looked up at Mitch, waiting for him to make his next move.

***

"Come on! Come on! Pick up, goddammit!" Christian yelled into his phone as silence met his ear once more. He had spent the last half an hour openly breaking the law as he drove at high speed to the Hall. He was desperately trying to call his mother-in-law on his mobile phone, but the call was not being connected. The road ahead seemed endless, and he felt like he was trapped in some never ending loop. Thankfully, the snow storm had eased, and had almost completely stopped after ten minutes of hitting the road. It was proving difficult to drive in these conditions, the tyres feeling unresponsive and skittish due to their lack of grip on the road and the snow. The windscreen wipers were still going at full pelt as the snowflakes struck the windscreen, keeping in time with Christian's now pounding heart! But, regardless of this hindrance, Christian was undeterred as he had to be somewhere fast, and he would be damned if the weather was going to stop him!

Throughout the journey, Christian had repeatedly been trying to call Lydia, but her mobile phone was unresponsive and her landline was completely dead! No matter how many times he called, there was no answer. He concluded that something was very wrong with this situation!

Filled with concern and desperation, he reluctantly called his wife. He didn't wish to cause Susanna any concern or distress, but he felt he had no choice. She deserved to know what was happening, and perhaps she could keep trying to call her mother, then he could concentrate more on his driving.

"Hello?" Susanna asked, as soon as she picked up the phone. Her tone was tailored and formal, as she spoke to him with her so called 'telephone voice'. A habit she had picked up from years of working in a professional office with high-end clientele. Both Christian and Jessica would tease her over it on occasion, but it seemed that old habits die hard, and this one harder than most.

"Susie, love!" Christian called.

"Christian? What's going on? You never call me this late. Are you alright?" she spoke down the unstable line, making herself sound far and distant.

"I'm fine. But I need you to listen very carefully to me," Christian began to say.

"What's that noise? Are you driving? Are you coming home?" she requested to know.

"Yes, I'm driving, but I'm not on my way home. I'm driving to Carnation Hall to get to your mother! Listen, Susie. I've found something out, and Lydia was right! Something very bad is going on at that Hall!" he attempted to explain.

"Tell me what's going on!" Susanna demanded to know.

"Okay, but you have to promise to stay calm. I need you to stay calm! Do you understand?" Christian insisted.

"Just tell me!" she raised her voice, and Christian sighed before speaking again.

"It's those two people that run the Hall. I think Lydia was right. I've found some evidence that points to some of the residents' deaths not being purely accidental. I think Lydia might be in trouble, but don't worry, I'm on my way to get her and the police aren't far behind!" he explained as calmly as he could.

"Oh my god!" Susanna suddenly sobbed down the phone. Christian felt his heart ache at the sound. He couldn't bare the thought of his wife feeling any distress or anguish.

"It'll be okay love, I'm almost there. She'll be fine! Trust me! Okay?" Christian insisted, trying his best to sound reassuring and comforting, "but Susie, I need you to do something for me. I need your help. You need to call your mum and let her know that I'm on my way. I've been trying to call her, but there's no signal! You should have better luck with the landline. I'm going to hang up now so you can try to call your mum. Call Lydia, okay? Can you do this?"

"Yes. Yes, I'll call now!" Susanna whispered, and that was all Christian needed to hear before ending the call, reluctantly cutting her off! He hated leaving her that way, but he had no choice. The Hall wasn't far now. This would all be over soon enough. He just hoped the police were as fast at driving through the snow as he was.

***

The phone wouldn't stop ringing from within Kelly's office. The bell aggressively chirping, demanding the attention of anyone close enough to witness it.

Kelly unlocked the door to her office, and opened it with excessive force making it shudder violently on its hinges. The noise of the wretched phone had disturbed her from her otherwise peaceful evening. She had been sat down enjoying the peace and quiet since Mitch had suddenly wandered off. He was probably hiding from her to avoid being handed more chores to do. She half expected to find him concealed away beneath the stairs, in order to watch the rest of the football match in peace. If that was the case, Kelly didn't mind, at least he would be out of her hair for a while instead of sulking in the corner like a naughty puppy.

The phone continued to call out from upon the desk as Kelly stood before it. A brief glance towards her watch informed her that this was an extremely unsociable hour for anyone to be calling. This caused Kelly to hesitate for a moment before picking up the phone. It was late at night, and certainly well beyond business hours, telling her that whoever it was on the other end of the line, they weren't just making a social call. It had to be serious for someone to be calling at a time like this. Her first instinct was that it may be the police, calling to question her further about Kate's accident. But, if that were the case, surely they would have left calling until the morning, or simply just arrived unannounced. Curiosity was quickly getting the better of her, and Kelly couldn't resist the urge to find out who was calling. With one frantic move, she lunged towards the desk and raised the receiver to her ear.

"Hello, Carnation Hall. Kelly Miller the manager speaking, how may I help you?" she spoke confidently into the phone, urging herself to sound as professional as possible, despite her distrust of the situation.

"Oh Kelly, I'm so glad you picked up," a woman's voice, one that she vaguely recalled, responded.

"Can I ask who's calling please?" Kelly questioned, as cheerfully as she could muster.

"It's Susanna. Susanna Pearson. I'm Lydia Jones's daughter," the voice replied.

"Oh hello, Susanna. How lovely to hear from you again!" Kelly exclaimed pleasantly, "is there something I can help you with?" she added after a moment's pause.

"Yes, actually there is," Susanna spoke with surprising speed, "I've been trying to call my mother all evening, but I can't get through. Her landline doesn't seem to be working, and her mobile phone is going straight to the answerphone. Would you happen to know anything about this?" the woman questioned abruptly.

"Me?" Kelly gasped, faking polite offence, "I'm sorry, but I have no idea. Perhaps she has simply mislaid it. People around here are always losing track of their keys and phones. However, the landline is an issue. I will have my husband look into it tomorrow. He will find the fault and fix it," Kelly returned, trying to sound as reassuring as possible.

"Hmm . . . I suppose you could be right, but that doesn't sound like my mother at all. She's always been very careful with her mobile phone," Susanna said, and Kelly picked up a hint of suspicion in her voice, "would you mind going and getting her for me? I haven't been able to reach her all day, and I'd really like to speak to her," Susanna requested.

Kelly glared into the phone at the words, wondering who this woman thought she was ordering her around. She was the manager of a successful business, not a maid doing house calls!

"It's rather late. Wouldn't you be best leaving it until the morning? Your mother is more than likely sleeping now," Kelly replied through gritted teeth.

"I doubt it! My mother has always been more of a night owl. But even if she is in bed, she wouldn't mind you waking her up for me," the woman on the phone insisted, Kelly's face becoming more unpleasant with every word. "Please!" Susanna added after a moment's thought.

It now occurred to Kelly that this woman was not going to let this drop, and the simplest solution would be for her to give in, and go and grab the old bag out of bed. Then, maybe she could get back to the peaceful evening she had planned.

"Just a moment and I'll go up and see how she is," Kelly informed, realising she now sounded just as put out as she felt, "I'll fetch dear old Lydia and get her to call you back as soon as possible," she couldn't even be bothered to hide her discontent now.

"Thank you!" was all Kelly heard from the other woman, before she had a chance to put down the phone.

Minutes later, Kelly was standing in the hallway outside Lydia's apartment door. Her face was turning red with the outrage she now felt, her hot breath huffing out into the air. It was barely contained rage that possessed her, as she arrived at the woman's apartment to discover the door ajar, and the apartment itself being vacant of life. Even with every room unoccupied, Kelly was now left gasping with what she was witnessing within. She could see the wooden board lying widespread across the coffee table, its surface painted elegantly with faded gold lettering and numbers. Kelly recognised the board from several films she had seen, but she had never actually witnessed one in reality. It was a spirit board! The fact that the room was also surrounded by still burning candles, confirmed to Kelly that this was no doubt the scene of a séance. Fury was now beginning to boil within Kelly. Lydia had lied to her, and she obviously knew far more than she had been letting on. Why else would the old woman be attempting to call out to the deceased so late at night! What made the realisation even worse, was that if Lydia wasn't there, then she had to be snooping somewhere else within the confines of the grounds.

There was only one thing for it! Kelly didn't relish the thought of having to act again so soon after the last one, but she knew what she had to do! She couldn't risk this old lady escaping to the outside world with the knowledge that she now possessed! Kelly was left with no choice! No choice at all but to handle the situation in the only way she knew how. She would have to stage another accident! This time it was to be for Lydia Jones! A tragic situation, as Kelly had actually grown to like the plucky old woman. But, there were simply no cards now left on the table. No method of making this situation quieten down without drastic action! The decision was made, Lydia Jones must die! And, as soon as Kelly could locate her, then her fate would finally be sealed!

***

"Why are you here?" Mitch bellowed, stooping down over Lydia from above. She was shaking with fear and shivering from the cold, lying on the dusty floor of the old work shed. Lydia ached deeply as she shuffled her body backwards, moving away from the bulking man before her. She kept moving until her back hit the stone wall. Tears were still falling and stinging her face where his large hand had struck her just moments before. Knowing she had nowhere left to go, Lydia hunched to make herself as small a target as possible. She cowered beside one of the old workbenches, desperately wishing she could disappear through the ground below her.

Mitch just watched her movements, his face a mix of emotions ranging from outrage to disappointment. He looked conflicted and angry all in a single glance. He seemed both pained and intent on inflicting pain, without his expression changing an inch.

"Why did you have to be here?" Mitch shouted out again, leaning over Lydia even further, meeting her eye to eye! "Do you have any idea what you've done?" he yelled at her angrily, yet his face displayed pity.

"I'm sorry!" Lydia whispered, fresh tears welling in her eyes, "please? I didn't mean to!"

"That doesn't matter now. It's too late!" Mitch spat at her, "you should have just stayed out of our business!" he declared, before swiftly lunging at her and grabbing her roughly by the arm, raising her to her feet. Without thinking, and fuelled by pure instinct, Lydia kicked out at the man holding her. This blind attack caused her knee to rise up and knock hard against Mitch's body. A gasp of pain escaped the large man, and his grip on her arm went slack. Mitch momentarily lost his hold on Lydia! That was all the chance Lydia needed before making her escape and racing towards the work shed door. In one swift move she yanked the door open on its rusty pivot, and was met with a rush of cold night air, splashing against her already chilled skin. Yet, before she could continue her escape, she found the doorway was already occupied! Kelly was standing before her, blocking the only exit and halting her way out!

The younger woman was a terrifying sight to behold! Her hair was a mess, pointing in all directions thanks to the strong bellows of wind outside, her face and skin glowing red from the irritation of the cold. She was neither dressed or prepared for the icy weather, wearing only a thin cardigan covering her shoulders, and a pair of dark blue jeans as protection from the chill. Her eyes should have been the most disturbing part of her facade, wide and wild as they glared at Lydia with discontent. But no, the thing that was really chilling Lydia to the core was held within Kelly's hand. She held a knife, a large kitchen knife. It was hanging loosely at her side, her fingers slack and uncaring as its blade glistened in the dim light.

"And just where do you think you're going?" Kelly demanded to know. A broad smile graced Kelly's face, but her tone was venomous like a serpent. Lydia stepped back as Kelly advanced. She was fully aware that Mitch was looming somewhere behind her, as she was now left sandwiched between these two menacing individuals.

A long and drawn out screeching noise drew Lydia's attention from behind! She turned around, just in time to glance at Mitch dragging a large claw hammer across the workbench towards her. Its heavy metal head scraping across the wooden surface was the source of the ear-piercing sound now filling her ears.

"You know we can't let you leave!" Kelly stated, sounding sorrowful as she looked at Lydia with pity in her eyes, "you should have just left this alone. You could have stayed out of this and everything would have been fine. But now . . ." Kelly paused to sigh heavily, "you've brought this on yourself," she announced, her gaze now cold and emotionless, as she suddenly reached out to grab Lydia with her free hand. Before Lydia could process what was happening, the knife in Kelly's other hand was being thrust towards Lydia's upper body. It was with instinct that Lydia raised her left arm to protect herself from the slashing blow. The blade cut into her forearm, and crimson liquid began to leak from the fleshy wound. It was a second or so before the stinging pain became apparent, growing sharply in its intensity! Lydia was unable to hold back a cry as the cold metal met her frail skin. Yet, shielding the blow had effectively prevented the knife from making direct contact with her neck, and in doing so had saved her life from its deadly touch.

Now in pain and starting to panic, Lydia threw herself to the side, lunging for the nearest workbench. She was intent on arming herself with anything she could find within reach. Blindly, she grabbed an object, a large screwdriver. She raised it out before her, her back leaning against the bench. Her eyes were darting wildly at the two people stood rigid in front of her. She was now ready to attack!

"You're just making this harder on yourself," Kelly soothed, inching her way closer to the distraught woman, "this doesn't have to hurt! Just close your eyes and we'll make it quick! It'll all be over soon, I promise!" Kelly said, in the most reassuring and gentle voice Lydia had ever heard. She could almost cry at the sincerity in the sound of it. As if Kelly truly wished to help her and bring her nothing but peace. But, the sight before her eyes betrayed this message. These two figures with deadly weapons were stalking her, as though she was prey trapped between two wolves. The knife in Kelly's hand was still held up, sluggishly dripping Lydia's lifeblood onto the ground below. Lydia could not be fooled! Not any more! If she was going to die tonight, then she was going to die fighting! She would not let these two parasites end the battle, and bury her memory in an eternal stony tomb!

"You won't get away with this!" Lydia declared bitterly, staring at her adversaries with contempt.

"Don't be a fool Lydia!" Kelly huffed at her, a tinge of amusement lining her voice. "Mitch, grab her!" Kelly ordered, with an insisting wave of her knife.

"Yes, my love," the unthinking oaf of a man said, before lunging forwards to carry out his orders. To the best of her ability, Lydia slid sideways along the bench, dodging Mitch's outstretched grasp. She lashed out at his arm with the screwdriver, but only met open air with each lance, while her other free hand felt its way long the bench, reaching for anything that could aid her. Finally, her hand met something solid and ceramic. She grasped it firmly by the rim, and without hesitation hurled it towards the intimidating and advancing man. An echoing crash followed, as the ceramic plant pot made direct contact with Mitch's forehead, sounding out a sickening crack as the mighty goliath fell to the ground. Mitch was sent billowing backwards in a dead faint, crashing down against the dusty floor where he now lay, unmoving upon its surface.

For a moment, Lydia couldn't move. She was paralysed by the realisation of what she had just done, and the damage she had caused. Lydia had never hurt anybody before in her life, and now, a man was lying prone and unresponsive at her feet. She felt sickened by her actions, yet quietly relieved by the result.

This moment of hesitation was all that Kelly needed to lash out. She grabbed the older woman firmly by the wrist, taking advantage of the slip in concentration, and seemingly unconcerned about her husband. In one swift move, Kelly spun Lydia around, thrusting her face down against the workbench, whilst twisting Lydia's left arm painfully up behind her back. Lydia's right hand holding the screwdriver was now pressing firmly against the surface of the workbench, forcefully trying to push herself up and to freedom. Kelly swiftly halted this action by striking through the woman's hand with her knife! Lydia let out a gut-wrenching scream as she watched the palm of her hand become impaled on the wooden bench by the metal blade, releasing the screwdriver from her grasp! She was now pinned down, with a slow trickle of blood welling to the surface of her hand! At first, Lydia didn't feel any pain from the wound, just a nauseating feeling in her stomach at the grotesque sight of her hand! It was only when she attempted to move, trying to raise her trapped appendage, that the pain and agony finally hit her. Like a red-hot poker, the pain burnt through her skin and ascended up her arm in waves. So excruciating was the pain, that the edges of her vision faded to black, as her mind threatened to abandon her body altogether. But, the adrenaline in her blood refused to let her surrender, and a moment later her vision returned. Broken sobs slipped from Lydia's throat as she lay there, pinned against the workbench, trapped and seemingly helpless!

"You shouldn't have made me do that!" Kelly stated, her voice low and dangerous, whilst she stood back and watched the older woman struggle and writhe. "This could have all been so simple, but now . . ." she hesitated, looking firstly at Lydia's impaled hand, then at her husband lying motionless on the ground, "now you've made this complicated!" Kelly informed, looking far more irritated than annoyed. With that she stepped away, the heels of her boots informing Lydia that the distance between them was now increasing. The sound of metal scraping and objects being thrown about followed, filling Lydia with the dread of the unknown! She was listening to the sounds of Kelly rifling through the work shed in her apparent search for something. Lydia couldn't even guess what the other woman was looking for, her mind was too flooded with terror and pain to calculate Kelly's sinister intentions.

With all of the excitement going on within the work shed, none of the occupants had noticed that the temperature had begun to rapidly drop. Even through their struggle with Lydia, neither Kelly or Mitch were taking note that their breathing was beginning to cloud, causing goosebumps to bubble up on their skin beneath their clothes. Nobody even noticed the thin layer of frost spreading across the small window, or the tiny flecks of ice crawling their way around the door frame. The lock on the door had now become set in ice, sealing it shut and trapping all the occupants inside. The Millers were not aware of their entrapment, as they were too preoccupied with ensuring the containment of their sinister secrets. They were also not aware that their surroundings were slowly being invaded by a supernatural presence. Not even Lydia was aware of the static tension now slowly beginning to fill the air, causing it to crackle and pulse around her with ethereal power.

Not one of the three residents in the work shed realised that they were no longer alone, as invisible spirits began to enter and invade their earthly plane.

The only light within the work shed, the single light bulb hanging from the ceiling, began swaying ever so slightly above them. Its gentle movement went unnoticed in the innocuous breeze. Below the light, Kelly was huffing in annoyance as she continued her search through the work shed. She eventually found what she was looking for, a lone red jerry can. It was sitting all the way at the back of the work shed next to Mitch's dormant chainsaw. The blonde woman grabbed it with a smirk of achievement, its heavy weight letting her know that it was almost full. There was a shimmer of glee in her eye as her latest plan was now starting to take form!

Over to her side, a grunt suddenly drew Kelly's attention, and she glanced over towards its origin. It was Mitch now coming round, lolling his head in her direction. The oaf frowned at her, seemingly confused as he raised a hand to his now throbbing temple.

"Get up!" she spoke sternly to him, "I have a job for you!" she ordered.

Mitch was a little unsteady, so Kelly offered him her hand to help pull him to his feet. Still dazed, it took Mitch a moment to interpret her words before accepting her outstretched hand, he then clambered upright to his feet.

"What the hell happened?" Mitch questioned, one hand still resting against his head as he looked around his work shed, the confusion on his face clear as he caught sight of Lydia's sobbing form.

"She attacked you, so I got even!" Kelly stated, "you're bleeding!" she added, noticing the small gash on his forehead, and the line of blood leaking its way down his face. She threw him a handkerchief that she had in her pocket. "Clean yourself up!" Kelly told him, wrinkling her nose in disgust at the sight of him mopping his own wound.

"What are we gonna do now?" Mitch asked, still watching Lydia, hearing her struggled gasps.

"Only one thing we can do," Kelly informed, as she once again lifted the jerry can.

A few moments later, the smell of petrol began filling the room, making their eyes water in the enclosed space.

"We're going to burn her?" Mitch questioned reluctantly, "but all my stuff is in here!" he said sounding confused.

"No other choice. We have to hide the evidence!" Kelly replied coldly.

"But my tractor!" Mitch stated sadly.

"I'll buy you a new one . . . now shut up and help me!" she hissed at him showing no compassion, just thrusting the can into his arms.

It was then, just as Mitch began to pour petrol around the perimeter of his work shed, and as Kelly was vigorously searching for a box of matches, that a force began to build up in the work shed. The light bulb was starting to swing more wildly on its chain, causing the light in the room to dance, and the shadows to move around rapidly from the movement. The sudden change was impossible to ignore, and Mitch halted in his tracks to look up at the aimlessly swinging bulb.

"What the hell is that?" Mitch asked, though the words didn't seem to be aimed at anybody in particular.

That's when Lydia's senses awoke, and she suddenly felt a rush of supernatural energy surround her. It felt dark and threatening like an uncontrollable rage being carried on the wind. Fresh fear began to eat away at Lydia, as the spirits now occupying the space around her grew closer and stronger. Finding a wave of renewed strength, Lydia placed her free hand upon the hilt of the knife, and with one agonising cry, she pulled the blade free from her flesh. She fell to the ground in a mixture of agony and exhaustion. Her legs gave way below her due to the strain, and her damaged right hand fell uselessly to her side. Blood was now beginning to flow freely from her injured hand, causing her to feel light-headed and faint from the sudden blood loss.

The commotion had been enough to attract Kelly and Mitch's attention. But, before either of them could advance upon Lydia, and once more restrain her, the room was suddenly plunged into complete darkness. The light above them let out an electrical whine, and then completely failed as the power faded out!

Dazed and confused, Lydia took advantage of the temporary distraction. She used the sudden darkness as a shield and drove herself unknowingly towards the far corner of the room. Completely blind, she crawled on her hands and knees across the floor, using her blooded hand to feel its way across the ground. She was completely unaware that she was leaving crimson stains of blood in her wake.

"What happened?" Mitch shouted out in the darkness, causing Lydia to halt all movement and pause. She became petrified upon hearing his voice, realising he was far closer to her than she had expected him to be. For a moment she was terrified to move, too terrified to even breathe and risk giving away her position. She was fully aware that she was practically kneeling at his feet!

"The power must be down!" Kelly groaned, "find a light! I want this ended!"

"On it! I think there's a torch on the shelf near the hatch," Mitch replied, and Lydia finally let herself breathe as he stepped back, moving away in search of a light source.

"Well . . . grab it!" Kelly spat impatiently. Lydia could just imagine her standing in the dark with her arms folded angrily across her chest, waiting for her orders to be carried out.

"I'm doing my best, but I can't see!" Mitch hissed back at her in annoyance. His voice sounded sufficiently far enough away now, and Lydia very carefully continued her journey across the dusty stone floor.

Reaching out with her good hand, Lydia continued to feel her way along the ground, being very careful not to knock into anything as she went. Her fingers then came into contact with a large object that felt cold and firm. Whilst feeling along its surface, she felt what appeared to be dirt and mud, and then hard rubber. She had discovered Mitch's tractor at the far end of the work shed. This wasn't where she was hoping to be! The darkness had disorientated her greatly, as her intention had been to reach the main door, but she would not let that discourage her. As quietly as she could, Lydia rolled onto her back, and proceeded to use her good hand to shimmy and pull herself under the motorised monster. Once beneath, she curled herself up on her side, attempting to become as small a target as possible. She raised her undamaged hand to her face, covering her mouth and nose in an attempt to buffer out the sound of her own heavy breathing.

Lydia had only settled into her hiding spot for a few moments, before the light bulb above suddenly powered up, flooding the room with light once more. Although the light in the room was rather dim, it now felt painfully bright against Lydia's eyes due to the momentary darkness she has just endured.

"About time!" Kelly stated, speaking to no one in particular, "we'd have been here all night waiting on you and that torch!" she rolled her eyes.

"Where did she go?" Mitch demanded to know, no longer seeing Lydia's prone form before him.

"Find her! She can't have gone far!" Kelly demanded, stalking across the room, and whipping up her knife from where she'd left it abandoned on top of the workbench.

Lydia's heart began to race as she listened to the pair hunting for her. She could hear her own pulse pounding in her ears with each beat, the pressure enticing a headache to strike her down. Lydia closed her eyes, just for a moment as she attempted to calm her breathing. But, as she forced herself to open them again looking out for Kelly and Mitch, she could hardly contain the gasp of fright that escaped her body. Luckily for her, she had been muting her voice with her hand, otherwise she would have surely been discovered by the sound. What had shocked her was the appearance of more limbs standing within the work shed, surrounding those of Kelly and Mitch! It looked as though four more figures had entered the building, all of them appearing to be made up of some sort of static energy, definitely not human! They were jittering uncontrollably where they stood, silently watching Kelly and Mitch's movements as they were probing around the room. The Millers were clearly unable to see, or hear these lifeless visitors that were now sharing their space, but Lydia could see them! She could perceive the feeling of anger within them, raining off them whilst they just stood there motionless. They were watching and waiting!

***

Kelly felt beyond irritated, as she watched Mitch scurry down the ladders of the hatch, checking to ensure the old woman hadn't sneaked down there to hide. Each of the wooden steps creaked loudly under her husband's weight as he descended.

Shaking her head in dismay, Kelly continued to scan the room above ground. She purposely made each of her footfalls as light as possible, as she continued to skulk around the back of the work shed. She herself was on guard in case Mrs Jones made the mistake of trying to strike out against her from the shadows. The smell of petrol that had spilt onto the floor was now quite overwhelming in the confined space, and it was making

Kelly's nose wrinkle in disgust at the unpleasant odour. Her eyes were now scanning the dark gloomy corners of the work shed, and she was contemplating joining Mitch in the pit when something caught her eye. The surface of the workbench where Lydia had been pinned to was still pooled with blood. The blood was running like a steam to the edge of the bench, then sluggishly dripping down to collect on the floor below. It resembled a gruesome type of waterfall, but, what really grabbed her attention, was the stone floor itself and the bloody handprints smudged and smeared across its surface. She knew these markings would lead her directly to Lydia!

Cautiously, Kelly inspected the floor at her feet, carefully following the faint trail as it led across the work shed. Ahead, she spotted a fully formed handprint of bright red blood thrust upon the side of Mitch's tractor, surely giving away the old woman's position. Kelly quietly laughed to herself at the other woman's naivety. Did she really believe that hiding would save her? Yet, Kelly had to respect her tenacity, and it almost seemed a little sad to watch her go this way. But, now wasn't the time for any sentimentality.

Quickening her step, Kelly marched across to the side of the tractor, and in one swift grasp she reached underneath. Her hand could feel soft warm flesh, so she grabbed it firmly and started to tug at it. She had a firm hold of Lydia, and was now attempting to yank the now screaming and struggling woman free from her hiding hole.

"Mitch, get your arse up here! I've got her!" Kelly yelled, wrestling Lydia to the best of her ability, whilst the old woman bucked and twisted in her grasp.

***

Lydia panicked the moment she felt Kelly's cold skin on her arm. She had attempted to push herself away and slip out from the other side of the tractor, but Kelly's grip had been too strong, and Lydia had become too exhausted from the continued blood loss. But, that didn't mean she wouldn't try and struggle. As Kelly was pulling her free, Lydia kicked out, screaming and shouting whilst the other woman attempted to manhandle her into a tighter hold. Her attention was waning, but Lydia felt sure she had managed to leave some bruises on Kelly from her blind kicking and punching. It was all to no avail, as Lydia's energy had now been sapped from within her. She could resist no longer, and Kelly swiftly dragged Lydia onto her feet. Before Lydia could resist, Kelly was pressed up against Lydia's back with an aggressive hand threaded through her hair. She yanked her head back, exposing Lydia's neck to the warning blade of a large knife! She could feel the cold metal biting into her skin, just deep enough for a sliver of fresh blood to spill and run down the blade. Lydia didn't dare move, she was beyond terrified as she watched Mitch's bulking figure emerge from the room below. His rounded face childish with excitement as he lifted down a large pair of garden shears from a hook on the wall. He proceeded to storm towards

Lydia wielding the weapon, each of his heavy steps echoing dully as he marched forwards.

Lydia felt the urge to cry due to the helplessness of her situation. Her body was trembling with fear as she watched Mitch steadily approach her. Behind him, in the far corner of the work shed, she glimpsed a spirit standing motionless, appearing to be just watching the horrific event about to unfold! It seemed that it was there to witness Lydia's imminent departure from mortality! As she stared at the spectre through her tear-filled eyes, she could see its image flickering in the half-light. She could see that there was something eerily familiar about this being, the way her hair was hanging, and the constant pattern of ethereal water running from her body. It was Elizabeth! She was standing and staring intently at Lydia, her face impassive as she watched the horror unfold. Her white eyes were beaming into Lydia with a look of possible disappointment, or perhaps just a hint of pity. Their eyes met for a mere moment, before Elizabeth finally moved. The spirit slowly raised her arm, her fingers still forever dripping water as she pointed straight through Lydia! Her eyes appearing to burn, as the ghost now stared at Kelly with a look of hatred! As Lydia looked on, she could see Elizabeth's lips begin to move, carrying on a silent mantra that nobody would ever be able to hear or understand. She was emitting a look of both desperation and anger, making a connection deep within Lydia as her adrenaline started pumping once more.

With one last desperate attempt to escape her fate, Lydia suddenly decided to throw back her head using as much force and power as her humble body could muster. The back of her skull made instant contact with Kelly's face, and the woman screeched down Lydia's ear at the pain. Lydia was instantly released by both of Kelly's hands, as she used them to try and protect her own pulverised nose. In a state of shock, Kelly fell to her knees behind Lydia with her hands covering her face!

Hearing his wife scream in agony, and laying his eyes on her bloodstained face, Mitch was now filled with rage! Grasping the open shears firmly in both hands, he set upon Lydia, charging towards her like a knight carrying his lance and ready to joust. But, as he advanced, the room went black, the power being cut once more! However, the darkness did nothing to dilute the aggression within Mitch, as the goliath continued to gallop forwards. His weapon was held firmly in his grip, ready to strike down the woman who had dared to harm his beloved wife!

Lydia was oblivious to what happened next as she was standing there in the dark, panting heavily and silently waiting for the inevitable excruciating blow that was to befall her! Disorientated and unable to move in the pitch black room, she suddenly felt a strong force against her shoulder. The sensation of an ice-cold burn sped down her arm, as she felt herself being pushed sideways to the ground! She fell with a thump, landing heavily against the hard stone surface.

A second later, a frightful yell could be heard as the light flickered back to life, Lydia daring to raise her head and gaze up from the dust below. What met her eyes next would haunt her for an eternity. Stood exactly where Lydia herself had been just moments before, was Kelly, her posture rigid and her body shaking violently! Directly behind the blonde woman stood the wraith-like figure of a different spirit. It was the familiar form which Lydia could only refer to as 'MOTHER'! The spectre's scrawny thin hands were wrapped firmly around the back of Kelly's neck, after forcefully raising her to her feet, bracing her like a puppet in its tight and paralysing grasp. The spirit's head then turned to face Lydia, its limp neck hanging loose as it grinned at her triumphantly! It continued to stare at Lydia, as though it was demanding her to share in its sickening delight.

An agonising cry fell from Mitch's lips, and Lydia's attention was then immediately drawn towards him. There was such anguish in his voice, that Lydia just couldn't ignore it.

"No!" the man cried out, "no, no, no!" he repeated, completely distraught at the sight before him. That's when it hit Lydia! Her eyes finally allowed her to see what was truly standing right before her. She could see Kelly's terrified face, her eyes wide open, staring directly ahead towards her husband. Her body was shivering as she let out a painful rasping sound with each rise and fall of her chest. Two sharp and pointed pieces of metal were protruding out from behind her torso Her hands were clutched around her abdomen, holding onto the handles of the sheers with just a feeble grip, as if attempting to pull them loose, but to no avail!

The realisation of what had just actually happened started to set in upon Lydia. A quick glance behind her shoulder revealed Elizabeth's spirit watching from her side, jerking viciously into existence. This confirmed Lydia's theory. Mitch had been aiming for her, intending to strike her down in the dark with his weapon, but the vengeful spirits had other ideas. The cold force that had pushed Lydia from her footing was Elizabeth. This spirit had safely removed Lydia from harms way. The other spirit holding Kelly from behind was 'MOTHER'! This spirit had summoned its power to forcefully drag Kelly to her feet, and into the path of the deadly blow! Mitch had been helpless to prevent the fatal strike upon his wife, his razor-sharp shears gliding their way through her stomach and bursting out from her back. With one mighty blow, Kelly was left standing there, dying and paralysed in the spirit's supernatural hold!

Lydia could only watch as Kelly opened her mouth, oozing out gurgling and gagging noises, leaving her throat devoid of the ability to form words. An ever growing pool of blood was forming at Kelly's feet, running down her back and stomach, then rhythmically dripping onto the floor. It was spreading rapidly as it ran along the channels in the stone, creating a gory mosaic-like artwork below her. The harrowing sound of a wet spluttering cough soon followed, blood splattering forth from Kelly's mouth. It began to trickle down her chin, her cheeks already speckled by the crimson substance.

Kelly's eyes continued to follow her husband as a lone tear fell forwards. The look of agony and betrayal on her face was now meeting one of anguish.

"Why?" Kelly eventually whispered. The words fell from her lips as heavily as her body was now falling, as the spirit finally released her from its hold. She slumped to her knees, one hand desperately reaching out for Mitch, whilst the other continued to grasp the handle of the shears!

"I'm so sorry!" Mitch howled, himself now dropping down to his knees alongside his dying wife, "I didn't mean to do it . . . I'm sorry!" he whimpered!

To their side, Lydia was still frozen in place and unable to move, as she watched the ghastly scene unfold before her. Kelly's skin now looked deathly pale and Lydia knew she couldn't be long for this world. The blood loss was too great and her wounds too severe to stand any chance of survival. Mitch was now weeping openly, watching his wife expire as her breathing became more and more shallow. The shivering in her body was now beginning to subside. Seconds later, and this time without any glamour, Kelly collapsed to the side, landing with her arm splayed out on the floor and blood running from her mouth. Her chest had ceased to rise, and Lydia knew in an instant that she had finally perished! She could feel a shift in the atmosphere as it happened, the crackling force of energy surrounding them steadily fading out into nothingness! At that moment, Lydia almost cried with relief, feeling no sympathy for the woman who had tormented so many, bringing misery and death to countless old and vulnerable individuals. Lydia had never believed in heaven or hell, but at that moment, as she watched Kelly Miller take her final breath, she wished that she did. She wished she could force herself to believe, and comfort herself in the fact that this woman, this vain manipulative liar, would be spending the rest of eternity burning in hell for her sins!

"You did this!" were the words that dragged Lydia back to reality. She looked up to find Mitch glaring at her with abhorrence from where he knelt by Kelly's side. "You did this!" he repeated, but this time much louder, the edges of his front teeth showing as he growled out his words.

"I'm sorry!" Lydia told him, genuinely feeling some pity for the man.

"It's your fault . . . she's dead because of you! You did this!" he bellowed, the anger rising quickly in his voice, "you killed her . . . not me . . . it's all your fault!" Mitch stood up, his eyes burning down on Lydia with detest. "I'll make you pay for what you've done to her!" he slowly whispered, before lunging forwards with both hands outstretched. Before she could move, Mitch was on top of Lydia, his hands latched around her neck, his fingers wrapped tightly like a nest of snakes slowly crushing the life from her.

The light above them now began to flicker, at first slowly and then building in pace. The pair were coupled, thrashing around on the cold ground. Lydia's fisted hands were hammering frantically against Mitch's arms as she tried desperately to loosen his grip. Her lungs were burning from the lack of oxygen, and she could feel the blood welling up under her skin where her aggressor's fingers were pressing upon her with enormous force. She could feel bruises starting to form as she gasped for breath and began choking! The sight of Mitch's enraged face was now beginning to fade as her vision became hazy. The trauma that Mitch was now inflicting upon Lydia's throat was crushing her windpipe, and a loud ringing noise started to fill her ears. She was almost totally consumed by the darkness of unconsciousness. Then, suddenly, Mitch's clutch loosened, and looking up through her tear-blurred lashes, Lydia could see his face transform from rage to confusion! His eyes were staring open wide, his mouth uttering out words she could no longer hear or understand over the static in her head. Raising her gaze, Lydia could see the cause of his torment, as not one, but three spirits were now surrounding him! They were flickering in and out of visible existence, perfectly in time with the strobing light high above. Lydia had never perceived any of these spectres before, but she surmised that they must all be past residents from the Hall. Their lifeless eyes were cast upon Mitch as they watched him nervously glancing around the room. He could sense impending danger, but his eyes were unable to glimpse the threat that was lurking patiently behind his back!

Lydia could only look on as the first spirit reached out and grasped Mitch by the upper arm. The spirit was an elderly gentleman dressed in a suit and tie, his sunken eyes heavily rimmed and glazed over with the fog of age. Mitch let out a grunt of pain as a handprint began to appear on his arm, the skin becoming blistered and bruised before his unseeing eyes.

Not a moment had passed before the other male ghost sprang into action. This spirit was large in stature, grotesquely bloated around the gut, with rotten and swollen skin. It looked as if his body had swollen into one large infected boil. With little effort it lashed out at Mitch, and with a swing of the arm knocked him cleanly away from Lydia's prone form. The spectre met her eyes as she caught the air back into her lungs, feeling them swell with joy as they fed her beating heart once more.

"Thank you!" Lydia wheezed, her voice broken beyond all recollection. The ghost then turned away from her and advanced upon Mitch once more. He was now huddled and quivering in the corner of the work shed, nestled in as tightly as his goliath form was able. Only the spirit of the woman took the time to look back at Lydia, her eyes looking sad as it nodded to her in silent gratitude.

The light still continued to dance in and out of reality, as the spirits marched towards the cowering man. With each flash of the light, it seemed as though even more spirits were appearing, each filled with the desire to pour harm upon their previous tormentor. Lydia could now barely see, as the flickering of the light and the jerking of the ghosts was becoming too painful for her eyes. They were now stinging and watering as they attempted to focus in the darkness of the room. She pushed herself up onto her forearms using her exhausted limbs, scurrying as quickly as she could along the floor in the half-light. She was desperate to put as much distance as possible between herself and the angry army of spirits before her. Soon her back made contact with the wall, and she slumped against it wearily. Her body agonised with every breath after the torture she had endured, her head pounding from the buzzing in her ears. She was now feeling faint from her blood loss! Completely debilitated from the nights events, there was nothing Lydia could now do but to close her eyes, raise her bloodied hands to cover her ears, and wait desperately for it all to end as the horror continued around her.

Mitch's screams continued to ring out into the night, each one more harrowing than the last. The ghosts were patiently taking their time to inflict insidious and fatal torment upon the man, in ways Lydia was unwilling to see, as the tension in the room continued to rise.

A few moments later, the tension in the work shed finally reached its climax. Lydia could only cower against the wall, as she heard the sound of a heavy metal object strike something soft and flesh-like. A dull thud echoed out, accompanied by a sickening squelching sound. This was followed by the sound of dripping, as though large raindrops were landing upon the stone floor!

Suddenly, the lone lightbulb overhead lost its fight against the surge of ethereal power within the room, causing heat to rapidly build up within. The fixture began melting inside, triggering a short circuit in the connecting wires. A small fire started to break out and spread across the dry and dessicated wooden beam. It was swiftly spreading, galloping unimpeded across the timbers, stretching out to engulf the rest of the work shed. As the flames grew, sparks began spitting out, circulating around the room within the turbulent ghostly wind. Some of the sparks encroached upon the petrol-covered floor, igniting the vapour and filling the space with flames.

Lydia had been too afraid to move, terrified by the array of loud and violent noises that assaulted her senses. She was not immediately aware of the flames growing around her, until an orange glow flashed before her closed eyes. Lydia was forced to raise her head and open her eyes, exposing herself to the nightmare she was now trapped within.

The flames were now starting to engulf the room, licking hungrily at the petrol-soaked surfaces and eating away at anything within its path. Lydia could only stare in shock at the inferno raging around her. The gruesome image of Mitch's body was now illuminated from within the darkness. Lydia had to swallow back the bile rising in her throat, as she saw what fate had befallen the man. His lifeless body was propped up with his back against the stone wall, his arms lying limp at his side. His head was hanging forwards, his chin resting against his motionless chest, with the long handle of the claw hammer protruding sideways from the crown of his head. Blood was oozing sluggishly where the steel talons of the hammer had penetrated his skull, soaking and staining the material covering the dead man's shoulders as it dripped.

Lydia wanted to look away! She wanted to cast her eyes anywhere but upon the grotesque body before her, but she couldn't do so.

The spirits appeared to have now fled the building, their quest for justice finally over. Lydia's fate was not their concern and they had all now seemingly abandoned her, or so she thought! Beside Mitch's lame corpse stood one lone spectre. It was the spirit of Elizabeth. Her sad eyes had been watching the elderly woman as she shuffled away, flinching from the rising heat within the work shed. She witnessed her skin being scorched and her body being engulfed in smoke, causing Lydia's eyes to redden, and soiling her lungs with its choking thickness. The ghost now started to approach Lydia, moving across the room unhindered, her translucent form totally unaffected by the turbulent red-hot flames lapping all around her. She came to a halt before Lydia's battered and shuddering body. She looked down upon her, and for a moment their eyes met, each filled with a sadness and mutual understanding. Elizabeth's voiceless mouth began trying to communicate once more by mouthing a few brief words. This time, Lydia was able to read her lips and interpret what she was trying to say to her, despite the constant jerking movements of the spectre.

"I'm sorry!" were the soundless words that Elizabeth was attempting to convey, her ethereal face filled with sympathy. Lydia wanted to cry as she watched on, feeling disheartened as Elizabeth's spectral body began to fade away. The form was starting to crack and shatter before her, slowly disintegrating. Now, only a few sprinkles of dust remained in the air, falling slowly towards the ground and then disappearing into the void.

Lydia knew that she wouldn't be able to escape the inferno. Her only exit being the door at the entrance of the work shed, far from where she now sat. A wall of deadly flames blocked her path to survival, and the heat was becoming almost unbearable against her already pain-filled body. Lydia now just wanted to sleep! She felt she had known from the moment she entered the building, that she would never be leaving, well at least subconsciously! It now felt almost poetic, to die here alongside her enemies, the curtain finally falling on their tragic tale, once and for all!

The villains would never be able to harm anybody ever again! Lydia had accomplished what she had set out to do. Now, she just wanted it all to be over, and to escape this hell one way or another. Once again, Lydia's thoughts turned to her husband Robert, as they had done every day since his death. Whenever Lydia was alone or afraid, her husband's smiling face would enter her mind. Just seeing him in her memory was enough to make her chest ache in mourning. The hollowness of being without Robert was all-consuming, and she now told herself that she had to put these thoughts aside, and concentrate on the present.

She couldn't let her emotions distract her from the perilous situation she now found herself in! Lydia's yearning to see Robert again was so strong, that if this truly was the end for her, then she was finally ready to accept her fate! If she was destined to perish in the old work shed, burning in the blaze of fevered flames, then so be it! She would at last be reunited with her beloved husband once more.

With no more hopeful thoughts, and a single tear slowly trickling down her cheek, Lydia allowed her eyes to finally fall shut. She wanted to block out the horrific scene of the approaching inferno. The dense smoke was now encasing her, and it was becoming increasingly difficult to inhale. Her chest was wheezing with every shallow breath she was taking, and she knew there would be no sense in trying to fight it. She was extremely tired, exhaustion hanging on to her far greater than any sleep would be able to cure. Full of sorrow, she sighed and let go of herself, slipping into the darkness that was now consuming her world! It was only a matter of seconds before the flames would find her, but she prayed she would be gone before she felt their arrival. The black smoke would soon suffocate her harrowed lungs and end her breathing. It would all soon be over. But, until then she would dream of Robert smiling down on her one last time!

***

Christian finally arrived at the Hall, his entry being hindered by the barricaded iron gates at the entrance. Mitch had made sure that the property and its residents were securely locked away from the outside world. Christian had honked on the car horn several times, trying to grab somebody's attention, but no help arrived! He exited the car and tried pulling against the metal structures, but was failing to gain access. A large padlock wrapped around a metal chain mocked him gleefully as it kept him out. The house became visible beyond this trap, as if it were teasing him with what he wished for most, but was not able to obtain.

Precious time was now being wasted, as Christian's attempts to gain entry through the elaborate gates was proving to be fruitless. He decided to accept defeat, return to the warmth of his car and wait impatiently for the police to arrive. But, as he stood before the snow-dusted metal barriers, a distinct smell began to rise through the air. The smell of scorching wood met his nostrils, and for a brief moment, Christian humorously thought that somebody had lit a bonfire in the woods. But, as the scent increased around him, he spotted a distant glow somewhere behind the Hall. He then deduced that it was actually coming from somewhere within in the grounds of Carnation Hall!

He felt a sudden spike of panic shoot through his body, adrenaline mixed with fear suddenly running through his veins. His heart was now beating violently within his chest, and before he knew it, he was back behind the wheel of his car. He threw the vehicle into first gear, and revved up the engine as if he were in the starting grid at the Grand Prix! He was poised like a wild animal about to strike!

It felt almost like an out-of-body experience as Christian instantly let go of the clutch, accelerating forwards and ramming the front of his car against the mighty iron gates! A flurry of snow fell from the top of the old metal structures as they buckled against the force of the intrusion. Inside the car, Christian had braced himself, gripping the steering wheel firmly as he prepared for the impact! Seconds later, a gasp of surprise escaped him as his head rocked back against the headrest. The car had come to an abrupt stop, the gates still standing proudly before him! He felt the pain in his neck from the sudden jerk, but now was not the time to complain. He felt compelled to find Lydia, and nothing, least of all a pair of rusty old gates, was going to stop him from reaching his goal. The overwhelming urgency to find and protect her felt like a primal urge. He just knew that she was in imminent danger, the rush of nausea in his stomach informed him so every time she entered his mind.

With renewed urgency, Christian quickly threw his now battered car into reverse, retreating backwards and away from the buckled gates. Taking one last breath to calm his nerves, he once again drove forwards at full speed. The accelerator was pressed all the way to the floor for maximum power! With an almighty crash, the car then breached the mighty iron gates! The links on the metal chain snapped open, leaving the tall metal structures swinging wildly as they bounced off the body of the vehicle. The two deformed metal barriers were now bowing pathetically, as they strained against their rusted hinges.

Finally free of the gates, Christian had no time to look in his mirror and assess the carnage left behind in his wake. He continued at full speed to race up the snow-covered driveway, barely stopping the car before leaping out and dashing across the grounds of the Hall. Paying no attention to his severely damaged car, he continued to trudge through the blanketed field of snow. The origin of the smoke-filled air was his only destination, and ensuring Lydia was safe was his only concern!

It didn't take long before he reached the work shed, and wasted no time in rushing for the door. As he approached he could see the smoke permeating through the door frame, its wooden surface offering little or no protection against the raging fire within!

An ill-conceived grab of the handle revealed the immobility of the door, and earned Christian a searing burn mark across the palm of his hand for his efforts.

With alarm rising within him, Christian ignored the sudden pain in his hand and took to ramming the door instead. A few well placed kicks from his black leather shoes soon had the door conceding a few inches of movement, as it reluctantly pushed a little more inwards. Even outside, the smoke was now starting to burn at Christian's throat, causing him to cough and choke. He continued to rain more kicks upon the old door, each one with as much force as he was able. Finally, he conceded to try and ram the door with his shoulder, putting all of his weight into each strike, until eventually the wooden door caved in!

Without hesitation, he stepped through the doorway, raising his jacket up and over his mouth to try and form a makeshift mask against the thick cloud of smoke that was engulfing him. The heat was unbearable, reminding him of the furnace they used at the morgue, a sensation Christian never wanted to experience first hand! The density of the smoke made it difficult to see very much at all, and the painful bright orange glow of the flames dancing through the air left Christian practically blind. He quickly stooped down to his knees, deciding to crawl forwards instead of walking, as the smoke layer was thinner nearer the ground. This was a tip he had learnt a long time ago during a hospital fire drill. He had never expected it to serve him so well all these years later.

Ahead, only a few metres away, Christian thought he had glimpsed just a hint of coloured clothing. He struggled to see through the flickering flames, but he knew instinctively that it was Lydia! An unknown voice in his head was telling him so! But, he couldn't reach her, his path was blocked by the wildly burning fire. For a single moment, Christian contemplated running back to his car in order to retrieve the small portable fire extinguisher. He always kept it there in case of emergencies. But, with the ferocity of the flames before him, he knew it would be a pointless endeavour. The extinguisher in the car would hardly make a dent in the inferno rapidly surrounding him.

Then, before he could even begin to conceive another plan, something strange began to happen. The flames that were blocking the way between himself and his mother-in-law, suddenly began to simmer down right before his eyes! A cool spirited breeze began to work its way around the back of his neck as he watched the fire start to miraculously subside. The intense flames were somehow being pushed back, parting the pathway before him in order to gain access to Lydia! It was as though a superior force was giving him permission to aid Lydia. It was like a scene from the bible when Moses parted the waves of the Red Sea, creating a safe passageway for his people to cross the ocean floor to safety. Christian seized the opportunity and scurried forwards, watching cautiously as the hungry tendrils of fire threatened to pounce back upon him at any moment, and without any warning! Reaching the next clearing, and with a fleeting glance behind, Christian was relieved to find that the path ahead still remained clear. Despite the intense heat, he continued to catch sight of Lydia's limp body straight ahead, lying on its side against the wall. Her eyes were closed, her face blackened from the ash, and her chest barely rising and falling with each slow lingering breath.

"Lydia! Lydia! Can you hear me?" Christian shouted out, raising his voice as loud as he was able with his smoke-damaged throat, and mouth as dry as the Sahara.

The old woman did not stir. She didn't even flinch as he shook her shoulders in an attempt to rouse her from her slumber. Desperation was rising, and Christian began to fear he had arrived too late to save her!

"Lydia! We have to get out of here! I need you to wake up! Please . . . can you hear me?" he explained, still shaking her roughly in his hold. In a blind moment of panic, Christian raised his hand back and then slapped his palm harshly against her cheek, before yelling, "wake up!" directly into her ear.

In all honesty, Christian hadn't expected that to work. He assumed the smoke inhalation had probably set in too deeply for her to be roused from her catatonic state. But, after a moment of silence, the old woman suddenly lurched forwards, seized in a violent coughing fit, as she fought to take in the limited air left inside the room.

***

Lydia's first thought when she reopened her eyes, was that she had died, and that she was now residing in hell! The fire raging all around her, and the dull ache she felt all over her body, helped to confirm her theory. But, after a second, when her vision and memory began to return, she suddenly realised she was still alive!

"Lydia . . . are you alright? Can you hear me?" a voice spoke to her, sounding both near and far all at the same time. Lydia opened her mouth to reply, but was unable to speak! Her body had been savaged by her incessant coughing, her throat attempting to expel the plumes of smoke and ash now firmly sitting inside her lungs. After a few moments she started to calm down, and she slowly rolled onto her back feeling intense relief at being found. A tiny smile graced her lips as she gazed up at Christian kneeling over her, his face flooded with concern as he held her steadily by the shoulders.

"I didn't expect to see you here!" Lydia spoke, her voice haggard and hoarse.

"We need to get you out of here!" Christian stated. He didn't let his relief at seeing Lydia conscious deter him from the serious situation within which they were both still trapped! "Come on!" was all he added, before he wrapped his hands around Lydia's frail wrists and yanked her up on to her feet in one fell swoop!

The sudden movement made Lydia's head spin, but Christian had hold of her tightly! With surprising ease, the man threw her uninjured arm over his shoulder, holding onto her wrist firmly to keep her up, whilst wrapping his other arm securely around her waist. As quickly as they were able, the pair began to move. With Christian as her human crutch, Lydia stumbled forwards, flames licking dangerously close to her fleeting form as they moved towards the door. Neither dared to look behind as the fire began to resurrect itself, now consuming the space they had just left in their wake.

***

It was like stepping through a waterfall, as Lydia and Christian all but fell through the open door of the work shed and out into the open world! The mist of smoke cleared instantly as they raced across the threshold, the crisp cold air flooding over them like a tranquil wave of refreshing cool water after enduring the stifling heat within.

Christian was practically carrying Lydia along. The exertion was weighing in on her so heavily, she could hardly move her own feet through the thickness of the snow. The wound through her hand was still sluggishly leaking blood, marring the perfect white of the snow behind them as they trudged along. A brief glance over his shoulder informed Christian that they were now far enough away from the burning building, and were now in a place of relative safety. The air around them was mostly clear of the toxic fumes, yet the fire continued to burn in the distance, emitting an amber glow that held the blackness of the night at bay.

Lydia let out a sigh of relief as Christian lowered her down onto the cold ground. She cared little as her back rested up against the plinth of a faceless statue. The cold touch of its surface felt soothing against Lydia's heat-seared skin.

Christian wasted little time tending to her injuries, using his own belt as a tourniquet on her arm to slow the still-falling blood. He then reached up and removed his neck tie and started wrapping it around the savage wound in her hand, using the strip of fabric as a makeshift bandage. For the moment, it was all he was able to do to stop the bleeding until help arrived. Despite his comforting words, Lydia remained mostly unresponsive, gesturing only with short gasps of pain as Christian's prodding hands aggravated her wounds.

Christian could have kicked himself as he realised that he had foolishly left his mobile phone in the car. It was sitting on the passenger seat, a decision he instantly regretted. The device hadn't been his primary concern as he was dashing from his car earlier. The doctor was just about to make a run back to the front of the building to retrieve it, when the faint sound of a siren met his ear. The whirling and whining grew louder and more intense as they approached. With an exhausted sigh, Christian pushed himself up onto his feet, feeling his back groan and protest against the sudden action as he stepped away from Lydia.

He looked her over carefully, her skin appearing a sickly pale colour in contrast to the grey slab of concrete against which she was resting. Dark circles were evident around her eyes, and her face was marred with drying blood, crusting up against her cracked lip. Dark bruises were already setting in below her pale skin, prominently shining even in the dull light. Her vision seemed unfocused as she stared straight ahead, eyes locked and barely blinking as she gazed upon the still burning building. It seemed as though she was looking straight through Christian as he stood right before her, intently watching something that only she could see within the burning flames.

Fearing she was now slipping into a state of shock, Christian made a snap decision. He would have to leave her here. He didn't wish to do so, but he had little choice. He lacked the strength or energy to carry Lydia any further, and the most rapid method of getting her aid was for him to lead the authorities to her.

"Lydia . . . I'm going to go for help . . . the police are on their way! I'm going to meet them and tell them what's happened . . . I'll be right back! Okay? You're going to be fine!" he told her, his voice flooded with strained reassurance. But, he gained no reply, not even a firm hand on her shoulder could jostle her from her feeble and vapid state. With one last reluctant glance towards his mother-in-law, Christian urged his legs to move, forcing himself to run through the dense snow that had settled around the grounds. The sirens were now wailing constantly, filtering up the road and telling him that their arrival was imminent. Christian had barely reached the front of the house before he was greeted by a flood of cars trailing up the gravel driveway. An array of flashing blue and red lights were reflecting off the white snow as they came to a halt at the main entrance to the Hall. Three police cars had arrived outside the Hall, closely followed by a brightly coloured ambulance.

Before Christian's feet were able to land on the gravel driveway, two policemen in full uniform were already stepping out from their vehicles. One by one, the sirens powered down, the flashing lights remaining lit, illuminating the darkened building as they reflected off the blackened windows.

Without hesitation, Christian approached the men, wasting no time rushing around their vehicles to meet them, his mouth already moving and spitting out everything he knew about what had occurred this snowy night.

***

Lydia was sitting solemnly as she watched the fire burning, the flames flailing and dancing in slow motion amidst the sparks of fire discharging from the blaze! The heat from the engulfed building was still catching her face. At this distance the heat felt quite comforting, a pleasant warmth brushing softly against her cheeks, preventing the cold from further seeping into her old bones. The work shed continued to burn before her eyes, its mostly wooden structure having already succumbed to the raging flames. The main beam was now collapsing as the whole roof began to buckle, before finally crashing down amidst a torrent of flames. Something else, however had consumed Lydia's complete attention, the fire being just a mere sideshow to what she was now truly witnessing. She was peering intently, directly through the flames and into the space beyond. It was as though only she could see what was happening! A lone spirit emerged from within the falling building, swiftly rising up into the night sky with an air of majesty, continuing to accelerate in a heavenly direction! A faint blue glow was encasing its form as it ascended skywards, reaching higher and higher into the blackness of the sky, until it finally faded away from its earthly existence! Lydia could feel the power that it was emitting, the ethereal energy was prickling her skin as she watched it fly, until suddenly, all sensations disappeared! The spectre's energy appeared to dissolve into the air surrounding her, all forces withering away and out from existence. A single lone tear began to fall from Lydia's cheek, as she realised what was now happening. The spirits that had become tormented victims, trapped within their stone-like tombs, imprisoned as mere decorations standing amongst the living, had now finally broken free from their chains binding them to earth. Now that justice had finally been served, they were free to move on from this world of torture and torment!

Before Lydia could process what she had just witnessed, another light began to rise up out of the ashes, again ascending up into the sky in a similar fashion. Then, rapidly followed by another, and another! Lydia held her breath at the unseen beauty of what she was now witnessing. All of the spirits, each and every one that had been wronged, finally moving on to the next world that awaited them. This vision resembled a poetic firework display, like Roman candles rising up from the ground and ascending into the night sky in a bright flash of colour, before fading away peacefully into the darkness.

Lydia could only watch on wearing an exhausted smile upon her face. She could feel the joy the spirits now held, as opposed to the spiteful anger they had filtered into the air before. With Kelly and Mitch finally gone, the spirits were now at peace for the first time since their lives had been snatched away from them in such a cruel manner. Lydia watched them all disappear, content that she had played her part, despite the personal losses she herself had also endured. She began thinking of her dear friend Kate, and despite Lydia not being a religious woman herself, she prayed that her friend's spirit had also moved on to a better place.

As the seconds ticked by, the flow of spirits began to slow down, and soon only a few stragglers remained waiting to take their journey up into the clouds. Finally, just one spirit remained! Lydia's eyes were beginning to close, the peaceful ambience abundant in the air lulling her to rest. But, from the corner of her lidded eyes, one lone remaining spirit caught her attention! If questioned, she would probably not have been able to explain why, but without hesitation, and despite the pain and her exhaustion, she pushed herself up onto her feet.

Standing shakily and leaning heavily against the statue, she forced her eyes to focus on the lone figure standing before her. This spectre was not at all like the others she had previously seen, she knew this from instinct alone. Its appearance was a blur of shadowed features as it stood. Its evaporating evanescent body seemed unsteady as it looked in her direction. Lydia limped slowly forwards, advancing towards the waiting spectre. She couldn't yet see its face, its astral body too agitated and jittery for her eyes to focus upon, but Lydia did not need to see this spirit clearly to know who was now standing before her!

"Robert!" Lydia gasped, her voice barely a whisper in the night.

The spectre merely nodded gently, raising his arm slowly towards her, as if encouraging her to move closer.

Lydia stepped forward, now only an arm's length away from him.

"Why are you here? You were supposed to have moved on . . . I thought you had gone!" Lydia whimpered, sobs beginning to shake through her chest.

Again, the ghost said nothing, voiceless in his current state of existence. Silently he raised his other arm towards Lydia, beckoning her to come to him.

Lydia looked at Robert for a moment in sheer disbelief, tears flowing freely down her cheeks leaving lines as they fell. She hesitated only a moment more before falling into Robert's open arms. Ethereal static brushed against her skin, making it tingle at his touch, as Lydia leant into the ghostly form. She had barely touched him, before the figure began to slowly disintegrate in her arms, fading out of existence with increasing haste. Lydia couldn't see it, but she knew Robert was smiling, a fact that just made her weep even more. As quickly as it had begun, their reunion was over. Robert's ghostly form shifted upwards out of her grasp and began to fade away, becoming weaker and weaker as it blended into the night sky high above. His spectral power dissipating until finally fading from existence!

Lydia fell down to her knees! A torrent of uncontrollable sobs overtook her body, with an avalanche of emotions overcoming her mind. She continued to cry, not even noticing that Christian had returned to her with a policeman at his side, asking waves of questions she just couldn't hear. She didn't even react when the paramedics arrived and began tending to her wounds, or even when they lifted her up and manoeuvred her into the ambulance. The rest of the night would pass as a complete blur to Lydia. She was later unable to recall how she even arrived at the hospital, or remember her beloved daughter Susanna racing to be by her side, hugging her mother tightly. Nor, would she remember the green hue that tinted her daughter's face, as Susanna watched her mother's injured hand being sewn up by the nurse. The only thing occupying Lydia's thoughts until the next dawn was Robert! He was now finally gone! She knew that she would never see him again, at least not in this lifetime! But, she was eternally grateful that he had visited her just one last time!

CHAPTER 17

Epilogue

After the paramedics had taken Lydia to hospital, Christian decided that he would spend the rest of the night at the Hall aiding the authorities. The fire service had arrived at some point to extinguish the blaze at the work shed, but there was barely anything left to salvage from the fire. The entire building had been burnt to a cinder, with only the old stone walls remaining standing. The roof had buckled and collapsed after the fire had roasted away the aged wooden beams. Now, as daylight approached, all that remained was a smouldering ruin of what once was.

The officers on the scene had discovered two completely burnt and charred sets of human remains within the work shed. The bodies had been taken away to be examined by a team of forensics, and Christian felt confident that their dental records would confirm them to be the caretakers of the Hall. After a thorough search, the police had not been able to find Kelly or Mitch anywhere on the property, and all of the vehicles that the Millers owned were still parked at the Hall.

The forensics team were currently scouring the property and grounds for more evidence. Christian watched on as several boxes containing papers and documents were being carried out of the house. Even the statues in the garden were being prepared for removal and further examination, presumably to analyse the suspicious components that lay within. Vanessa had kept to her word by immediately contacting the police, and upon arrival at the Hall, the officers had already been fully briefed about the alleged crimes that had been committed on the premises.

As the police continued with their work, the paramedics assisted the remaining elderly residents, whilst Christian spent his time wandering around the Hall. He had the foresight to head directly to Lydia's apartment, packing her a bag of essentials that she may need whilst recovering in the hospital. He gathered together some of her personal belongings, and then dropped them off at his car. He then continued to walk around to the back of the building, and was just about to enter through the back door, when he glanced at a small bundle of black fur lying in the snow near the dustbins. Upon closer inspection he discovered that it was a black cat, lying dead beside a ripped open bin bag, the contents having spilt out across the neighbouring ground. The sight of the dead body caused a pang of pity to bubble up in Christian's chest as he passed the sad-looking animal.

He then continued into the building, through the kitchen heading towards Kelly's office. He wanted to see if this place could offer any more clues as to what had been happening at the Hall. Kelly's office had been a major point of interest to Christian. He had heard Lydia speak about finding evidence in there, so now he wished to visit this damned room for himself. The police had already swept through the office by the time he had arrived, and it appeared that they had already removed most of the files and books that could have been of interest to them. However, a few papers remained lying scattered across the floor and desk, seemingly unimportant to the police at this point. Feeling a wave of exhaustion, Christian threw himself down into the chair behind the desk, trying not to feel nauseated by the horrors that this very room had been protecting. He slowly gazed around the room, his eyes carefully scouring the walls for anything that would give away some of its secrets. It was completely by chance that something then caught his eye lying on top of the desk in front of him. Christian would never know what possessed him, but he singled out one lone envelope that was lying harmlessly amongst the pile of others.

The envelope seemed innocent enough at first sight and was addressed to a *'Mrs K. Miller'*. With more than a hint of curiosity, Christian pulled the letter from within its paper casing and began to read it starting from the top. The date and address gave nothing away, however, as he continued to read the words his jaw began to drop. The mild nausea he had been feeling had now been replaced by a fully fledged revulsion. The letter read as follows:

Dear Kelly,

I would like to thank you so much for showing me around Carnation Hall earlier today. The place you and your husband manage is amazing and a credit to you both. The apartment you showed me was wonderful! I think it would be the perfect place for my wife Lydia and I to spend our future together, and I hope that we will be making the move very soon. I have decided to keep this venture a complete surprise for my wife and the rest of our family. We are not getting any younger, and we do not wish to become a burden to our family in our old age. Thank you once again for your hospitality towards me today. I will surely be in touch with you very soon.

Yours sincerely
Robert Jones

P.S. I loved the home-made cupcakes you served me with tea this afternoon, they had such a wonderful and unique flavour, I can't wait for my wife to get the opportunity to enjoy them too!

Christian was in shock upon reading the letter, and it took him a while to process what he had just read. It was then that the actual date of the letter brought a firm lump to his throat! It was dated as being the very same day that Robert had died. Lydia's husband had no doubt visited the

Hall, and spent the afternoon discretely viewing the apartment and grounds. He then must have taken tea and cakes with that psycho woman Kelly Miller! Later, Robert had even gone as far as to write and post her a thank-you letter. In the letter Robert had actually mentioned eating cake, and had eaten it not long before he perished! Christian felt sick as the final pieces of the jigsaw fell neatly and sickeningly into place. Another level of the mystery was now beginning to unfold before his eyes.

Kelly had murdered Robert! She had deliberately poisoned Lydia's husband, and all this time no one even knew about it! The world truly was a twisted, cynical and sardonic place. Perhaps, it was best if Lydia was never to know about this last cruel twist of fate. Christian was well aware of all the torment and heartbreak that the poor old woman had endured, and she did not need the burden of this terrible knowledge weighing down upon her soul. With that thought in mind, Christian slipped the letter into his jacket pocket, patting the area gently to confirm its safety, before exiting the office and the building.

As he finally drove away from Carnation Hall, Christian grasped one last fleeting look at the building through his rear-view mirror. His car then continued to limp along, slowly passing the remains of the entrance gates, before turning onto the long tree-lined road that concealed the property. He then made one final vow that he would never again return to these haunted grounds!

THE END

Printed in Great Britain
by Amazon